THE ALIEN
in MY E-MAIL *and*
Other Stories

THE ALIEN
in MY E-MAIL *and*
Other Stories

WOLFGANG NIESIELSKI

iUniverse, Inc.
Bloomington

THE ALIEN IN MY E-MAIL AND OTHER STORIES

iUniverse books may be ordered through booksellers or by contacting:

iUniverse
1663 Liberty Drive
Bloomington, IN 47403
www.iuniverse.com
1-800-Authors (1-800-288-4677)

ISBN: 978-1-4759-0990-6 (sc)
ISBN: 978-1-4759-0992-0 (hc)
ISBN: 978-1-4759-0991-3 (ebk)

Printed in the United States of America

iUniverse rev. date: 04/28/2012

To my loving wife, Ebele.

Writing Columns

"Man Bites Dog, Cat Eats Woman." Here I am crafting the cleverest of expressions, words, and literary devices, with such spellbinding power, they would cause anyone reading to swoon and faint, assuring me that, even if I have no nominations for the Nobel and/or Pulitzer prizes, at the very least, I have the admiration and awe of those around me (and perhaps a few folks down the street). Then I put my work aside to sleep on it. Perhaps in my haste to fashion the most perfect of sentences I might have overlooked a minor error or two. Naturally this would be a pleasure to work on and correct tomorrow and chisel into an even greater piece of flawless perfection, I think.

The next morning, after making myself a nice strong cup of coffee, I cheerfully open my writing machine to take another look. What is this? This is not what I wrote yesterday! Someone got into my computer somehow and changed everything around! This is absolutely the greatest piece of pathetic, silly, childish, self-aggrandizing horse manure I ever had the displeasure to look at! And I wrote this? It can't be! But before I have a chance to delete the idiocy my wife sneaks up to read it.

"This is absolutely the greatest piece of pathetic, silly, childish, self-aggrandizing horse manure I ever had the displeasure to look at!" she exclaims. "Who wrote this?"

"I have no idea," I reply. "I thought maybe you had something to do with it."

"Oh, sure," she says in a mocking tone, "I have a habit of waking up in the middle of the night to turn your brilliant narrative into this piece of pathetic, silly, childish, self-aggrandizing horse manure. Sure I do."

Well, alright, I can take a bit of sarcasm but I am still at a loss as to, why something that seemed so good yesterday would turn into an absolute disaster today? "It seemed a lot better when I wrote it yesterday," I confess, crying on the inside. "And now . . . just look at the mess."

"Oh, poor dear. Maybe you should have written it in a language that people actually speak nowadays—English would be helpful," my wife suggested, not at all sympathetic.

"But I did!" I protested, choking on my inner tears, as the dire prospect immediately hit me that, instead of living off enormous literary prizes, I would be forced to change back to my original plan—that of winning the lottery.

"Quit whining and write something worthwhile," my wife, a great advocate of the *Tough Love* movement, urges me.

'This is my dog, Spot', I finally write. 'See Spot run! Run, Spot, run!'

"There you go," she said. "This is a thousand times better than that garbage you produced yesterday. Just keep going."

Fine. But my dog Spot, frolicking quite innocently, suddenly hits a wall, taking me right alongside with him and smashing me against a writer's block the size of Mount Everest. At a complete loss, I just sit and stare. Then I get up to make some more coffee. Then I sit and stare some more. This time, due to caffeine overkill, I also quiver. Suddenly a brilliant idea hits me—talking about dogs, how about a dog biting a man or a man, in retaliation, biting the dog, or dogs eating dogs, while some of them find new, creative ways to skin the cat? Ideas spill out like turnips from an open truck. Feverishly I pound on the keyboard to finish an absolute gem of a literary masterpiece. It has everything, excitement, adventure, humor, immersed in dazzling eloquence—something probably not seen since Shakespeare. Proudly I show it off to my wife.

"Dogs?" she says, wrinkling her nose. "Didn't you do something on dogs the other day? Well, I don't know . . . uh . . . mm, I guess it's okay."

And you thought it was easy being a columnist.

CONTENTS

CHAPTER ONE

The Alien in My E-Mail and Other Stories

Author Bruno Bronson discovers the source of his writer's block.

THE ALIEN IN MY E-MAIL

A few days ago, I was happily sauntering through cyber space, accessing all the various messages from friends, family and *very concerned individuals* whose sole mission in life seems to be to rescue me from all sorts of quandaries, like bankruptcies, impotence, baldness and below-par bosom measurements. I even had developed an increasingly intimate relationship with an extremely friendly former big government honcho in an African country who, in desperation, had seen no other choice but to seek me out to deposit millions of dollars into my bank-account—the only piece of information lacking in his pursuit of selflessly providing me with untold millions was that he needed to know the number to my bank account. Although lately, the government honcho had become increasingly absent after I suggested meeting him somewhere and, since my car is quite large, picking up the lucre in cash.

I had actually planned to inform the aforementioned individuals and their organizations (who were worried sick about my financial status), that I would have to decline their offers, since considerable time would now be allocated to facing the vexing problem of lack of space, due to tropical bags brimming with cash, littering my house, when my e-mail went out.

When I tried to access my e-mail account, the automated reply stated in violent red letters—"E-MAIL CANNOT BE ACCESSED DUE TO FAULTY ACCESS CODE." This was a curious development, since I had used that same code to access my mail for 3 years. But I always have a contingency plan for plausible deniability and I had had my wife pick the number, figuring I could always blame her if something went awry, such as forgetting a number I had been familiar with for a long time. In this case I didn't have to exercise this prerogative because I had cleverly posted this exact number right in front of my eyes, on the desk-top in big black letters. I resumed typing the correct sequence into the box provided for that purpose. After proceeding several times, with the same result, the endeavor seemed to be a sure sign of insanity and I think I was close to getting picked up by the friendly folks in those nice white coats, when I finally relented.

That was when I discovered that an evil Cyber Presence had invaded the sanctuary of my e-mail account. It might not be the kind that habitually pops out of your stomach at the most inopportune time during a dinner date but more in the vein of stealthily invading your brain, causing havoc with your synapses and initiating a speedy descent into madness. It is not without reason to assume that the abstract concept of "cyber space", a vast, mysterious and perhaps "unknowable" place, is populated by equally enigmatic creatures, operating beyond our human comprehension and logic. I was convinced of that after frantically searching all over cyberspace to find a phone number to contact the e-mail proprietor personally.

No sooner had I dialed the appropriate number, than an "extraterrestrial" voice informed me that my wait would be substantial and suggested hanging up and trying later. Apparently the aliens needed considerable time to transform themselves from scaly, tentacle-laden creatures into forms capable of speaking English. But since I ignored the offer and hung on, it cost me several eternities, where I was treated to elevator music without the elevator—an obvious prelude to purgatory. Finally the agent of the *Evil Presence* descended upon me. After first trying to entice me with her charming drawl, her voice turned sharp and tinny, which I assume was due to her overly long, alien voice passages. She curtly informed me that my birth date, which she needed for identification purposes, was wrong. I assured her that my mother had always complained about my reluctance to see daylight and that *that day* had been burned into her mind forever. A long time ago my mother had passed this information on to me, along with the correct date. But to no avail, not being familiar with human motherhood, the extraterrestrial agent was not impressed. My birth date was wrong, she proclaimed, and she would not release any information on my e-mail account without it. The evil game, lasting several more eternities, began. I tried to convince her that amongst human beings we always find ways to work things out and that perhaps there was another way to confirm my identity. But the creature always paused, mimicked listening, and then always repeated the same answer—perpetually, ceaselessly, without end. Fearing the familiar slide into insanity I again yielded. I was not about to provide comfortable lodgings inside my mind for aliens unfamiliar with human logic. Instead I slammed down the phone and decided to change my e-mail to another provider and a brand-new set of aliens.

Unfortunately my African big government honcho friend might not be able to locate me now and I find myself sloughing away without the comfort of a large bank account. I wonder though, giving away millions to a stranger doesn't correspond with human logic either. More than likely he is also from outer space.

HOW TO BEAT THE NEWEST E-MAIL SCAMS

For some reason these e-mails from faraway lands, promising me riches, have become quite sparse. I used to receive several a day, now I'm lucky if I get one or two per week. What have I done to deserve this snub? Or has my Spam filter improved that much now?

The e-mails usually start out addressing me as: "Dearest One,"—quite endearing, isn't it? No one around here uses that kind of arcane language anymore, at least not since ink quills went out of fashion. Who also has time to compose a long letter these days, or even read them anyway? Nowadays you'd better make your case within a sentence or two or lose the reader. Maybe that's why the authors have to resend the same e-mail over and over again. Since very few people actually take time to work through any lengthy piece of mail, if I were in a position to advise them, I'd tell them to cut to the chase.

This is how the e-mails should read: "Please, send me your name, address, bank account and social security number and I'll hand you ten million bucks. If you can find it in your heart to add your secret codes, even better, I'll increase the loot to a couple million more."

See how short and to the point that was? None of that flowery, whiny stuff necessary, about some rich dad dying in a plane crash and an evil uncle now conspiring to get his hands on dad's millions. And don't be so stingy with your imaginary millions; you could even turn the "m" into a "b" and really make an impact.

But no, of course no one listens to me. Instead, I can see these poor souls sitting down, sweating over their extensive e-mails. Remember, when your mother used to make you write a thank-you letter to Aunt Mary for your birthday present? It's probably just like that. You just couldn't write, "Thank you, Auntie Mary, I really like that woolen sweater you sent me", and be done with it. No, you were expected to elaborate in long, drawn-out, fancy sentences how you appreciated the incredible appropriateness of the handsome, handcrafted piece of clothing, and marvel about how Auntie Mary was able to predict the change of weather, just in time to provide you with protection from the cold winds of autumn (and you didn't dare complain about how scratchy the darn thing was).

As you can see, I can definitely identify with the stress and anxiety that is associated with the composition of a successful e-mail, perhaps one so finely calibrated that it would woo the recipient into viewing the writer with a sense of ever-increasing generosity. Maybe, in the case of Aunt Mary, a more brilliant narrative might have been able to touch certain areas in her psyche that may have caused her to abandon future shipments of coarse garments, and veered her instead towards the idea of sending toys? Naturally the art of fine-tuning the subtleties is key, because any off remark might persuade Auntie to shine her newfound benevolence more to the direction of competing nieces and nephews.

That's why I'm so disappointed with my newest get-rich-quick Nigerian correspondent. He went all out in his flattery and praise of me, emphasizing his immense appreciation for my "exceptional good nature" that would make it possible for him to put his fortune of several million dollars into my bank account. But then he signed the letter as Miss *Julian* Justin. MISS? See, in his haste to craft the perfect letter, he must have completely forgotten what gender he was. Again, if I had been his advisor, I would have told him that there are ways to make sure by checking in the right places. At the very least he could have asked his friends.

You blew it big time, Julian! Now you have to sit down and do it all over again. This time, make sure to cross all your t's and dot your i's, and please keep the new e-mails brief.

WHY AUTUMN IS NOT MY FAVORITE TIME OF THE YEAR

Give anyone a word-association test providing the word "autumn" and invariably most people will come up with "leaves." Perhaps because as leaves fall off trees by the ton during a time of decreasing temperatures and increasing number of months, leaving the crowns meager and bare, they prominently remind us of the impending bleakness and decay that a harsh, cold winter promises and we shiver at that thought. Although the bright beautiful colors the leaves display just before tumbling to their demise might provide some fleeting solace for folks who have been piling up bills for luxurious vacations and other frivolous purchases made during the untroubled, carefree, warm days of summer, most of these folks realize quickly once the last of the leaves hit the ground that they will be faced with the hopelessness of added gigantic bills for Christmas presents, which regularly facilitate vacuums in bank-accounts, inflated balloon payments and bursting credit maximums.

Naturally, instead of sticking it out through the harshness of winter, like the rest of us, the cowardly foliage takes the easy way out and commits suicide. I suspect the beautiful work of art that trees flaunt just before the dastardly act is just a clever psychological ploy to make us feel sorry for them and guilty. Perhaps they expect us to send them to a warmer climate during winter, like migratory birds. Consisting of nothing but wood, these dumb plants have no idea of the expense that would be incurred to truck them south, as well as the enhanced contribution to the depletion of fossil-fuel. Shortsighted and foolish as they are, not one of them considers the fact that, in this case, we would also be forced to use *them* for fuel again, so that we don't turn a different color, wither and drop ourselves.

Fortunately not all the trees are so dense, spineless and selfish. The leaves of fir trees, for example, courageously make it through the winter without complaint. That is why we celebrate them by chopping them down and putting them up in our living rooms as Christmas trees, causing them to drop their needles all over the carpet after all anyway (some of us realize that irony and purchase trees made of plastic. Of course this, in turn, contributes to the impending oil-shortage. Is there no end to this downward spiral?)

Independent of the motives of cunning trees, the vibrant splendor encompassing our landscape during the fall months has been indispensable for eons now in creating the source of inspiration for artists, poets, writers and similar layabouts. The rest of us are confronted with marauding gangs of pintsized extortionists, disguised in cute costumes, who roam the neighborhood demanding payment in the form of sugar-based, high-caloric foodstuffs or threatening unpleasant "tricks" in retaliation for non-compliance. A protection-racket, which, I'm sure, is whole-heartedly co-sponsored by dubious elements in the candy and dental industries. Some of the mischief featured as "good-natured" pranks or "tricks" include the pelting of raw eggs and decoration of leafless trees using up large amounts of toilet paper. Again I wouldn't be surprised if a certain milieu within the poultry and tissue industry had something to do with the creation of such bedlam.

In my opinion, it just fits into the theme of the time of year—damage and loss. The demise of foliage and the lack of good dental protection seem to feature paramount as a subject matter during this latter part of the year.

But come to think of it, if so many—from poets to chicken-farmers to pintsized snot-noses—stand to profit from this time of the year, what chance do I have of getting a consensus on feeling bad and lamenting the passing of summer?

LOST WITHOUT A LAPTOP

My laptop, an ancient, five-year old, steam engine-powered writing device, finally collapsed into a heap of smoldering plastic and chips. Apparently the *sissy* couldn't take the little bit of pounding I subjected it to every once in a while. Instead it quit in protest, but not before sneakily sending smoke signals to warn other computers to stay away from me. That seemed to be the reason I was unable to find a new one fitting my budget. As soon as I hit the computer store they had all been forewarned and quickly hoisted the prices of those tiny computers (small enough to fit on one's lap), beyond the lofty cost of the burgeoning big ones that usually sit on giant desks of important highfliers.

Confronted with the burden of being forced to change current habits—I wondered if I could put my thoughts down employing the archaic mode of actually scribbling a variety of lines onto paper with a tiny, old-fashioned ink-dispensing tool—I got a hold of a pen. Ancient memories returned with a vengeance, of bending over a school desk, sweating profusely while a spinster of a teacher swung a menacing foot-long ruler cautioning me to stay within the lines. Lacking this kind of cheerleader, I gave up sooner than anticipated after realizing that not only was the act of writing enormously arduous but actually deciphering the mess afterwards was even more laborious.

But it had not been that long ago that I prided myself on proficiency in this very skill. I had been able to write long, drawn-out sentences in quick pace, scoffing at those newfangled writing and calculating machines. However, sooner or later when it became apparent that I would probably end up being the last person on earth without the ability to push the "on" button on a computer, I was coerced into shelling out almost the equivalent of an entire stationary store to purchase one of these "word processing" units.

The time it took though, coordinating the symbols on the keyboard with the actual letters on the screen was reminiscent of those early, unsettling days under the diktat of the alphabet teacher, and I often broke down realizing that although I was able to produce symbols of the alphabet on the screen with enormous speed, that act was completely fruitless, unless I was able to organize them into actual words and sentences. I have a huge respect for those enormously dexterous people whose hands become a blur as they fly across the keyboard hitting the appropriate letters in mind-boggling speed while using a mere two fingers. But I was somehow unable (using this method), to locate suitable symbols in an alphabetic ocean quickly enough to form a word and then an entire sentence, before my train of thought became fatally derailed.

The learning curve of mastering the skill of typing with ten fingers, which I arduously adhered to later, turned into a mountainous, treacherous ascend before I found myself proficient enough to dare writing a few lines without the aid of a teaching program. And although I was sure that I had completed the entire course, I am still unable to this day to unearth the more exotic symbols, like the semicolon for example, without actually looking at the keyboard.

But now, fairly practiced at it, as a dweller inside the 21st Century, I find myself at a loss without this modern device. Barely a decade removed from the days of writing with longhand I am incapable of composing anything remotely considered intelligible without the aid of a computer. Writing, as math without a calculator, seems to have gone the way of the horse buggy. And the once highly valued craft of calligraphy is nowadays appreciated as little as the skill of tracking and clubbing a boar, and taking it home to the cave to feed the family.

Come to think of it, I wonder how people back then, armed—not with "input" but with "knockout" devices—would have dealt with a noncompliant laptop such as mine. I doubt if they would have been nice enough to expose it to a few silly bumps, as I did. And for certain they would have not caved in and paid a colossal bill, the size of a mammoth, after hunting down another one as I finally had to do.

BABY NEWS

The most merciless creature on earth doesn't even have any teeth, it is not a boa constrictor, a ferocious leopard or some other nasty critter with a mouthful of sharp teeth, because registering absolute zero on the pity-scale is not a wild beast but a tiny, cute little baby.

If you doubt me, just put your face close to a baby's tiny, little hands as I did, and experience them turn into a fearsome vise, with a squeeze tight enough to transform a plastic toy back into liquid-dinosaur. It starts when you happily exchange "googoo-gahgahs" with the child, and then he or she will grab a hold of your mustache with lightning fast moves and won't let go until you're on your knees, tears shooting out of your eyes and are about to pass out! And don't even think about looking for help from mom or anyone else around, as they usually enjoy the cruel spectacle as much or even more than the little one, spurring the baby on to even greater feats of capriciousness, such as aiming for the nose. That organ will then be ripped off with one swift move, especially when you start to nag about certain baby smells emanating from the opposite end of the little critter.

It seems that for some reason little tots attend to zero in on me as a target. Perhaps they sense the weakest link amongst the adults around them—someone totally unable to resist these little people with their potent charm that adults like me don't have any defense for—being small, cute and adorable. I know that I would be completely useless as a kindergarten teacher, for instance, because in no time at all the kids would surround me, tie me up and set fire to my shoes and I would be unable to utter even a whimper. For example, when my niece was three or four years old, my duties as an uncle included becoming a horse, each time I came to visit. Immediately after a few short preliminaries (like pretending to be paralyzed) I was conscripted into getting on my hands and knees and scooting all over the place with her on my back urging the lazy beast of burden on to go faster. Sometimes I was allowed to rest, since the child understood that no animal can go on forever without munching on some grass. Unfortunately that meal consisted of foul-tasting green plastic, which my little tormentor fed me because, of course, a horse can't do much on its own since it lacks opposable thumbs as well as a brain to outsmart the little rider (not to speak of the guts to say no).

Now my wife's cousin just had one of those cute, little babies, a healthy, sweet and lovable girl. Hearing the good news, my knees shaking, we went out to look for an appropriate baby gift. I immediately voted for a baby blanket or perhaps a bib. Cognizant of how the baby-toys manufacturing industry works and keeping my own protection in mind this seemed to be the safest choice. I'm sure these companies go through great pains making the toys as safe for infants as possible. Precautions are taken to make sure toys can't be swallowed because they are crafted without sharp edges or any other features exposing the child to danger. But then, I wonder, how is it possible that with all these safeguards in place whenever I pick up a baby somehow I always get viciously poked in the eye?

Sooner or later I will have to face the new baby. Born into a new millennium that doesn't appreciate a bushy mustache, I'm sure the little one will aim directly at mine. Well, it's time for a modern, bald look anyway.

CHAPTER TWO

Round The World in 30 Days

"If you want my opinion, we're flying way too low again."

LAS VEGAS

There are three main reasons to avoid Las Vegas: too much heat, too much neon and too many Elvis impersonators. While heat and light can be avoided by dodging inside air-conditioned and dimly-lit casinos, Elvis clones have a habit of pursuing you at all hours of the day or night, lips pursed, sideburned, collar upturned, sneering with an attitude that they are "all shook up." But what motivates anyone in the first place to *drive* to Las Vegas in the middle of the summer when the upper area on the thermometer is running out of digits? Especially at a time when gas-prices were in hot pursuit, clambering higher and higher towards a dizzying summit?

Maybe it was temporary lunacy, or maybe it was just the longing for black-dyed, duck-tailed hairdos and second-rate rhinestone-studded, hip-swiveling jumpsuits, but whatever hankering my wife and I had for "hunka-hunka burnin' luv" crash-burned as soon as I opened the door of my comfortable, cool, air-conditioned car at a gas-station in the middle of the desert on our way to Las Vegas this Labor day weekend. I'm not clear which sensation was responsible for sucking the air out of my lungs—the bake-oven heat or the fact that I was just about to spend a sizable amount of my life's savings on liquefied dinosaur remains. Gasping for air and contemplating crawling under any rock for a smidgen of shade, I realized though that I had no choice but to continue on our journey to Vegas, as a mirage of ice-cold *free* drinks waiting for me at the slot-machines, appeared suddenly.

The realization that those "free drinks" were indeed an illusion hit me later on as I plunked myself in front of a slot machine and stuffed a twenty-dollar bill into a yawning black hole while waiting for a "free" two-dollar beer. In fact, illusions are what created Las Vegas. From celebrity impersonators to disappearing white tigers on a magician's stage—nothing seems to be real—except of course the ever-increasing vacuum in your wallet. But since that is an abstract concept (at least until the reality of credit card bills hit home), it remains as intangible as the perception of your having fun "gaming" away your nest-egg. It seems a brilliant marketing move by the industry, leaving out the letters "bl" and turning "gambling" into "gaming", although it requires only a small amount of time and money to figure out who the "game" is and who the hunter is.

The standard ritual in Las Vegas seems to be that after a streak or two of bad luck (and when the empty feeling stemming from your stomach seems to equal the burning hole in your pocket book), many people in a desperate attempt for new ideas try rerouting from the beckoning blackjack and roulette tables to slot machines until finally, the sign "buffet" seems to do the job. "Buffet?" One of the many misconceptions about Las Vegas is that the food is cheap because as the reasoning goes, "they want to keep you inside the casino." But of course the proprietors of the castle-sized casinos are always a step ahead in the business of extracting money from unsuspecting customers and have therefore wisely placed their operations in the middle of a scorching desert. Naturally no one dares to venture outside, at least not without gallons of iced alcohol pulsating through oxygen-starved veins (which causes people to do strange things, including demanding to have Wayne Newton sing "Danke Schoen" one more time). My wife and I only became conscious of this after a bone-tiring hour-long wait, inching ahead in a line of ill-tempered hungry gamblers, when another inconspicuous sign suddenly appeared proclaiming a multifold price-increase for the buffet. Any thoughts we may have had of changing restaurants were discarded quickly since hunger pangs trumped concerns over deflating bank accounts as we, alongside serious eaters and other professionals, dove onto heaps of meatloaf and roast beef. Luckily after spending considerable time feeding on the vast variety of dishes, one eventually manages to grow a thick-enough coat of blubber as protection against the bone-chilling, air-conditioned cold permeating the casinos.

Finally, after a few more nights of fending off scores of middle-aged "Keno-girls" and busting one more blister, punching

Poker machines, we were finally ready to pack up and head back home for another drive through sand and sun.

But why am I telling you this and complaining? Perhaps I ain't nuthin' but a hound-dog cryin' all the time.

TRY NOT TO FLY ON A FULL STOMACH

Sitting in a plane on my recent trip to Europe I was just chewing over the fact that I had, indeed, foolishly indulged in too many of the Old World's culinary treasures when the stewardess approached me. I had barely squeezed myself into a seat at the back of one of those smaller-type airplanes called "City Hoppers" when she asked me, very brusquely, if I could move towards the front on the *other side* because it would "balance out the aircraft better." I know it would probably have been a greater insult if I had been required to move from port to starboard on an ocean-liner because of the captain's fears that the giant ship might keel over due to my padded waist, but this came pretty close.

Is it my fault that I'm addicted to smoked sausages and bacon, dumplings, sauces, chocolate, cookies, cakes and pies, ale and beer and all sorts of other delicious calorie-laden delicacies? To be honest, I had pampered and coddled myself during my stay in Germany to the point of becoming extremely cuddly; perhaps some malicious people might call it fleshy, stout, hefty, tubby or chubby. But shouldn't the airline industry be aware that people do eat these things and shouldn't they prepare for it by building tougher aircraft engines and more sturdy planes, able to hold up a few people who cheated on their New Year's resolutions?

Digging my fingernails into the armrest I was now completely petrified that we would spin out of control and crash into one of the farms below, instantly turning a healthy herd of cattle into sausages and burgers. I almost grabbed one of the stewardesses to hold on for dear life, someone who, I'm happy to report was anything but scrawny, but was actually quite healthy-looking herself. To tell the truth, this fact causes me now to suspect that, very selfishly, the City-Hopper cabin crew demands that its passengers be skinny so that they can afford bulky staff without having to worry about obstructing hopping ability—why should *they* be the ones always to suffer, foregoing holiday poultry, rich sauces and scrumptious deserts, the thinking probably goes.

I was supported in my assumption that the crew had probably been carried away by the holiday spirit and was now suffering because of it, because what happened next was a bit unexpected. In my experience, the usual practice after takeoff on the short one-hour flight between Hanover (Germany) and London was that the pursers tossed a tiny bag, usually containing exactly half a dozen peanuts, in front of you and then supplied you with a beverage of your choice. The drinks were served in plastic cups and were quickly snatched away from you after a few sips because soon after you receive them it is already time to land again. But that never seemed to matter because they were free of charge. On this trip however, after I ordered a simple cup of coffee the stewardess continued to hover over me. Her continental accent blending in with the noisy engine confused me and I was unable to make out what she wanted from me, causing me to assume that, sensing my severe food-withdrawal symptoms, she just wanted me to have a sandwich (a complete altruistic, selfless, humane gesture).

Little did I know that sky-personnel have turned from friendly, concerned folks trained to spoil passengers, into money-hungry predators, as I was required to surrender a substantial amount of colorful Euros to pay for my very small cup of coffee. Soon after I had searched through my pockets to hand over the correct change, there was an announcement that it was time to land, and my coffee and goodies were snatched away from me without mercy.

I guess they wanted to give me an opportunity to own up to my New Year's resolution to drop a few pounds from the Old World.

TEN DAYS IN EUROPE

Resigning ourselves to the hassles of the long, tedious ten-hour flight to Europe, my wife and I plunked our apprehensive rears into our seats on the airplane. To our dismay the aircraft was so jam-packed that, conceivably, even timid sardines (the kind accustomed to being squeezed tightly into tin cans) might have objected vociferously. My wife, usually kind and unobtrusive, had immediately elbowed me out of the way to get to the window seat while I was struggling to shove the hand-luggage into the overhead compartment—a rough reintroduction to the brutal, dog-eat-dog world of airline travel. I was reminded of unsettling tales about normal, everyday folks turning into voracious beasts, ripping arms out of the sockets of fellow travelers just to get to the sparse peanut bags, casually tossed in front of them by complacent flight personnel, which by the way contain—I counted and recounted them—exactly *six* peanuts (I stopped counting finally because I suddenly sensed burning, ravenous eyes all around me). Soon I realized why I had received the sharp-elbow treatment from my wife, my mate who supposedly is linked to me by virtue of the soul and mind, but apparently makes a distinction when it comes to the body—the seat next to me was still empty. Nobody easily volunteers to sit next to another, possibly disagreeable body, unless it was somebody like me—supposedly my body would embody the physical ability to withstand the close proximity of anybody's body.

The remaining stragglers slowly filed in and I was left to guess who my seatmate for the next eternity might turn out to be. An attractive, young woman showed up. She definitely was someone I wouldn't have minded rubbing elbows with, although it might have earned me another elbow coming from the other side. But she unfortunately passed by. Another candidate was a smart-looking young fellow, who seemed like an intelligent conversation companion while presenting himself at the same time as a sturdy tag-team partner in the rough-and-tumble battle for peanut snacks. But no, it turned out to be a shuffling, profusely sweating, heavyset chap, languishing in the last stages of middle age, accompanied by an equally perspiring wife, as well as a moist smoker's cough. The presumably longsuffering wife, who very wisely must have demanded a sizable space between herself and her life's partner, seated herself across the aisle, while her husband rammed his elbow into my ribs as he worked himself into the chair next to me.

Well, I thought, as soon as he ordered a bottle of wine about half an hour into the flight, more than likely he is a borderline alcoholic who will soon be coaxed into deep slumber by the peaceful cumulous clouds outside the window. Unfortunately, the higher we soared, the friendlier the skies became for him, a perfect atmosphere to let me in on the ups and downs of his life story, which spanned several centuries. Fueled by more wine and an apparent speech impediment that permitted pronunciation of certain consonants, like "f" and "s" only if accompanied by liters of moisture, he complained about his "fffive wifffesss", which included the one across the aisle who was almost "deafff." Well, good for her, I thought and tried to play dead. But of course he was on to my ploy immediately as he demonstrated his skill in bringing back the departed by hovering over me and pointing at the blue sky outside. "Ssso niccce, that sssky!" he marveled. In desperation I attempted to address his spouse, reminding her of her wifely duties that should have included keeping her husband occupied. But of course, she was almost "deafff."

My wife, who had no idea of the dire straits I was finding myself in above the Atlantic Ocean, slept like a baby. As I ordered something more potent than wine I looked resignedly at the "niccce sssky", which now seemed completely without a hint of moisture.

DAY ONE—LONDON, ENGLAND

There are several brands of taxis roaming the streets of London, England. One is the kind you see in British movies and TV shows. It's black and operated by surly cabbies with Cockney accents who usually reach back through their open windows to open the door for people like Judy Dench and Geoffrey Palmer in British TV series like *As Time Goes By* without ever leaving their seats. Although romantic and fitting the London scenery, I was warned ahead of time to avoid the London "black cab" at all costs because (as I suspect) the meter is turned on as soon as the driver even suspects a hint of your intention to use his services. Other types of cabs which I became familiar with during my recent visit to London ranged in all kinds of makes and colors, the choice of which I suspect probably depends on the driver's taste or maybe even his wife's, rather than a cab company's. On my first day in England, as we raced through the streets in a multi-colored cab, it felt as though we were sitting in a friend's private vehicle (most probably because that was what it was—someone using his own car to make some extra money). Except that anyone charging us an arm and a leg for short rides like that cabbie was, would not have remained a friend for long, I can tell you that. Besides, sarcastic remarks about the incredible mess inside the vehicle would have prompted any friend to refuse to take me anywhere in the first place (Good thing I don't have any ambition to offer my car for taxi services).

The important difference between the black, boxy-looking taxis and the other ones which are expensive as well, is that not only are you able to negotiate a firm price to your destination beforehand with the multi-coloreds, but the driver also offers to carry your suitcases in and out of his trunk. This is an important advantage for a tired American traveler, especially if you travel with someone like my wife who must have inherited the genes of Louis XIV, a traveler who refused to budge without bringing along the entire Court packed in suitcases. The driver of the black box, on the other hand, just uses your battles with bags as a cheap source of entertainment, probably reporting your foibles to fellow cabbies later over a few lagers and raucous laughter at the local pub, as he passively watches your every move with bemusement from his driver's seat without moving a muscle.

You can also opt, as we did initially, to get from the Heathrow Airport to the Paddington area (downtown London), for a speedy train, a short 15-minute ride costing just a fraction of a taxi fare. Or you could take the subway, called the Underground in England, saving a fortune, but spend an eternity meandering slowly from station to station amongst the strange natives of London. This might not be so bad if you're rested and have time and an idea about the logistics of traveling in this immense city. But arriving after a bone-tiring ten-hour flight, which in retrospect, may have facilitated hallucinations about sudden wealth, we subsequently settled on a taxi to take us to our hotel, a decision costing us more than 50 pounds. That's *pounds*, not dollars! Head this advice, as soon as you hit the ground at the airport in England—multiply everything by two. So if you're thinking fifty bucks for a ride is quite steep but maybe you could swing it, think again. It's a hundred smackers! People speak English over there, maybe causing you to be lured into thinking that everything is pretty much the same as over here, except perhaps for so many people talking with a lisp or sounding like James Bond. Don't be fooled, especially if you have a leaky memory and may perhaps forget to double prices in your mind. In that case it might be a very good idea to win the lottery first before venturing back to the Old Country.

THE IRISH ARE GREAT FUN

After spending three days in England, and enduring seemingly endless rain, my wife and I decided to take an overnight trip to Ireland. Dublin was just an hour away by plane. Right in Dublin City Center, around O'Connell Street across from the famous General Post Office is an incredible landmark called The *Dublin Spire*. It's about 120 meters, or about 390 feet high, silvery and shiny and looks like a gargantuan sewing needle, reaching way out into the sky. What's the meaning of this, I wondered after arriving. Maybe Ireland expects an invasion of green giants needing holes in their socks repaired? Our hotel was located just about half a block from the Spire. And, although the locals tell you not to worry about the fact that the thing sways back and forth in the wind, I lay awake all night anxious that any minute we would be turned into gigantic shish kabobs, which, of course, could be offered as an appeasing snack to any potentially ill-tempered giant visitors. But that's the way Dubliners are, kind and always worried about the well-being of important guests.

Contrast this to the haughty, big-city attitude of Londoners that we experienced just the day before. Previously, before arriving in Dublin, my wife and I had decided to try out a restaurant in London's Paddington area. Because of jetlag, a condition that produces delirium and the tendency to crash head first into the bowl of soup while attempting to fend off fatigue and hallucinations, we missed the universal time period commonly assigned for lunch. Naturally we assumed after stepping in, that the place might already have closed, especially since it was completely devoid of guests. Our tentative inquiry about the state of business was met with an impatient, disdainful motion towards a notice saying, "open." With a sneer the proprietor added, "Why do you think we have such a sign displayed at the door?" Well, we were hungry, felt sheepish and swallowed our pride, as well as, subsequently, the meal of tasty Indian dishes, which did include some sheep and actually turned out to be quite edible. Fortunately for the owner I didn't experience any of those blackouts leading to a violent facial contact with soup dishes at this point. At least in Dublin the waiters appeared to be pleased to have us spend some time and our money in their facilities (even though it must have meant cutting into their important period of catching up on gossip with each other).

Since we're talking about money, it is important to note that Ireland and England *are* different countries and so instead of pounds, in Ireland you're pounded by Euros, which actually look dangerously just like multicolored play-money. They come completely without any of the stern-faced monarchs printed on the bills warning you to spend it wisely and you therefore might be tempted to throw the money around the way you would buying up hotels at Park Street in a Monopoly game. But if I could buy a hotel in Dublin I would be tempted to at least change one item—the water delivery system commonly known as faucets. Maybe it makes sense for Dublin hotel proprietors that, since hot and cold water are delivered in separate pipes to the rooms, they therefore must be discharged from different faucets also. But I believe that we in the 21st Century have come a long way from assuming that hot and cold water cannot be mixed. They can! With this surprising technology we can now enjoy soothing, comfortable water temperatures, instead of being shocked by icy liquids or being scorched by piping hot water. Or maybe I just missed a peculiar sense of humor only known to the Irish, because when I called the front desk of my hotel to complain that there was no water coming out of the faucets initially, I was advised that all I had to do was turn the handle all the way up and wait. I'm sure experienced Dubliners naturally assume that no one would be foolish enough to leave tender hands underneath faucets designated for scorching hot water. Funny people, these Irish—always joking and cutting up.

HOW FRUSTRATING CAN A HOTEL ROOM BE?

What is the most frustrating incident you have ever encountered? Well, you've topped me if it involves hanging upside down from a tree staring directly into snapping jaws of gigantic, hungry crocodiles while listening to the suspicious sound of a breaking tree branch. I admit that this kind of experience might be a bit more anxiety-provoking than mine which was: sitting in a hotel room, the one I paid top dollar for, in the freezing cold while frantically trying to coax the thermostat to move a few digits upwards! You might even agree that my experience comes pretty close to yours, especially after I pounded on the thermostat until it registered 95 degrees but nothing but ice-cold air whooshed out of the metallic grid (which was highly mislabeled as a "heating vent"). What was even more annoying was listening to the equally ice-cold, patronizing voice from the front desk after I called them, lecturing me about the significance of certain arrows on said thermostat.

Second-guessing my sanity and intelligence, I ventured back to the contraption on the wall going over the procedure again and again, assuming that I, perhaps, had missed something. But soon (around the time frostbite was beginning to turn a few extremities into a bluish color), I picked up the phone again and dialed "zero" with my still functioning index finger. It is amazing how the mere emotion of anger is able to heat up the human body enough to survive a bit longer, at least long enough for the brain to conjure up a stream of invectives to direct at the hapless person hiding behind the number "0." Lucky for my wife and I, this time the operator at the other end, trained to sense the minutest of discomforts in hotel patrons, promised to send someone to investigate the situation.

A knock on the door finally cut a seemingly endless wait in the arctic winter room short. Two awkwardly grinning gentlemen entered and immediately rushed to the wall to inspect the faulty thermostat. After conferring with each other in hushed tones, their pleasant demeanor changed into the serious miens of surgeons before a heart-transplant. First there was confusion as to which direction we wanted the temperature to go. Apparently one of the guys, a heavyset fellow, who seemed to have hauled himself and his very heavy tool-belt up several flights of stairs instead of taking the elevator, was under the impression that our room needed to be *cooled down*. Since he seemed completely confused, face flushed with perspiration, his companion, utilizing both hands, motioned towards the ceiling to make him understand that the residents of the room were encased in a thin sheet of ice.

After removal of a wall panel, a nonstop session of hammering, probing with screwdrivers and earnest swearing and muttering which lasted deep into the night, a sheepish, "It should work now", finally ripped me out of my nightmare of being chased by polar bears. At once I rushed towards the wall, running my hand over the vent, testing the crew's workmanship before they had a chance to disappear into the darkness. Concerned about the pained, beleaguered expressions on their tired faces, I conceded that—yes—it did almost feel as if there was a bit of lukewarm air now seeping through the metal grid. Of course, as soon as they departed the tepid current turned into a howling polar wind.

Why am I telling you this tale? Naturally I am concerned about you and only retell it for your benefit, in case you should find yourself in a similar situation. A bit of advice—take your time and be sure to fill yourself up on the free breakfast buffet the management, racked by guilt, offers you the next day. Make sure you feed yourself until a nice, thick sheath of blubber covers your entire body. You will need it for protection because the next room they offer you, after you've complained again, will be placed in the same artic vicinity as the last one.

A FEW LESSONS TO BE LEARNED ABOUT HIGH-PRICED HOTELS

Just ask anyone how he or she would envision a life of luxury and, aside from the villas, fancy cars and yachts, "residing in posh hotels" will always be part of it. So, recently, due to hardly any effort on my part, I was bequeathed with the honor of becoming a privileged resident in one of the most luxurious hotels in the world (well actually, in simpler words, someone won a prize and handed it to me because he couldn't collect on it himself), and my wife and I ended up shacked up in some "fancy pad."

Tired of being condemned to the bargain basements of life, I figured a bit of opulence might be just the right antidote against the fatigue that run-of-the-mill mediocrity has to offer. Hobnobbing with the upper crust and indulging in a life of luxury was just what I needed to charge up the batteries.

My wife did put her foot down though on my fantasy of sprawling leisurely on expensive furniture, clad in a tuxedo while puffing on a fat cigar and making slight swirling motions with a glass of expensive brandy in hand. And she started having convulsions when I began to stiffen my upper lip, looking down my nose at her in my best David Niven impression (or perhaps Sean Connery in the service of his Queen, as agent "Double-o-seven"). I had wondered in the past how a public servant on a government employee salary could afford to lounge in the casinos of Monaco, lavishing rolls of gambling chips worth thousands on beautiful, malicious double agents in slinky dresses. But now I don't care anymore how *007* did it. Who knows, perhaps he too won a prize? But this was the life I yearned for myself and I'm sure, given the chance, I too can squander enormous funds on extravagances with the best of them.

My first lesson, which I learnt quickly enough as soon as I pulled up in front of the luxury hotel, was that as a "man of stature" you cannot be trusted to squeeze your own car inside the white lines at a hotel parking garage. Immediately upon arrival an entire squad of uniformed men descended upon me, demanding my car. The first time I ever heard the term "valet parking" it sounded like "ballet parking" and I always imagined unshaved goons in pink tutus gingerly tiptoeing towards guests scaring people into surrendering their car keys. At a posh hotel, you quickly realize that you have no choice in the matter and that you are <u>required</u> to add the equivalent of several standard motel bills to your tab (and also include a tip for measure) for the privilege of housing your motor vehicle overnight.

Entering the ornamental reception area of the hotel, I was in for another disappointing surprise. There was not one dinner-jacketed aristocrat to be seen anywhere. No one was swirling and sniffing overpriced beverages and the slinky, elegant ladies must have "slinked off" somewhere else. All I saw were normal looking people, sweating day-trippers, lined up and being hustled by hungry-looking reception staff who appeared to be begging them to stay additional nights because the hotel appeared close to vacancy. It seemed the "upper crust" had completely disappeared—or maybe famished tourists had gobbled "it" up? Perhaps the program of distinguishing upper breeding from the lower kind had been abandoned in favor of treating everyone alike? How was I now supposed to hobnob with them if they were indistinguishable from the Bermuda shorts-clad common folk? The effort of practicing my high society English accent and casually clasping an extravagant nicotine-dispensing device in between two dainty fingers would now surely go to waste!

Then I checked in and learnt yet another painful lesson—the only difference between normal hotel rooms (where you can get free Internet service) and the high-priced room is that Internet service in your fancy room usually costs the equivalent of an entire normal hotel room rate. In addition to that my high-priced room looked exactly like any ordinary hotel room, the only difference being that now someone had carefully tied a pretty little bow around the toilet paper roll. But I suspect the scheme to give ordinary rooms to ordinary guests was to keep the riffraff away from consorting with nobles who, I'm quite certain, are quarantined in exclusive, exquisite superior suites somewhere within the vicinity, and I intend to find out where exactly.

All I need is someone to bankroll my obvious need to squander enormous funds on excessive extravagances.

THE PERILS OF FLYING

Aerodynamic laws demand that airline passengers be packed in as tightly as sardines without the benefit of oil, which—unlike people trapped on planes—enable the lucky fish to move around a bit. Supposedly even the narrowest of spaces between travelers must be closed airtight or the plane risks a fiery crash from the unfriendly skies. That is why there is absolutely no oxygen available on planes. One is advised to pump a sufficient amount of oxygen into one's lungs before each trip or face trying to retrieve it from the bubbles of stale beer that is served irregularly and usually only after being able to demonstrate a need for it—like the certainty of death by thirst.

Of course these aerodynamic laws only pertain to the Tourist Class. First Class passengers are exempt from any and all discomfort deriving from lack of space, a fact I discovered during my recent trip abroad. As a matter of fact during that trip rumors were abound that these privileged First Class passengers frolicked freely through the halls, holding classes in ballroom dancing. Naturally I was unable to verify this since any attempt at catching a glimpse by peering through the forbidden entrance of "First Class" was matched by the menacing glares of the flight personnel. Apparently the staff is trained to display friendly smiles, which automatically turn into snarls if any attempt is made by mere mortals to substantiate gossip of vast differences between First Class and Tourist Class, as for example that there is actually edible food to be found amongst the privileged.

It seemed that the food handed to me on several occasions might have been of the same substance it was served on—cardboard. Come to think of it, that is actually a pretty clever idea, since it may well save the airliner an incredible amount of money and bother. The manufacturer of the food-containers may actually have supplied our dinner—it had a somewhat chunky consistency that could have been either fish or chicken. I opted for the "cardboard chicken", reasoning that fish are not made for hurling through the air and might not blend well as we hit the various air-pockets that seem to spot the skies in abundance.

The very bumpy ride and whispers of "air-pockets" kept me awake. What exactly are "air-pockets"? They must be filled with something, more than likely—air. If they are filled with air, why then are they unable to sustain the plane? Are they made of a different kind of air, a substandard one perhaps, unable to carry anything above the weight of birds? It seems that these flying critters are never bothered by "bumpy rides." But maybe these "pockets" are really tiny "black holes", the kind that suck in any and all things, including complete star-systems, even light, and of course airplanes filled with people without access to classes in ballroom dancing. I desperately tried to sleep my way through several romantic comedies on my eleven-hour flight around the globe. The romantic comedy of fellow passengers seemed much more entertaining than anything displayed on the movie screen.

Once hitting ground overseas, I came to regret my reluctance to use my idle time on the plane to sleep because a substantial amount of my life was slashed off—since our part of the globe is seriously lagging behind in the path of the sun. This phenomenon causes Americans to be, on the average, six to nine hours younger than the average European, resulting, of course, in much younger, healthier-looking teeth.

Aging nine hours was enormously taxing on my system and I spent my entire visit to Germany sleep-walking and drowsy, unable to cope with the enormous, sudden jump towards retirement age. That is why on my return trip to San Francisco I seemed better able to manage the hazards of air-travel, ignoring the bad food and inability to move, and contemplating instead signing up with classes in ballroom dancing, designed to limber up aging bones.

HOW EQUAL ARE WE IN THE AIR?

You would think with all the talk about social equality and the fact that we are supposed to be a thriving democracy, that there should not be any evidence of class divisions anywhere. Well, that might be true on the *ground,* but be aware, as soon as you step across the threshold of an airplane you'll enter the tyrannical world of a caste system.

I understand that captains of ships have historically been granted quasi-autocratic powers. They even have the authority to marry people. But just imagine the eternally long voyages of the past with tight, crammed quarters, and the idea of wedding bliss seems less attractive. Maybe that's why there were so many mutinies. Since divorces were not in fashion then, the captains, facing retribution, were forced to walk the plank at the point of the sword. Come to think of it, the cool, soothing ocean waves might have been better than having to listen to spats and squabbles of newlyweds all day long for months on end. But make no mistake, absent such a mutiny, the captain was in complete charge and had absolute power, something he was not shy to demonstrate by liberally making use of his infamous *cat-o-nine-tails.*

It makes sense that in the even smaller, compact spaces of an airplane such an enforcement instrument might not be as practical because there is absolutely no place to swing a cat. But I can imagine that airplane engineers are laboring right this minute, to redesign this tool, perhaps cutting down on the number of tails so it might work better.

Venturing on another eleven-hour flight to Europe the other day, tired and crammed, trying desperately to get some sleep I was drifting in and out of nightmares. Hunching down on an aisle seat, unsettling flashes of disturbing dreams made me imagine I was Charlton Heston in Ben Hur, chained to an oar as a galley slave. Instinctively I braced myself as I heard the footsteps of pursuers behind me, expecting any minute to taste the sharp end of the whip. And then I woke up, and as I looked around the airplane, I realized that even though none of us were being beaten (at least no one in my range of vision), the conditions in our "Tourist Class" seating hardly seemed an improvement over those in Ben Hur's time. I didn't see any living things wiggling in the slop the stewardesses tossed in front of us but then, very few creatures could survive in the clumps of ice that was so quaintly called "dinner." I suppose the reason none of us developed scurvy was because the trip was just too short.

Then while suffering the ravages of "Tourist Class," I learned that there exists a complete other world, a different universe in fact, one filled with privileges and advantages none of us could even dream of—the Nirvana of *First Class*! Usually no one of our kind is permitted near this forbidden place. But on a short flight between cities on a small airplane, there it was: I was situated smack-dab right behind a few rows of seats designated to First Class.

The difference was startling. While one single perspiring stewardess was laboring serving the thirty or so rows behind me, tossing a few peanuts around, two radiantly smiling, cheerful members of the airline staff happily offered a bounty of desirable and exotic goodies to the privileged class, most of who behaved quite grumpily, in my opinion.

Every once in a while, one of the pretty ladies almost ventured into my vicinity, although taking great pains never to make eye contact or completely cross over into the slum area. I could almost taste the gourmet snacks of Brie, caviar and other epicurean delights, whiffing past me, as I opened my mouth, hoping desperately for a morsel that just might trickle down. But the glaring sting of the most disparaging look I had ever received taught me to adhere to the parameters of my particular caste.

At least I didn't have to taste the cat-o-nine-tails.

THE ULTIMATE SOUTHWESTERN ROAD TRIP

My wife and I recently decided on the ultimate road trip through the Southwest, from San Francisco, passing through Southern California, through Nevada, and Arizona, culminating in Santa Fe, New Mexico, and back to San Francisco. During our trip, we decided to stop in Laughlin, a Nevada gambling town, right across the river from Bullhead City in Arizona. I learned that this particular spot has a reputation for really heating up in the summer. As a matter of fact, according to local lore, it gets so hot that even the devil shuns this place, preferring the much cooler region "down below." Consequently one could argue that without the presence of the "Evil One" no sin is committed while gambling. But don't listen to me. I'm neither an attorney nor a clergyman capable of correctly interpreting any document on such matters. Therefore you're on your own, especially while tracking down that special someone in charge of gambling success, someone called Lady Luck.

I'm not much of a gambler, myself. To tell the truth, I can never remember what exactly a royal flush is (which I suspect is so named because such a hand would make your face enormously flushed, shining beet-red through your pokerfaced mask—a dead giveaway). And I have no idea if or when it is proper to hit the dealer with a Blackjack. Or perhaps it is the other way around, the dealer is supposed to hit you, beating the "you-know-what" out of you at the "you-know-what" tables. Well, they're truly really and officially called "crap tables." But I want to be polite here, since I know I'm talking to a mixed crowd, which, hopefully, is not as mixed up as I am when it comes to risking money in a casino. My puzzlement in terms of casino games might give you an idea that my gambling largely depends on beginner's luck, a period, come to think of it, that actually spans quite a number of years now.

Coming from the tree-hugger, environmentally conscientious, smoke-free State of California, the nicotine-drenched atmosphere of a Laughlin casino floor is not easy to take. You might as well, along with your money, throw your heart and lungs at the roulette wheel also. Only the tough survive in that kind of place. And by the looks of the hollow-eyed, cigarette-puffing, hard-drinking survivors who were endlessly stuffing bills into the machines in robot-like fashion, it must have been a very tough battle indeed.

Since my wife's eyes were tearing, stinging from the smoke, we decided to take a walk on the boardwalk by the river. Early in the season, the evening stroll turned out to be very pleasant and soothingly warm. You can also take a river taxi, where you can ride in a boat from one end of the casino row to the other for less money than you could lose sitting in front of a slot machine in the same amount of time.

If you tire from the crap tables and decide to hit the buffet tables, make sure you don't carry any kind of bag because you'll become an immediate suspect in the crime of bringing your own food into the restaurant. Bewildered by Laughlin logic, why anyone would feel it necessary to bring food to an all-you-can-eat place, I confessed that my plastic bag consisted of nothing more than a rattlesnake refrigerator magnet I had bought at the gift store. I was released after promising that I would not remove any foodstuff from the buffet, except the kind found within the confines of my own body. After the ritual of stuffing ourselves to the rim, the eagle eye of the hostess immediately spotted an apple in the hands of a customer behind us as we exited the buffet. She had planned to take the apple to her room in order to wash it before consummation. The steaming-hot food police person furiously snatched it from her hands, reminded her that she had broken her promise to keep the buffet at the buffet tables, and took the apple back to its rightful place, within a basket of stale apples and oranges in a corner.

Fearing a new range of unusual rules, or a posse of an enraged Laughlin townsfolk, we left early next morning, heading for the Grand Canyon, a four hour drive.

JOURNEYING THROUGH THE SOUTHWEST—NEW MEXICO

After New York and Los Angeles, Santa Fe is supposed to be the third biggest art market in the country. I had no idea. There are over 200 art galleries and my wife and I must have visited each and every one of them during the few days we stayed there. At least it seemed that way each night after collapsing into bed, bone-tired, and foot-lame. We stayed at the Hilton hotel, around the corner from the downtown plaza. This is a dazzling square of old authentic adobe-style buildings, a place where the Navahos customarily spread out their beautifully crafted jewelry and ceramics on the sidewalk on one side of the square, underneath the block-long veranda of a historic structure, offering items to visitors like us who want to buy just about everything.

Your buying bone is assaulted on two fronts, first by the charming little old grandma, who matter-of-factly explains her skillfully crafted artwork without the customary pushy urgency of artisans experienced elsewhere, or the bold twinkle in the eyes of a talented craftsman on one hand, and the irresistible appeal of the astounding artistry and craftsmanship on the other. How can anyone resist? I had to physically drag my wife away from these alluring siren calls, or risk losing our nest egg and facing the bleak subsequent end result of poverty and despondency. Well of course, in this case we could turn around and sell our newly acquired pieces of Navaho art, but then again, I might just prefer to go to the poorhouse (which, I hope, will be located around the Santa Fe area).

If you ever contemplated becoming an artist at all, the visit to Santa Fe's enthralling artistic environment will force you to quit your hotshot law career, or your current work selling Silicon widgets and thingamajigs, and cause you to pick up pens and brushes instead to begin painting day and night. Needless to say you will eventually end up in the same poorhouse as me. But who cares if you can be an artist in New Mexico, an addiction similar to the one that turns ordinary accountants and paralegals into beach bums in Hawaii and various Caribbean islands.

Another hub of great Southwestern art is also found in Taos, a small town located an hour north of Santa Fe. This is an enchanting place that has attracted many famous painters, from Georgia O'Keefe, to Native American artist R.C. Gorman, to live and create there. But what was even more interesting to me than the town itself was the pueblo a couple of miles up the road. It is a hauntingly beautiful ancient terra cotta structure of several linked apartment-like dwellings that, astonishingly, has been occupied continuously since the mid-1300s by the Taos people.

I've lived in some ancient apartment buildings in my time and even though they usually featured leaking faucets and peeling paintjobs, none of them could boast any historic value at all. Maybe one of the reasons was that they weren't built to last more than 60 years, compared to the over 600 years of the pueblo in Taos. Aside from that, although I do remember strange noises in the night (something I now acknowledge was due to lackadaisical interpretations of building codes, or inebriated neighbors, instead of mysterious spirits), none of those buildings I lived in would have spurred the imagination of scores of artists, poets, and writers, like the enchantingly alluring and amazing Taos pueblo.

Intoxicated by the enchantment of art and beauty in New Mexico we were completely aware that we needed an antidote, or we would never leave. We decided that the gaudiness, flashy flamboyance, and fake reality of a replica existence that Las Vegas promised would be exactly what the doctor ordered, and that's where we headed next.

PAYING FOR YOUR VACATION

Somewhere it is written that any place deemed desirable by any more than an average number of people, means that the cost of just about everything automatically shoots through the roof. So, while a cup of coffee might still be affordable in a gloomy, desolate place like Novosibirsk, Siberia, in a nice warm vacation spot favored by more than a few resilient creatures you just may need to take on a second mortgage in order to supply yourself with your usual strong jolt of caffeine. Fortunately there are an untold number of businesses around that specialize in refinancing your home and bombarding you with offers from all sides, and those businesses might also be willing and ready to loan you the funds. My advice is—grab it at once if you qualify. You just may need that coffee, to be alert enough to make the plane out of your vacation spot on time (and perhaps the "loan sharks" might even be willing to waive some fees if you look desperate enough).

Also while on vacation, watching the family frolic on the beach and surf, be aware of the second rule of thumb—the closer the proximity of your hotel to seawater and sand, the more you can kiss the college tuition for your kids goodbye. For some reason excessive moisture and extra surplus of silicon deposits is murder on your savings account. Add a few cut-above-average rays of sunshine and you will find yourself selling your prized Elvis record collection in order to raise a few more dollars to pay for your holiday extravaganza.

The reason for my jaded view of vacation experiences is my recent holiday spree to just such a cherished vacation spot. My wife took a few days off work, and there we were! No sooner had we arrived, than I discovered a third rule of thumb—if you should entertain the idea of going out to eat, the higher the nostrils of waiters, positioned in relation to the ground, the greater the need to have a frank discussion with your family about the trials and tribulations of bondage and slavery. If you enter into a restaurant, and find yourself staring straight at nose-hair of snooty eatery employees, you might just turn over your firstborn immediately, without making too much of a ruckus. Chances are you won't make it past the soup without sacrificing at least some of your flesh and blood.

My wife and I entered into such a place while coming off a walk at the beach. Naively trusting a sign telling us we were entering a "bakery" and looking forward to a lunch snack of, perhaps, a sandwich and a coke, we were immediately surrounded by a gang clad in tuxedos. After a tight escort to a table in a corner another penguin-like waiter appeared, carefully cradling a bottle of wine. Right away I appraised the cost of this beverage to approximate the equivalent of the GNP of a smaller country and sheepishly declined.

Now here again is yet another rule of thumb—if the menu requires frantically digging into the part of your brain that conjures up images of your high school French teacher and forces you to make sounds engaging untrained nasal passages to order your meals, run as fast as you can. You have entered a French restaurant. A French restaurant at a beach resort, frankly, has a license to steal. Automatically the portions shrink to infant size while the prices of the dishes multiply. Perhaps the establishment is doing you a favor if you still feel hunger pangs after finishing your meal. Get used to it. You will need to train yourself to get by with less, in order to pay for that "dining experience" for many years to come.

But, on the other hand, there are always other alternatives if you want to save a few bucks on your vacation. I'm sure there are some spots available in places like the aforementioned Siberia. Or perhaps there are some choice areas obtainable even close to you, especially if you don't mind a few nuisances like the close immediacy of a busy freeway or a few wrecking yards. Nevertheless, at all times, keep an eye open for the positions of nostrils on snooty waiters.

CHAPTER THREE

It's My Birthday Again, No More Candles Please

"Don't worry Mr. Johnson. It's all in your head."

DON'T COUNT THE CANDLES
ON MY BIRTHDAY CAKE

A very important day passed almost unnoticed—The National Columnists Day, which according to my calendar was slated for Wednesday, June 18th—although it is actually supposed to be on April 18th, commemorating the death of famed war correspondent Ernie Pyle in 1945. But my calendar states otherwise, and that's what I go by, because if you can't believe your calendar, what or who else can you believe? It is a custom to take out secretaries on Secretaries Day, so it stands to reason that the same fate awaits a columnist.

Just in case tens of millions of readers are lining the streets ready to take me out to lunch, I skipped town as a precaution. My wife has put me on a diet, and ten million lunches would surpass my calorie allowance by quite a bit. I didn't have the heart to tell her though that I might have overstated my readership just a tad. This reminds me of the time when I told my 80 year-old mother in Germany that I had become a columnist. Her reaction was one of utter disappointment, as she recounted the times when we fled the regime in East Germany. It took me a while to understand what she meant.

"No, Mom—not a communist, I'm a columnist," I said, finally comprehending that she had misheard me. They're all the same—muckrakers and troublemakers—all of them, seemed to be her response. That's what happens if you just move a couple of letters around in a word—misunderstandings, mix-ups, and confusion. Bedlam, wars break out and mothers won't call you on your birthday. That's why as a columnist and as a calendar maker it's important to watch your p's and q's, as well as your m's and l's.

Since we're on the subject, I wonder whether I should trust my calendar on another date—my birthday, which happens to occur around this time also. Maybe that's all a mistake too, but what it would mean though is more lunches and more candles on a cake. To tell you the truth, being faced with the enormous amount of candles on my birthday cake nowadays, I could start a project like molding the entire Empire State Building from wax—it might keep me busy until my next birthday. It may well be a lot of fun but would also burn up the pages in the calendar in a hurry, racing me to that ominous next date in no time at all.

So maybe that is not such a good idea, besides it would be an enormous waste of material, put to better use for millions of candlelight dinners or lunches on Columnist Day. All this concern about waste of material and manpower has also made me wary of the new supercomputer at Los Alamos National Laboratory which I heard about recently. I have no doubt that it was constructed for the purpose of calculating my age, since no one in the history of mankind has ever been able to count that far. Its codename is "Roadrunner" and it is supposed to reach "petaflop" speed, which means 1,000 trillion calculations per second. Good luck counting, Roadrunner. I, myself, only make it to 39 usually and then I have to start all over again. But then I was never really good at math. Perhaps I was always better with words, being able to describe a problem by encircling it with a wall of dense and clever sounding words, so impenetrable that the dilemma seems impossible to solve, at least with the current unsophisticated technological means available. All I have to do is put it on the calendar for a later, more appropriate time to deal with. But since I can't trust my calendar too, who knows when I'll get to it . . . maybe the next year, maybe the following.

Do you smell something burning? Is it the Roadrunner? Did he finally give up counting too?

ONE BIRTHDAY TOO MANY

It is with relentless regularity that *that certain day* which is supposed to be a very personal, special one (celebrating the event featuring a complete stranger slapping you on the rear the moment you saw daylight for the very first time), keeps recurring with ever-increasing frequency. You barely have time to wipe off the last sticky remnants of your birthday cake when someone, teeth gleaming and face beaming, slaps you on your back (sometimes so hard that your head starts to swim), booming, "Happy Birthday" all over again. At least that is what it seems like to a person who has reached the age when one stops wishing to be older because—by jolly—that elusive goal has finally been reached (the reason why seasoned old-timers warn you to be careful what you wish for, because you might just get it).

For some reason, starting with that first painful experience of medical professionals causing harm to your gluteus maximus, slapping has become part of our birthday ritual. Many a youngster has experienced a painful "slap in the face" with the stark realization that he or she would be receiving nice warm underwear instead of the live pony desired for that special birthday. And in many circles you are required on your birthday to submit to your mates gleefully hauling off and introducing your rump to excruciating trauma for each year you have whiled on earth. This rite tends to find less favor after a certain number of years, not only because serious injury might occur to your backside but because it seems everyone recognizes that getting older is punishment enough.

Still, as the years go by, you may opt to continue the practice of "slapping" with ever-increasing vehemence, mostly by your own hand and aimed at your forehead when you realize that instead of getting that advanced degree, getting in shape or experiencing the pinnacles that life has to offer, you have mostly spent the years on your rear in that nice comfortable sofa, watching re-runs on television and not out there with the *in-crowd* as you had envisioned. It is at this point that one last slap to the frontal lobes activates a curious behavior in many middle-aged people, causing them to purchase red sports cars, tummy-tucks and ill-fitting hairpieces.

Looking into the mirror I noticed an angry mark right above my brows recently myself. Celebrating another birthday, I have entered my *late earlies*—or is it, horror oh horror, my *early lates* already? (Whops—there is another one to the old noggin, this time from my wife whenever my wandering eye focuses on a brightly colored motor vehicle, featuring sparse seating arrangements) How could I have possibly passed so many years without really being cognizant of them? Wasn't it just some recent Tuesday when I counted a mere dozen or two candles on the cake, instead of this gigantic forest of wax I seem to be facing now? Afraid that it might contribute to global warming, I quickly tried to extinguish the *enormous* flames, using up all available oxygen within the vicinity (I might have killed off acres of plant life, pushing us over the edge after all—sorry). Barring said or any other kind of disaster, it seems that we might be around for more of the same for some time to come. Since I do eat my broccoli and I exercise my right to say "maybe" to exercise every once in a while, I just might add a few more candles to that narrow space on top of that birthday cake also.

Or, wait a minute, maybe it's all just a bad dream and I'm really just in my *early earlies* after all . . . I need to wake up, someone please slap me!

DINNER & DANCING

My wife decided that for her birthday, we would go "dinner and dancing." But as I have discovered, there are several reasons to abstain from dancing. One of them is the inability to move your limbs in alignment to a rhythmic beat, which although reoccurring in regular intervals tends to catch many a participant totally unprepared. This in turn leads to certain sudden, awkward movements that may bring about massive embarrassment and ridicule to the person involved as well as his dance partner. The other reasons to abstain from dancing lie in the possibility of imprisonment and certain death!

The seeds for such possible carnage for me were characteristically planted hours before, during dinner in a fancy restaurant. Only in my case it wasn't seeds, it was snails. Snails, typically, are garden pests that most reasonable people try to either squash or poison as soon as they detect them. No one would actually ever think of picking one up and using it as a snack. But things change dramatically when the little critters are placed on a plate in an extravagant restaurant, a location where waiters are compelled to talk by forcing sounds through their nasal passages. This procedure is called "speaking French", and for some reason the government issues licenses to establishments demonstrating such abilities in order to permit them then to charge exorbitant prices for creepy-crawlies soaked in oil.

It seems absolutely imperative for every "fancy restaurant" to have their tables in close proximity to each other. As a matter of fact, the closer you come to sitting on some stranger's lap (someone you've never met before and don't care to meet in the future), the more valued the place is as a very, *very* fancy place indeed. In such places, eating utensils and dishes remain the sole property of the establishment throughout your dining experience, a fact the waiters are not shy to remind you of by constantly reshuffling your dining gear after you've just arranged it for comfort. At one time I was tempted to prevent a waiter from disrupting my fancy table arrangement yet again by attaching his hand to the table with a fork! Fortunately for the waiter, I had no idea which fork to use, since I had no intention of causing a faux pas by mistakenly stabbing him with the utensil used for salad instead of meat. Just thinking of it, this interlude might have earned me "seven to ten" in the pen for aggravated assault, as I was extremely aggravated indeed.

But all aggravation paled in comparison to my discomfort after receiving the bill. Snails (or "escargot" as they are called in fancy restaurants), cheesy, stringy soup, and a member of a fish variety, should not cost the equivalent of a down payment on a medium-sized island! An island that I could very well have turned into a snail-haven, making me completely "snail-independent" as I would raise the little slugs myself. And naturally *my* snails would be the free-range kind, as happy snails make for happy dining experiences—that's my opinion.

But moving from slow-moving snails to salsa dancing after dinner takes quite a step, one which it seems, my wife was able to take quite easily. Salsa is a dance that, for some reason requires that you display an expression of enormous disdain. You must look as if you viewed everyone with tremendous contempt, lower than an earthbound slug. At the same time you have to be able to move your feet speedier than a chicken pursued by a French chef armed with razor-sharp cutlery, someone in search for an alternative to slow moving critters.

Taking into account my recent dining experience, looking at everyone with disgust wasn't all that hard. But mercifully soon after my display of dancing dexterity virtually unknown on this planet, my wife, fearing twisted limbs, cardiac arrest or arrest for being a public nuisance, suggested we call it a day.

BUYING A PRESENT FOR "AUNT MARY"

What exactly is a "Salad Shooter"? Is it actually some sort of device that shoots at salad and wants it dead for some reason? Or is it advertised as a weapon instead, using salad as ammunition? Or is it in fact some kind of vegetable assassin that blasts back at you once you dare to approach the salad bowl with a fork? And is it covered by the Second Amendment?

These questions were shooting through my head because the sounds of holiday music permeating the stores these days coerced me to the bread-maker section of the shelves, passing the above-mentioned potentially lethal instrument in the world of salad-making. Just like Pavlov's dog which salivated at the ring of a bell, it seems we are conditioned to drop any item we meant to buy for ourselves and head immediately to the gizmo department of the stores to start on a long list of items for individuals we hardly know, as soon as we hear the first chime in "Jingle Bells." At once, engaging my failing memory, I clicked through a variety of names trying to find someone who might be a candidate for this Salad Shooter. Presumably it might seem perfect for a vegetarian, but perhaps one should be cautious if he or she has issues dealing with anger.

A huge variety of doodads and gizmos—from sandwich toasters to items that warm and light up your toilet seat—are now available for us to choose from (the last article, for example, might prove extremely useful for both vegetarians as well as meat-eaters). The vast majority of these items are created for people desperately trying to find one more gift for individuals like Uncle Harry, about two hours before he places himself under the mistletoe, lips puckered, for his annual smooch on the lips from his favorite female in-laws.

Aunt Mary, as we know, does not discriminate and deals out hearty, wet kisses to nieces as well as nephews. As a matter of fact, in her case, she does not even require an excuse such as mistletoe but rather chases terrified children down the hallways, her giant bright-red lips pursed and ready to smack anyone she can catch. That is why we have carefully selected her candleholder weeks or even months before this frightening moment, ready to thrust it at her before she has a chance to seize us in her clutches, even though we are now six feet tall and could easily wrestle her to the ground.

But now there is an entire industry in existence, specializing in ideas for gifts as a substitute for the obligatory tie or bottle of Schnapps (a bottle of booze, though, is always a good alternate, should something like a salad-shooter backfire). Also the doohickey business spends a lot of energy and expense to make the item look good on pictures on the package because it is an open secret that most of the time the thing won't even be taken out of the box.

According to the annual gift-exchange ritual, Uncle Harry will fiercely rip the wrapping off his present, lift the box up to his eyes, shake it and demand to know where the heck his bottle of liquor is. Aunt Mary will quiet him down quickly by threatening to reveal his secret—that his gruff demeanor is all show and that he actually completely wore out last year's gift, his baby-animal house-slippers. Then she will point at the picture on the package and indicate that such an "electric nail-file buffing system" would do wonders to improve his rough and battered fingernails. After some more haggling and complaining but full of enthusiasm and eggnog, everyone then will venture to the table and try out the new "electric knives and forks" on some hapless holiday poultry.

At the risk of creating violent images at the fest of peace, I have another suitable idea for gizmo-gifts. Since the salad-shooter appears to be made to cause havoc to vegetation, perhaps we can use it to shoot down the mistletoe before Uncle Harry has a chance to plant himself underneath it.

BUYING YOUR CHRISTMAS GIFT

An unappreciated gift was returned to me with such a force at one time that I actually had to duck, watching it land with a thud against the wall behind me. Escaping injury by a hair, the realization hit home that I had not been endowed with the "gift of giving", or at least with a clear sense of what someone might want for Christmas. I've since forgotten what the gift was that created this rage in my former girlfriend but she accused me of not knowing her and not finding out what she was all about. I think I may have given her a book—what was wrong with that?

As I learned the hard way, it apparently is not enough to take time out of your busy day, parting with a substantial part of your net-worth to buy a gift, but it is also required that you spend considerable effort in getting to *know* the person and empathize with his or her likes, dislikes and needs. Uncle Al should not need to worry about how to react upon receiving a coupon for ballet lessons, for example. We all know that he would have opted for a toolset instead had he been given the opportunity to express his wishes.

Maybe that is the crux of the problem in buying gifts for adults. Children have no problem noting their requests on long lists addressed to the kindly, portly fellow up on the North Pole. But since, as grownups, we don't believe in Santa Claus anymore we automatically forfeit our right to express, in longhand, what we *really* desire for Christmas. Besides, only in a fairytale will the wish of a shiny red Mercedes, accompanied by a curvy blond chauffeur be granted. In real life we must settle for a sturdy pair of warm underwear instead.

Many people are notoriously hard to buy gifts for even those we have known intimately throughout life—our parents, for example. We are usually more familiar with their dislikes, than their likes. My mother, for example, did not like my siblings and I to wear our shoes inside the house, dirtying her well-scrubbed floors. As a matter of fact, she absolutely hated it. That was why we pitched in as children and bought her a nice, robust mop. But apparently our father seemed to know her much better, since her eyes lit up brighter than the Christmas tree when he handed her a beautiful gold watch. This was very different from her reaction to our present. After gushing approval initially, she almost immediately began to complain that we should not have spent all of our pocket-money on an expensive cleaning tool. But she did not seem to have the same reservation about father's gift, perhaps assuming he had help from Santa Claus?

Usually we don't have access to Santa's help as adults and have to scrounge up funds great enough to purchase gifts for everyone, as well as our ability to gauge their wants and needs.

But are men less sensitive to individual needs than women? It is difficult to imagine that not everyone feels the same affection for things as we do.

Here are some hints gathered from painfully gained experience for buying Christmas gifts. It is pretty much safe to assume that your spouse is diametrically opposed to whatever you imagine to be the fulfillment of life. For example if you like sports, meaning a bunch of guys immersed in sweaty, muddy competition—think perfume. Should guzzling suds and eating fried chicken around a bar with your buddies be your cup of tea, you'd better think of financing a romantic vacation for two, sipping fine wines and sampling morsels of Brie. If heavy iron strikes your fancy, in the form of wrenches and screwdrivers or using same to hit golf-balls, you might want to think of precious metals instead—gold, silver and diamonds are always safe. Because of the enormous cost involved, no one would think of buying a tire-iron-sized bracelet, making these items definitely lighter in weight and only heavier on your wallet. But the advantage gained in case of rejection is tremendous. They don't make quite such a thud against the wall, after you've ducked to avoid them.

CHAPTER FOUR

Health and Fitness at the Right Time

Rather than physically exhausting himself, Ralph found it prudent to work on a healthy self-image.

SUMMER MAY NOT BRING A SLIMMER NEWER YOU

The bright yellowness in the blueness of the sky signals each year that sooner or later the excessive thickness around your waist cannot be explained away as bunched-up heavy winter clothes for too much longer. The tire-like shape wrapping around your middle torso, which you wisely constructed during the winter months just in case of a nationwide outbreak of famine, will now be visible to anyone interested in ridiculing you. Of course, unbeknownst to you, no one will care one way or the other because most people will be occupied with trying to hide their own imperfections from you. As summer begins, men will try sucking in their stomachs, drawing them as close to the spine as possible until they faint or collapse for lack of air, while women line up to buy oversized muumuus.

Certainly, as TV commercials inform you, no one needs to suffer. All you have to do is drink enough "Beer-Lite" and you can look as svelte as any of these underage high school athletes who pretend to drink it, as they frolic on beaches and prance around in night clubs. And then there is the billion-dollar diet industry offering to lend a hand. For a portly sum of money, the equivalence of multiple dinners, you are provided with a lunch menu of perhaps three leafs of lettuce, three baby carrots and three baby tomatoes (almost all the vegetables seem to come in infant sizes; an idea the fast-food industry has not had a chance to visit yet). But you soon recognize that this kind of food is only suitable for eating if you were provided with the bovine ability to chew cud. Therefore in order to eliminate spending precious time on a hillside, staring into space while chewing previously digested greens, you will be forced to cover the entire plate with thick, calorie-rich, tasty blue-cheese or ranch dressing. To satisfy your body's cravings for required building blocks, like protein, found in other foodstuffs you will need to ingest truckloads of this kind of fare. This will cause your body to blow up to the shape of a large weather balloon and still leave your body and soul yearning for sorely needed diet essentials, which you will attempt to still by quickly diving into the pie-store and helping yourself to large pieces of cheesecake with chocolate toppings.

By now summer has arrived, your fainting spells (caused by your reluctance to breath normally in order to prevent your protruding midsection from interfering with normal human intercourse) have come to the attention of the authorities at work, and muumuus are frowned upon even on "casual day." The date of the company picnic is looming. You are aware that large desks, capable of hiding your sizable girth are unavailable at this site, instead you might be required to jump up and down at a volleyball game or be made to sit in a "dunk-tank", skimpily attired and exposed to ridicule and fastballs by *backstabbing coworkers*. The absolute terror of this image will force you to go out and at once, purchase a treadmill. Since the salesperson has you convinced that greater investment into the bells and whistles of the most up-to-date electronic equipment will pretty much eliminate the need for your own physical participation, you shell out the equivalent of a small army tank. The soreness that follows the attempt at daily training will turn the treadmill into a convenient depository for a collection of size-increasing muumuus after about a week or so. This action will cause extreme depression, only to be alleviated by digesting more cheesecake and gallons of strawberry ice-cream.

The date of the picnic will come and go and will only be hazily remembered as a day of bellying up to people with oversized muumuus, while drinking excessive amounts of "Beer-Lite" and digesting enormous hotdogs and ice-cream.

Again another year will come to an end and you will repeat the same process over next year with the only exception being that you now start with the handicap of having increased several sizes in the meantime.

FABULOUS ABS

Paramount amongst all the pressing concerns that we should be worried about these days—wars, billion-dollar bailouts, the trillion-dollar deficit, the failing economy, mortgage crisis, looming unemployment etc.—what ranks highest? The worry about "fab abs", of course! At least that was what I was led to believe, as I was browsing through a bookstore recently. Making my way across the store, I bellied up to a section called, "Magazines, America Loves." Curious about the love interests of my fellow citizens I looked it over and a flashy magazine popped into my view, one called "Abs, The Guide" or something like it. Judging by the title of this periodical I initially had to assume that there must be people out there who have trouble finding their midsection and need a map to guide them to the exact location. I would have thought that most people do as I do in the mornings after waking up—yawn while simultaneously scratching their bellies? So what is the problem? That's where it is, folks!

Hang around for a moment, instead of "Abs, The Guide", let *me* be your guide. Abs are found in the same general area that serves as the depository for all kinds of things, like cheesecake, pizza and beer, for example. To give you another hint; it frequently features, depending on the individual of course, a more or less substantial bump. You see, it's easy to locate, so no need to buy a magazine and fool around with having to beef up on charts and graphs. If you still have a problem finding your abs, just stand in front of a mirror and locate the area that hurts the most, which is where the belt is cutting into you like a wire because you're thinking you're still sporting that svelte, lithe high school physique.

One wonders why locating this area is so important that publishers see a chance for a profit-making magazine, and unless it features a different belly each month, I don't see how portraying the same abdominal vicinity can arouse any interest time after time. Even different tummies each time must become boring, see one belly—seen them all, I figure. They are usually round, smooth with a bellybutton in the middle. That's all. No need to shell out five bucks.

But of course I didn't figure on what else can be done with a belly. It can be changed from a merely round and smooth one, maybe with a few soft bumps, into a solid, rock-hard wall. This stomach of yours, now called the "abdominal section" or "abs" for short, can be turned into a rippled washboard or six-pack-look in no time at all. All you have to do is buy the magazine. Soon after purchase you will be able to prance around, parading your stomach in front of all kinds of people who may or may not be interested in the show.

In times long past a man's worth was often gathered by the size of his girth; the ampler his abdominals, the greater his standing in society, although standing next to someone of sizable belt-size was not always a good idea. Individuals of significant dimensions, although able to push their weight around, many times knocked over expensive china. Maybe that's why, nowadays, abominable abdominals, the kind protruding outwards, are on their way out and deemed unacceptable—who could afford to replace pricey tableware all the time?

A better belly would be one with abdominal muscles the size of bridge cables running across your body. And that's where the magazine comes in. It hands you a set of exhaustingly strenuous exercises that you must repeat ad nauseum, until you're nauseous. You might want to try it because if nothing else, it does take your mind off things like wars, billion-dollar bailouts, the trillion-dollar deficit, the failing economy, mortgage crisis, looming unemployment etc.

CAN WE NOW BLAME OUR BUDDIES
FOR MAKING US FAT?

For once there finally is some good news—at least for folks falling short in the battle against that pesky padding around the waist. Now you can blame your *friends* for that unfriendly tire around your midsection.

I knew that would make you happy. I'm ecstatic myself! According to a recent study published in the *New England Journal of Medicine* (and who in their right mind would doubt such a study) obesity is actually socially contagious. Lucky you—now instead of merely giving your buddy next door the "evil eye" for bugging you about returning his barbecue tools, you have a very good reason to also give him a piece of your mind for making you fat. How dare he! Were you not sleek and slim when you moved into his neighborhood? Now look at yourself. Finally you have proof—it's all his fault.

So who can we blame for our weight issues? In my case, the most paradoxical thing happens when I check myself out. I find myself looking perfectly fit and trim when I look into the mirror. But all hell breaks loose as soon as I step on the scales because the numbers don't correspond with the reflection in the mirror. I've now come to the conclusion that it must be all the heavy, iron-rich air I suck in, trying to pull in my stomach each time I look at myself.

Naturally your friends will use the ironclad facts from the New England study to try to turn things around and blame *you* for the fact that they have jumped a dozen sizes since knowing you. They might even send you a bill itemizing exorbitant expenses for ever-increasing costs in tent-like clothing. But you didn't hold a gun to their heads making them inhale super-size pizzas, large beers and high calorie drinks, did you?

Can we now actually blame each other for ballooning up? Maybe the cause is some kind of "fat virus", as some suggest;

a bug that is passed from one skinny person to the next, which, instead of swelling up your sinuses, enjoys working mostly on your midsection and thighs. But I doubt that theory, mostly because it might actually let your friends off the hook. It is much more convenient pointing a finger at your easy to spot, heavyset friends, instead of looking for tiny, indiscernible germs.

You might as well blame the jumbo squid, multiple sizes bigger than our domestic species (that recently invaded California from the South) for your weight issues. Maybe observing this obese beast splashing around the waters in Monterey garnered some fatty tissue around our waists as well? After all, it would save us a fortune in floatation devices. But don't think this squid invasion is all peaches and cream. Who knows, as soon as our tiny domestic squid starts palling around with this fatso, from what we know now, sooner or later they'll increase to gigantic sizes as well. Very quickly they will run out of food and then watch what will happen! Will they attack us? Remember the movie *Jaws*? That would be a picnic compared to what will happen to beachgoers if events happen that way, and it will definitely be a picnic for giant squids feasting on slow moving, portly swimmers. And when they run out of party food, they might even emerge from the waters and invade our towns and cities, coming after you and me (although I expect that the afternoon gridlock may slow them down a little).

Well, what lesson can we glean from this? As for me, I know I have to cut down on high-calorie midnight snacks, avoid my overweight friends, and refrain from watching B-rated horror movies.

FIGHTING THE HOLIDAY FAT

I recently discovered an article, which named "eight foods that fight fat." Fantastic, I thought, just in time for the holidays! Naturally it immediately conjured up images of brave chickens in mortal combat with overstuffed turkeys or heavily armed, knife-wielding produce goring outgunned slices of pizza.

Facing the stark possibility of inflating girth-sizes during this time of more than plenty, we would definitely need something on our side—loyal foodstuff, valiant and courageous enough to "fight the good fight" for us. 'Let's get it on,' I thought. I can definitely imagine myself ready for warfare in food fare with the help of maybe some tough-looking turnips, menacing mushrooms or burly barley. I trust that is actually all it would take—send these brave soldiers into battle, as they so nobly and selflessly make the ultimate sacrifice so that we can continue to stuff ourselves with scrumptious holiday feasts.

But of course, nothing is so easy as someone doing you a favor like dying for you in battle, while you sit fat and happy and do nothing. Supposedly, there are eight foods that fight fat, but the problem is that you actually have to eat them! And the battle doesn't take place on your front yard, it happens inside your body and it's not a pretty sight, let me tell you. What are the eight foods? Almonds, berries, cinnamon, mustard, oranges, soybeans, sweet potatoes and, of all things, Swiss cheese—not exactly the tough gang I was expecting. I had hoped for hardened warriors capable of doing some real damage, a bloody rare steak, perhaps, or at least a half-pounder burger. But no, we're left with wimpy, scrawny scraps of soybeans, sweet potatoes, cinnamon etc.

And how is this supposed to work? We are told that, for example, calcium-rich foods like Swiss cheese reduce fat-producing enzymes, or turmeric, the spice that gives mustard its color, may slow the growth of fat tissue. Well, okay, after stuffing myself with Thanksgiving turkey-stuffing, buttery drumsticks, mashed potatoes, a mighty slice of cheesecake or two, maybe I now shove down an industrial-sized bowl of mustard to get rid of the fat built-up, right? Not so fast! It apparently takes time. You don't eat almonds by the pound, for instance, you *nibble* on a few, or sprinkle them over some salad. Or, instead of munching down a gigantic chunk of Swiss cheese, you put an occasional thin slice on your "lean chicken sandwich."

How disappointing is that? Doesn't that remind you of that strange contraption in your bedroom, that you assumed would turn you into a muscle-rippling hunk after looking at it for a week or so (remember that machine that now provides a convenient clothes hanger for your next-day wardrobe)? You actually have to follow the program for days on end, maybe even years. Instead of gorging yourself on this stuff you have to use it *sparingly*, in addition to cutting down on fattening foods beforehand.

Holy cow—no more meat? What happens to that buttery turkey you ate on Thanksgiving? Where did it go? More than likely it will show up on your belly and thighs tomorrow, unless you used some precautions. What we need to do is go the extra step and show who's boss. I have an idea; maybe we can wear some menacing t-shirts that display terrifying images of these fierce fat fighters. Pictures of bad-dude berries or sadistic soybeans should do the trick. Just like security warning signs on your front yard, these depictions showing them cutting down flab in nothing flat, just might cause the same to shrink in horror and help reduce it to nothing but cowed babbling puddles of blubber.

I think that strategy could go a long way towards preventing any larceny-minded lard from entering your body in the first place.

ONE DAY AT THE GYM

Just walk into any bookstore in search of something to spark your interest—like a barbeque cookbook—and your path will invariably be obstructed by an impenetrable wall of literature claiming to show you how to pack on mountains of heft on one part of your body while losing it on another. Whereas in the past a substantial girth-size was the sign of wealth and good living, this feature is frowned upon today, and such individuals are sometimes reviled by scores of the "young and buffed", riled up by the latest "fitness books."

Gleaming faces with perfect teeth, hair and glistening muscle-bound, bare bodies on the covers of these fitness magazines will cause you to pick them up to determine why your "glutes, trapezius" and "abdominals" need so much improvement. Besides gathering trivia previously only of interest to professionals in the field of medicine, you are now beset with a sudden compulsion. Why shouldn't *you* be able to unbutton your shirt and reveal a bronzed set of steely strings of muscle in your midsection? The only requirement is—something usually omitted—you have to be between 18 and 25 years of age, lift several tons of weight for up to six hours a day and ingest chemicals originally intended for racehorses. Ignoring your own concerns that a workout schedule of such proportions would cut into your timetable for getting rich by investing in that real estate, or interfere with the strides you have made following instructions in "winning through intimidation" or improving your vocabulary, you make the decision to finally get the body *you always wanted but were afraid to ask for.*

At once you join a fitness club where youngish, cheerful instructors inform you that no one has ever managed to get into shape without first purchasing several sets of the club's fitness garb and jars of dubious white, powdery substance called "supplements", aside from paying for additional lessons. But more than likely, after a week or two of instructors barking at you daily to do one more "rep", you are so sore that you labor just to make it onto the scales at the end of the day. Then you realize that instead of losing, you have actually gained several pounds. Immediately various unemployed lawyers gather around you, offering to represent you in a lucrative lawsuit, while the gym proprietors swear that the weight you gained consists of nothing but solid muscle. Quite sheepishly they explain, in addition to hoisting tons of dumbbells, you must now also do aerobics (which is an innocent sounding term for painful, sweat-drenched hours of feet-pounding on an endless conveyor belt, while at the same time being exposed to equally painful Jerry Springer re-runs).

It is at this point that you begin to watch "exciting" commercials on television at home, featuring aliens who seem perfectly bronzed and sculptured, while working on fitness machines that lack the cumbersome heavy weights but instead are equipped with seemingly easy to manage strings and cables, and then you opt to give *them* a try. Compared with the endless hours of sweating at the gym, the promise of working out for only twenty minutes a week on a machine costing just "twenty-nine ninety-five" a month, in order to attain the body of a Greek god, seems like a bargain. The weeks following the delivery of said instrument are taken up with constructing the machine from scratch, taking you away from your previous workout schedule. This, of course, means that the fitness gains achieved during your time in the gym will be completely lost when you are ready to begin on your new contraption.

Soon you realize that this machine, taking up sizable space in your bedroom, could also be utilized as an apparatus for hanging up next day's wardrobe. In no time at all this function will surpass its original intent. Therefore next time you spend time in the bookstore you will steer clear of the "fitness-books" section and finally purchase that barbeque cookbook you had entered the establishment for in the first place.

HOW MUCH SLEEP DO WE NEED?

Just how many hours are we required to sleep at night? With the possible exception of sharks which need to move constantly so as not to sink to the bottom, most living creatures do require a certain amount of *sleep*. It would be quite a scandal in the shark community I expect, if it became known that one of them drowned because it was snoozing on the job. That is why image-conscious shark families continue to drive each other on—swimming continuously most of the time, night and day.

One can only imagine the incredible amount of caloric intake necessary to maintain the vigorous physical condition of this gigantic ravenous predator! I wonder what all the fuss is about developing potent shark repellents. Next time you venture into shark infested waters it might be a good idea to take along one or two super-sized bottles of your industrial-strength sleeping pills and then, very inconspicuously, let them have a glimpse of the objectionable drug every once in a while. Knowing that they can ill afford to take any time off for sleep, the beasts will naturally avoid you (and while you're doing this, it might also be prudent to place your calorie-rich physique inside a steel cage, just in case the sharks are not familiar with sleeping pill commercials).

Aside from the sharks, the only other living thing that I'm aware of that goes without sleep—is my wife. While I definitely need my 6 to 8 hours of sleep (mostly leaning towards the 8-hour period), as recommended by very alert sleep experts, my wife always seems to be awake. Something usually happens to wake me up at two or three in the wee hours of the night and—voila—I find her reading a novel. More than likely it's something like Tolstoy's War and Peace, a gigantic tome of a book, which she might inadvertently have dropped on my head, while plowing through the exiting parts that contain descriptions of war. My advice that she should concentrate more on the "peace" sections, hoping that more soothing pages might put her to sleep, goes largely unheard. As I frantically look for headache medicine and then immediately drop off again, she roams throughout the house for the rest of the night like a ghost, haunting the visitors of a medieval castle in a B-rated horror movie.

Then in the morning, looking completely refreshed, she goes to work. There she continuous to read, not novels but briefs, which to my surprise have nothing to do with underwear labels but are rather legal papers filled with a foreign language called lawyerese. I continue to go on with my daily routine as well, which mostly involves activities like bumping into walls due to lack of sleep. Lucky for someone like me, another potent drug is available to keep me from dozing off right after getting out of bed, and this comes in the form of a hot black liquid called coffee. My wife doesn't drink coffee because, she says, it keeps her awake all night. Oh really?

Maybe for me it works the other way around because quite often coffee doesn't seem to do its job of keeping me alert *during the day*. I can usually tell that coffee was sleeping on duty again when I suddenly perk up in front of my laptop and realize that I have written multiple pages. But the screen is filled with an incomprehensible language—page after page full of inexplicable letters like "tyutyut." At first I assumed it was a mysterious code—perhaps extraterrestrial beings were trying to contact me? Or ghosts, haunting my house, were trying to tell me to get the hell out because they have trouble sleeping, with me tossing and turning all night? Unfortunately I usually realize that the letters signify nothing otherworldly but instead indicate the exact spot where my nose hit the keyboard when I dropped off.

Perhaps I should take a page from sharks and go for a midnight swim, an activity which would result in a ravenous appetite. Then, unable to sleep on a full stomach I could, along with my wife, haunt our haunts all night and maybe hunt down ghosts and extraterrestrials as fodder for my writing.

FINDING THE RIGHT WAY TO DIET

Sometimes your mind plays tricks on you. As for example, when you're on a diet and your mind tells you that chocolate cake is healthy nutritious food and good for you. It sometimes even goes through elaborate schemes of providing proof especially when you read that scientists have determined in recent studies that chocolate is definitely *crucial* to human survival. Or perhaps your mind convinces you that, for example, beer is "liquid bread" and has all the ingredients necessary to sustain a person throughout the day. Should certain essentials still be missing, it reasons with ironclad logic, they could always be added by ordering appropriate toppings on one or more extra-large pizzas.

That's your treacherous mind for you. Why is it always sabotaging you when you try to do the right thing, staying on the straight and narrow? Well, it is because the mind does not have to negotiate the tight corners and narrow spaces a body is forced to do. Instead it just sits there and snipes at you with sarcastic remarks after you fall for its siren song and munch down an entire pizza by yourself. Never trust that treacherous mind, instead trust your wife to put you on a diet, as mine did some time ago.

There seems to be a law that once the lady of the house makes up her mind to go on a diet, everyone within the vicinity must automatically go on one too—even common household pets. As a matter of fact should there be any other critters like pests, bugs or vermin lurking in dark corners, depending on leftovers and garbage for survival, they would be advised to leave the premises at once. There won't be one morsel of fodder available anywhere in the entire house! How could there be if each crumb of food, from then on, has a number assigned to it, called a "calorie-count"? At the end of the day the ultimate tally of those numbers will be recorded, which will determine if you have stuck to the new household program. Therefore to make things easier for you and to cut down on temptations and cheating, any foodstuff not essential for immediate survival must immediately be removed from the grounds. And in my case, no creature would be foolish enough to attempt to wrest even the tiniest piece of precious calorie-laden ration from me, since it would find itself in a *fight to the death*.

This also spells the end for that game-playing trickster mind of mine, at least concerning the subject of nourishment. Because, since each and every piece of matter that could be considered edible is dispensed with this calorie count, *no scam is possible*, especially if another, less gullible mind is watching over your own (as for example my wife's ironhanded, unbending one). You will not cross over the line of that specific calorie count that has been determined for you, no matter how lightheaded you become. And staggering through the streets doubled over by severe pangs of hunger will get you nothing but unbelieving ridicule because it is prominently written in one of your wife's diet-guru books that the human body can do without food for weeks. So why should anyone feel sorry for you if you black out? Instead you are required to go out into nature and not "worry so much about eating" but instead *breathe in* the healthy air—who needs food when there is so much oxygen around?

That is probably why you see so many guys today walking around with their mouths wide open. They are not really interested in breathing fresh air—they must have been put on a diet by their wives. What I suspect is that they are hoping against hope they might benefit from some airliner flying above losing a few candy bars by mistake. But unfortunately many airlines have cut down on serving lunches recently, which means that each and every peanut or piece of candy will be jealously guarded and fought over violently by the passengers. So better shut your mouth and stay with the program. Maybe, if you're lucky your mind will play a trick this time, not on you, but on your wife and tell you where she has secretly stashed those cookies.

IT'S ROUGH AND TUMBLE
IN THE FAD-DIET WORLD

You are what you eat. But, turning it around, if you ate what you are, wouldn't that make you a suicidal cannibal? The way most people eat, it wouldn't be all that nutritious anyway. No matter how you feel about cannibalism, you would be better served eating a balanced diet of protein, carbohydrates, fruits and vegetables.

The only exceptions to this rule are high fashion models who get by with digesting cotton wool soaked in orange juice. At least that's what I read one time. I have no idea why anyone would do such a thing. Perhaps working in the competitive fashion industry with emphasis on the emaciated look for models, produces not just immense pangs of hunger, but also a dislike of passé *cotton* cardigans. For the rest of us a wholesome meal should be comprised of the abovementioned ingredients, sans garnishment with garments, of course. Just make sure, if you should ever invite such a model to dinner, to keep an eye on the napkins.

There are all kinds of diets being offered these days boasting to help you carve out a happy, contented life, free from a perceived dependence on candy and cookies (something you had foolishly assumed you needed for your continued existence). You may come across something called the Cavemen Diet. It is hailed as a way to lose weight, and at the same time it is supposed to make you get in touch with your natural, animalistic instincts, probably assuming that pure animal instincts prevent you from the ravages of junk food (more than likely they have never had their campsites raided by raccoons looking for potato chips). Here's how the Cavemen diet works: Like the Cro-Magnon man of yesteryear you're required to subsist on all the *berries, nuts and roots* you can gather, as well as various *game* you've speared, which naturally, you are expected to share with the clan. More than likely, following strict guidelines that life during the Paleolithic Period stipulated, with this diet you may also be assured to enjoy the life expectancy of a caveman, who made it to the ripe old age of *30*, if he was lucky.

Come to think of it, why the wooly mammoth became extinct has never been answered in a satisfactory fashion. Maybe a closer look at Paleolithic high fashion featuring rail-thin cave girls who might have shown off skimpy animal skins at moonlight may just provide the missing link to the question. Although oranges must have been a rarity during the Ice Age there was enough wool for aspiring fashion models to live on, at least for a while.

Another diet that was all the rage some years ago was a very High-Protein diet. The way I understand it, you could pretty much gorge yourself on steak and pork chops but no carbohydrates whatsoever. Cotton was optional. Not many folks were able to hold out without cookies, pasta or cupcakes for too long. I've heard stories of people who were driven to insanity with desire for pasta and baked goods. They would camp out all night at bakeries and spaghetti factories and in the morning you would find their teeth marks on doors and at corners of buildings. But that might just be an urban legend.

I can imagine though that cheaters would be mercilessly hunted down, ostracized and banned from dieters' society, to roam around aimlessly until some other weight-watching group took mercy on them and fed them some calorie-restricted, yet carbohydrate-based nourishment. Let me tell you, it's not exactly all peaches and cream in the diet-fad world. It makes me wonder if roving bands of Cavemen, No-Carb and other fad-diet gang members ever crossed each other's path at the Supermarket. Now that would be a sight to watch, where members of the Cavemen diet plan might just pick up some clubs and duke it out with the All-Protein folks armed with sides of ham in a battle over diet turf.

It's a rough and tough world out there. Be sure to get enough roughage, you may need it.

HOW MANY WAYS ARE THERE TO EXERCISE?

There are renowned writers, Ernest Hemingway, John Steinbeck, Saul Bellow, to name a few, who, due to their enormous literal accomplishments naturally deserve to be admired. Their command of language, ability to craft plots and characters, as well as ingenuity and originality in style is adored and revered by readers the world over. Although I have nothing but respect for such authors, the writers I'm in awe of the most these days are the folks who write for theme magazines, like exercise periodicals for example. There must be a dozen of such publications out there, reporting on ways and methods to keep in shape each and every month.

Now imagine you're one of those writers, encumbered with the problem of how to describe building up your biceps in each and every issue for instance, and yet remain novel and fresh. How many ways are there to exercise this particular muscle? In my opinion, there are only two. Grab a weight and lift it up, that's one way. The other involves movement in the opposite direction, meaning, since you've got the darn thing already lifted, you might as well lower it down again. After that, repeat said motions until you're ready to shred the magazine into tiny little pieces but are unable to do so, due to exhaustion. See, that took a mere couple of lines and the subject of a bulging biceps is pretty much deflated. Now how do you write about this topic next month without repeating the same information?

Some years ago there was a best-selling book about running. It contained hundreds of pages explaining the best way to accomplish this feat, something I had assumed everyone was able to achieve soon after the diaper stage without instruction manuals. I never read it, but now I'm curious about the author's method of approaching the subject and his ability to fill page after page with teaching his audience how to run. To be honest, I probably would be at a complete loss after a few words of encouragement, and telling the readers to go outside and propel themselves forward by placing one foot in front of the other. And after coaching the reader on how to put on a pair of pants and socks, which would probably barely cover half a page, I'd be totally stumped on how to proceed. More than likely, the remaining yawning empty space of the tome would be filled with sparse directions, such as "put your right foot in front of your left, then repeat." And to make sure everyone is on the same page, I would continue with "left—right, left—right . . ." right up until page 325, where I would end it by advising the reader to go home and take a shower. Naturally I'd be terrified of being sued by readers who might run headfirst into a tree because they were reading the instructions while running. Or they just might mix up the sequence of "left" and "right", fall down and, voila, I'd be dragged in front of a judge in this case as well.

There are other magazines on all kinds of topics, like "brides", for example. How much is there to say about brides? Buy a nice white dress, grab yourself a groom, go to a church, temple, or mosque, and get married already, for crying out loud—end of story! That pretty much sums it up, doesn't it? Look at all these periodicals and books about decorating, cooking, and dieting. Next to your dinner table, hang a pretty picture, cook yourself a nice pot of spaghetti with meatballs, but make sure you don't eat it all at once. That pretty much covers all three subjects, doesn't it? What else is there to write about?

I think those writers deserve a special Pulitzer Prize for having to bulk up and repeat the same things over and over, but making them look completely original, fresh and new.

WHEN NOT TO BIKE

It had been decreed in my household, as a result of decisions made during a family meeting (it must have been the one that I missed) that from now on we will ride bicycles. Our immediate family, consisting of exactly two members, my wife and myself, apparently came to the conclusion that riding a two-wheel transportation system, one solely powered by yours truly, would not only help keep the polar icecaps intact but would also go a long way to keeping me in shape. Although I understand that this decision was reached after "debating" the subject quite thoroughly, I remember none of it. My wife blames this on my falling off the bicycle without my helmet on, which caused a condition that managed to block out entire decades from my memory!

But, aside from my apparent memory problems, riding a bicycle is supposed to be "good for you." Of course it is. What could possibly be better than sitting on a tiny saddle, one hard as a rock (and actually much too narrow for even the rear end of a greyhound), and one that causes you to anticipate being cut in half vertically any time? And who would raise a silly argument, such as the fact that driving the car would be a much easier and efficient mode of transporting one's self to any desired destination?

For some reason this reminds me of the British gentleman who recently completed a trip around the world, entirely on his own physical power. He accomplished this adventure by pedaling a boat across oceans, walking and bicycling. It took him a "mere thirteen years," a feat that would have eaten up a day or two in airline travel time. But having experienced red-eye flights, long delays and sleeping on benches at airports myself, I don't blame him from taking the long way.

One could learn quite a lesson from the experience of finding one's self in traffic protected only by flashy, silly-looking tights and deeply breathing in the exact gases that cause the destruction of the aforementioned icecaps. I can assure you that after exposure to this breathtaking experience, in conjunction with very close calls with speeding driving machines made of very tough steel, you will develop an abject, never before experienced hatred for anything on four wheels. In my experience such a rare, violent emotion can possibly only be felt after the loss of your favorite team, perhaps at the Super Bowl while you're trying to make your way out of the parking lot.

I once was personally the target of such utter loathing as I drove my motorized vehicle on the streets of San Francisco. I don't even remember the 49ers losing at that point but a red-hot, mad rider pounded on the roof of my car, totally enraged to find me on the same streets as himself, a privileged bicycler.

Well, we recently had another family conference (this one I know for sure I consciously participated in), and the chief subject discussed at the meeting was again bicycling—actually it was more about the inability to cope with the challenges of this activity. It turns out that my wife had not ridden or even touched a bicycle in a couple of years. Since then, her experience with velocity on wheels had only been conducted with the gas-powered kind, and fortunately the builders of such vehicles have the foresight to install mechanisms capable of immediately terminating your movement, should you tire of driving around whether up or down a hill. Although bicycles do feature such a device as well, it is not immediately available to an inexperienced rider filled with panic while racing downwards. Lucky for my wife, during her only recent attempt at bicycling down a hill, my voice, raised several decibels above the noise of traffic coming up from where she was headed, instructed her that, instead of *pushing* the pedal, she should *pull* the handbrakes.

Afterwards, our meeting was adjourned with the conclusion that, since the rainy season was upon us anyway, we would postpone bicycling until next year.

HOW I MISSED OUT ON SMOKING

During my movie-going years as a youngster you never saw the heroes of the silver screen sweat. You would never catch them even taking off their tailored suit jackets, much less their shirts, as today's action heroes do. Although there was a lot of fighting going on, showing up at a brawl unfashionable and underdressed must have been an abhorrent idea in those days. It seemed to be a given that battle garb consisted of a tuxedo or, at the very least, a dinner jacket. Watching the action in front of me (just as I have to fight the urge nowadays to warn the teen in a horror movie not to open the door of the closet), I always wanted to tell a certain Mr. Bond to take off his expensive silk tie because one of the bad guys would finally get the idea of grabbing hold of the thing and strangling him with it.

Clad in his elegant attire, the suave hero's manicured, yet masculine hand clasped a glass filled with a mysterious drink, which for some vital reason he demanded to be shaken and—God forbid—not stirred. And then, of course, there was his ever-present cigarette, which he stylishly posed with, and cool practiced moves as he dragged on it throughout the movie in order to gain more energy for his next battle I was sure. Since none of us could afford an expensive suit as young teenagers and nobody knew exactly what was in that drink (especially since none of us had any inkling what was involved in shaking or stirring the concoction), the item which to us cut the image of a dashing figure was the cigarette.

Using up a substantial portion of our hard-earned wages from various part-time jobs, we finally assembled behind the woodshed for our first smoke fest. But much to our frustration we were unable to light even one cigarette because the wind blew out each match immediately. Fortunately an older kid passing by, much wiser in adult experiences and adept at the skillful moves of a cowboy right before the OK Corral shootout, shamed us into the clever smoking technique of tough outdoorsmen which involved shielding the flame with our hands, and we succeeded in lighting up our first nicotine-delivering device.

Of course, it always looks so much easier in the movies. Smoking did not seem to be connected with any such discomfort when viewed from afar. Our lungs, formerly only acquainted with standard countryside summer air, seemed upset when suddenly assaulted by burning weed and each one of us began a wild coughing and wheezing fit. But since we were cognizant of the fact that we were being judged by the much wiser, older peer, as well as potential admirers of the opposite sex, we suppressed any inclination we had of ridding ourselves of the foreign object attacking our breathing apparatus. Smoking seemed to foster an easy passage into the mysterious world of adulthood. Everyone took to it as easily as a whiff of smoke drifting upwards in a crowded barroom.

The only exception seemed to be me. I cursed myself for never learning to draw the smoke deeply into my lungs and breathe out quaint lazy circles, as anyone else seemed able to do. Each time I tried I collapsed into another bout of violent coughing, which earned me nothing but ridicule. Aided by my father's caveat that he would "shove, not one, but the entire pack of cigarettes down my throat" if he ever caught me smoking, I was finally convinced to give up on the entire experiment.

But look what I missed out on—cultured, debonair sophistication and stylish elegance, an image that one can only attain by puffing on skinny rolls of tobacco clad in white cigarette paper. Had I only continued, I just *know* I could also have learned how to look like a suave double agent, even though I would be busy now hauling the ubiquitous oxygen tank behind me.

THE FORMULA FOR PEACEFUL SLEEP

My dentist tells me that I grind my teeth at night. Apparently instead of drifting off into a nice refreshing dream, I feel a need to go to work pulverizing tooth enamel which is a complete waste of energy of course, unless I find a way to use this downtime at night in a constructive way to make some money, perhaps grinding grain into fleur? Who knows, maybe milling a couple of pounds each night might actually pay for my lunch the next day.

So what makes one single tooth destructive enough to grate its fellow tooth into a stub? Is it tooth envy? Do I need a tooth therapist? Or is it all my fault? I always assumed I treated all my molars equally, little did I realize that there was a struggle of domination going on inside my mouth, turning chopper against chopper and molars against incisors, in a "tooth for a tooth" battle. I can only hope this unruly behavior does not spread to other parts of my body. I can spare a tooth or two but just imagine an eye for an eye kind of clash.

Hearing my concerns, my dentist set me straight on that fact, telling me that I don't really have to worry so much about the individual parts of my body, but about my "entire self." Quite casually, he told me that, while some people get high blood pressure, some other folks simply grind their teeth, seemly for the same reason—anxiety. I had no idea.

So now not only am I anxious about the things that made me grind my teeth in the first place, but I'm also worried about the fact that I *am* grinding my teeth. *What a grind.* This worries me so much that I have trouble sleeping. Each time I start to drift away, I jerk up immediately, terrified that I will begin the assault of yet another innocent molar. And the lack of sleep makes me so tired that I bump into things while awake and at present I'm in danger of knocking out the precious few teeth I have left.

In a determined effort to solve this problem once and for all, I strove to find the cause of my anxiety. Why was I hell-bent on destroying my own—quite healthy—set of teeth? It seemed that in my dreams most nights I fought gigantic sea snakes and saltwater crocodiles on a regular basis (although I seem to do all the damage to my teeth myself). Then it just hit me. Now I think I know what it is I fight with all night—it's not sea snakes—it's that darn quilt! Of course, that makes sense! My wife and I have been caught up in an eternal struggle with that quilt, a nightlong tug-of-war ending up with the blankets and sheets becoming twisted around my neck. I'm finally able to see that maybe, I do not wade through the swamps of an Amazon jungle each night after all but I am instead resting in my nice comfortable bed. The giant monsters I heroically fight in my dreams are just harmless twisted-up sheets. And what I assumed to be vicious bites by piranhas were nothing more than a few spirited kicks by my wife, designed—quite mistakenly—to calm me down.

So what can I do to save my teeth? Should I finally get rid of that quilt, as well as any other irritants disturbing my sleep? And then what—have boring, peaceful dreams about docile sheep perhaps? I don't think so. Well, is there ever anything good on TV? Of course not, and since the daily humdrum is generating nothing but depression and gloominess, there is only one choice:

Looking forward to more exciting adventures with dentures.

DENTAL ACHES

"It's like pulling teeth." Everyone has heard that phrase before. It's usually employed when facing a difficult task, or getting your husband to paint the kitchen, for example. My dentist, Dr. Lawrence, tells me that the job of pulling a tooth is actually no big deal anymore. As a matter of fact, I did have a tooth pulled one time—a wisdom tooth. The wise elders in my family had always warned me to be suspicious of doctors wanting to pull a healthy tooth out, especially one considered most likely to be of above average intelligence.

Hold on to any and all the teeth you can, I was told by my Grandma. Later in life, during times of dental scarcity, you'll be sorry about that hasty decision that caused you to abandon one of your precious teeth, filling you with sentimental dental regrets.

I'm not sure if it was due to my dental professional's gentle persuasion at the time or the effect of Novocain but someone made it clear to me that, unless I had the darn thing taken out, I would face ridicule from contemporaries because of a crooked frontal tooth. As I painfully had to learn, wisdom teeth are completely misnamed, and not so wise after all. Quite the contrary, in fact, they're very foolish, as well as nasty and greedy, selfishly pushing their weight around and crowding out other already established choppers. Just like sibling stragglers who are born after everyone else is grown, they turn into spoiled show-offs demanding to be seen. And since they're facing a life in a dark corner, way in the back of the mouth, I suppose the only way to make their presence noticed is to push the other teeth around.

At least that's what I think my dental pro told me. It, again, could have been the Novocain talking too. But nevertheless, the tooth pulling didn't hurt a bit and only seemed to take a few seconds. Actually, the dentist didn't do much pulling. Instead it seemed as if he pushed it out with some type of dental tire iron. I never actually saw the tool; it could have been a bloodstained rapier, for all I know. I never asked for any details either. It might have shocked me out of my blissful drug-induced stupor, had I found out that the instrument had been used to jack up a car previously. So I carefully refrained from pushing too hard for too much information. What could I have asked anyway? "Thouwowthoulough" only makes sense, temporarily, to someone under the ravages of painkillers. I also didn't ask for the tooth back, as sadly, I no longer believe in the tooth fairy.

In my grandma's day, things were not quite as sophisticated. Instead of a fancy dentist's office, if you suffered from a toothache, you were placed in front of a door. Then a string was tied around the offending tooth and connected to the door handle. As you sat there, hoping for rescue by the tooth fairy, the door was either suddenly shut or opened—I can't remember which, but apparently utilization of the proper technique was of utmost importance. Just imagine what could happen in the wrong hands? Instead of pulling, someone might slam the door in your face. You might end up with more than just a tooth missing, and add a broken nose as well. So, remember, don't do this at home without appropriate supervision of a professional grandmother.

In those days if your grandma failed you, the next choice was to send you to a real expert in dentistry—a barber. Apparently the thinking was, someone who fixed appendages on top of your head and around the chin area had more than ample opportunity to figure out how things worked inside someone's mouth. In addition, access to a variety of sharpened tools was a plus. A blacksmith for example, accustomed to unrefined blunt tools wouldn't be much help executing delicate operations, although he might have been able to assist in the area of anesthetics.

So as summer approaches, keep flashing those choppers. Things could be worse.

CHAPTER FIVE

The Tree in My Backyard

THE TREE IN MY BACKYARD

I call the tree in front of my house *Ol' John*, and I never did trust that big old tree. Not only does it enjoy dropping its leaves on my lawn every fall, suffocating the grass, it also relishes powdering my car with a thick layer of pollen every spring. Ol' John should have known that I have no intention of growing a forest on the hood of my car and that its efforts at furthering its own kind would meet a soapy end at the carwash. Nevertheless it continues to spread its seeds on my paintjob—a derisive display of mockery in anyone's book. Not only does Ol' John encourage all kinds of flying creatures to sit on its branches, training them to aim at my car while doing their dirty business (I consider this to be the height of all meanness), but it also seems to have afflicted my wife with a serious case of allergies. Last month, the real slap in the face occurred while being *really slapped in the face* by a branch as I exited my car—Ol' John had the temerity to reach down and whip me right across the old mug as I hurried to escape the rain. Finally, facing the humiliation of losing face—several vital pieces already hanging from Ol' John's branches like a trophy—I knew I had to confront this menace head on.

My neighbor, apparently an agent of plant life, tried to discourage me from cutting the troublemaker down, claiming that it must have taken decades for Ol' John to grow to its majestic heights. It took quite a few years for me to grow into my present dimensions as well but I would not think of insulting or physically assaulting a *tree*. I had even gone so far as substituting a life Christmas tree for a plastic one, using material from long-dead dinosaurs. This is the kind of respect I was prepared to offer to trees but I would not tolerate daily slaps across the teeth from any plant.

Gnashing my choppers I went to my garage, to view an array of cutting tools. I realized then that I lacked the appropriate gear, time, energy and beer supply to tackle bringing down a giant tree, therefore I opted just to trim Ol' John's lower branches. As I proceeded to hack off some of its offending extremities, Ol' John creaked mockingly. All I achieved was the cutting of some twigs, which apparently meant as much to Ol' John, as clipping the sideburns on an aging hippie. In no time at all its foliage would return to its former fullness and resume battering me about the face and body. Full of rage, I stormed back into my garage and returned with a saw and a ladder to reach some of Ol' John's sturdier limbs. What happened next I seem to recall only hazily but it apparently has solidified itself into my framework of painful lessons learned. I can vouch for the fact that I placed my ladder underneath the old tree and stepped up to begin sawing at the branch closest to its trunk. I worked feverishly, but as I managed to manually saw through a thick branch—some people claim this to be impossible—Ol' John viciously kicked the ladder out from under me. Holding on to the cut branch with one hand and my saw with the other, I landed on my rear, directly on the part of my body that nature would have slated for an appendage, in case humans needed assistance climbing trees at some future date. I realized at once that, again, I was far ahead of my time, as I had tackled this task without a tail.

I decided that climbing a tree without the dexterity and access to the natural equipment of our closest relatives, monkeys, was a perilous undertaking, an activity unsuitable for an urbane, civilized city dweller such as myself. Now, dodging swinging branches, I have finally entered into a pact with Ol' John—I shall leave it be, and allow it to fulfill its difficult, time-consuming endeavor of providing shade for me. Only once in a while am I reminded of its treachery, such as when some innocent-looking fallen leaves turned my sidewalk into a slippery slope during a recent rainfall. Then, as I stroked my throbbing backside yet again, dark thoughts of revenge returned with a thud.

Maybe displaying proof of purchase of a chainsaw might bristle the tree's branches. The game isn't over, pal.

MOTHER NATURE'S SECRETS

I forgot how to water the lawn. It completely slipped my mind, and now yellowing patches are appearing all over the yard because, after months of allowing nature to take care of my irrigation chores, I have become complacent, carelessly frolicking all over the grass without wasting one thought on the responsibilities that would face me sooner or later. Now nature in its eternal wisdom has decreed that my plate of tasks is not full enough and has provided little or no rain these past months, leaving me to deal with thirsty lawns all by myself. Perhaps nature did not see me as recently as last week, slaving over truckloads of receipts, forms and documents in order to get my taxes done on time? It should have recognized that my "plate" is not just a smallish dinner dish but actually a gigantic trough, overflowing with all kinds of unpleasant tasks that for some undetermined reason need to be done right this minute. But that's how nature is—*very unforgiving.*

Actually the act of watering the lawn is not something that I need to do physically myself because some kind of contraption located on the wall of my garage, is supposed to take charge of scheduling water dispersion. All I need to do is turn the knob to the "on" position and miraculously water appears from the ground to feed the slothful plants, too lazy to hunt for provisions themselves. But that is all theory. In reality Mother Nature doesn't work that way. That would be much too simple and easy and not at all entertaining for her wouldn't it? Instead she keeps all kinds of surprises in store for me, for example one source of amusement for her appears to be to remove the "on" mark from the face of that panel.

Also curiously the entire chart on that panel, something that I read and easily understood last year, now appears to have changed into a foreign language. I have a hunch it might be an obscure indigenous dialect from the Amazonian rainforest, spoken only by a few waterlogged folks who actually don't really need to know much about irrigation anyway. Recently I read about a mysterious Indian tribe called the Pirahã that baffle anthropologists and linguists from all over the world because of their peculiar use of grammar. Somehow I feel that *they're* involved here—what else can it be? This is the only way I can explain the confusion I suffer when standing in front of the mysterious gadget, its symbols an open book last spring but now incomprehensible hieroglyphs to me.

But I'm also quite sure that the Pirahã, spending much of their enigmatic lives amongst colorful jungle foliage, would find nothing wrong with a luminous, multihued lawn, flecked with a bit of yellow and brown here and there. We undoubtedly would get along just fine as neighbors. They might even help me hunt down the family of raccoons that has been pestering me ever since I moved into my home. We could have a block party, roasting game on a grill and drinking potent rainforest beverages. And if I'm really lucky, an accidental arrow or two might even bring an end to the incessant nightly barking of obnoxious neighborhood canines. This feat alone might be worth a couple of plane tickets from Brazil.

But this still leaves me with the problem of my lawn irrigation schedule. Fortunately Mother Nature, in her quirky April mood, has mercifully extended my time on this chore, suddenly deciding to provide us with more rain. But even with this additional rain, as I understand it, we might be in for a water shortage soon, which could force us to curtail our water use. Perhaps yellowish, brownish spotted lawns will become all the rage. And maybe my wife will quit bugging me to find out if there is a word for "procrastination" in the language of the Pirahã.

HOW GREEN IS YOUR GRASS?

Perhaps due to intricate, complex interconnections between the senses and emotions, visual distortions might cause a blurring of the line between reality and wishful thinking. That is probably why the cow standing amidst acres of luscious grass, strains her neck through barbed wire longing for that one strand of green beyond her reach. And that might be the reason why I peer into my neighbor's yard, full of envy because my grass always seems to suffer from perpetual yellow-brownish limpness while his lawn, in comparison, would have no problem—in its thriving green splendor—being featured as *the* national emblem of Ireland. For some time I rationalized that an optical illusion was the culprit, displaying a distorted view of my garden while enhancing his. In addition to the attack on my visual senses, I imagined the sounds of moaning when passing by my parched yard, and this strengthened my belief that—without a doubt—I was the victim of an inner game of psychological bamboozlement. It appeared that I now faced the choice of either surrendering to the friendly professionals in white coats or completely breaking down and watering my lawn. I decided to postpone both of these unpleasant options for the moment as I reasoned that the latter activity might involve severe physical exertion, which might prove detrimental to therapeutic development when ridding oneself of said mental dilemma, and rest and recuperation appeared to be of paramount importance in such a case.

So I decided instead to place myself under an umbrella and lounge restfully next to my lawn, with a cool drink in my hand. I figured that one should not make rash decisions when subjected to mental strain. After an afternoon of reclining and quaffing a variety of thirst-quenching liquids, I came to the conclusion that perhaps the grass *was* indeed greener on the other side of the fence and that my lawn would not only need severe irrigation but also the most advanced, up-to-date nourishment and sustenance known to modern meadow and garden science. Aside from the fact that my grass was quietly dying of thirst, I also discovered to my consternation, that there were trees abound in my yard, which I had wrongfully assumed were exotic desert shrub, but which (according to a friend), turned out to be formerly proud plants with solid trunks, once crowned with healthy foliage towering towards the sky. Because of human neglect though, they were now falling apart, crumbling into dried out shriveled piles of wood, as their wretched branches reached out begging for the tiniest amount of nourishment.

The shame of witnessing such disgrace caused me to quickly knock back a few more of the aforementioned swills, as various types of plant life seemed to gawk at me with envy and resentment. What did *I* care—this was a "dog-eat-dog", *"plant-devouring-plant"* kind of world, wasn't it? Weren't these creatures supposed to take care of themselves without human pampering every step of the way? Who has ever heard of Amazon Natives, for example, going through the trouble, taking time out of their busy day to walk through the forest and water certain plants? The sheer frustration of owning such helpless, feeble vegetation caused me to overemphasize the importance of keeping myself hydrated and I—in retrospect—carelessly absorbed a greater amount of liquids than I should have. The ensuing physical difficulties I experienced the next day were the result of—what else—vegetation, the fermented kind this time. Plants, I realized, seemed to be the cause of many of my troubles.

As I continued to suffer the consequences of excessive intimacy with vegetation (in liquid form), I contemplated for the briefest of moments, reprisal against all vegetation by continuing to withhold nourishment from my lawn. Naturally, full of human compassion, I changed my mind and refrained from such an inferior act of vengeance (something lower life-forms, like the grass surrounding my house, don't have the capacity of comprehending). Therefore as a member of the human race I did not lower myself to such extremes as revenge (although in the scheme of the universe I am not obliged to assume obligation for the prosperity of plants).

Because of this, maybe tomorrow, instead of procrastinating, I should just water the darn lawn.

WHEN IS IT OKAY TO SWEAR?

For some unknown reason I'm equipped with "furniture-finding toes." If there ever were a need to locate and hunt down chairs, armoires, sofas etc., I could make a pretty decent living hiring out my feet. They're specialists in finding all sorts of furniture, especially in the dark.

When that happens, I have found that screaming bloody murder and swearing a blue streak until I'm blue in the face seems to make the pain more tolerable. Each time I groggily stumble up at night and invariably stub my toe, I try to stifle an urge to curse that would make roughnecks and seasoned sailors blush. The reason, I don't want to wake up the entire neighborhood because I'm sure they would then alert the authorities, who would then have swat teams surrounding the house to bring down the culprit who made someone scream that much in pain. Quite a problem then I'm certain, because the culprit would be my own toe, an appendage connected to me.

According to a recent scientific study, swearing can actually make pain more tolerable (but it shouldn't have any bearings on tolerating mixing metaphors, such as above, though). Now they tell me! I had no idea. But with this study at hand, perhaps I could negotiate a ceasefire after the swat team bullhorn orders me out of the house with my hands up.

"I &$% can't walk because my &%#$# toe hurts but, according to a scientific study, I'm supposed to curse to make the %$#&% pain go away!" I would yell. I'm not sure, though if my lengthy explanation would have any effect on their decision to bust through the doors and arrest my toe.

The way scientists discovered the connection between experiencing agony and achieving relief in expletives was to test subjects with the help of ice buckets. They had one group put their hands into ice and permitted them to swear and curse all they wanted. The other group was allowed no access to any kind of coarse language or profanities whatsoever, even though suffering the same excruciating experience of having their extremities refrigerated. Guess what—the vulgarity gang won. They reported less pain than the others.

Well, I take that with a grain of salt (placed on the rim of a chilled Margarita glass would be just great). Just imagine the scene in the lab of individuals with their hands in ice buckets experiencing pain, while surrounded by folks in lab coats scribbling notes on clipboards. If it were me, I would call these so-called scientists every name in the book (and insult their kin as well), just for making me go through the excruciating experience. What would happen then? Someone surely would snap and punch me in the nose, thereby adding an extra wrinkle to the experiment. Could they really remain objective then, differentiating between different kinds of pain?

But anyone who has lived in snow and ice can tell you that the period of your limbs freezing doesn't hurt as much as when they have a chance to thaw. I remember the excruciating agony I suffered as a child, after playing in the snow all day with my fingers frozen solid inside soaked gloves. After coming inside and warming them on the stove I often wanted to scream. Of course, at that time a young boy's inadequate vocabulary excluded most of the abovementioned choice of words that could have helped to alleviate the pain (I wonder, in lieu of this exclusion, if someone can make a case for child abuse when adults refuse to allow children such scientifically appropriate terms of pain relief).

More than likely though, having access to swear words and expressing them in order to alleviate pain might not have been as gratifying as a child anyway. The reason, at least in my case, was that after having my kiddy fingers frozen, the additional discomfort visited upon my backside with the use of adult fingers might just have canceled out any benefit I would have acquired from expressing foul-mouthed grownup terminology.

MONEY IN MY FRONT YARD

Lucky for me there is a money-tree in my front yard. Just the other day as I was backing out of my driveway, I spotted a brand-new dollar bill brimming on the lawn. I slammed on the brakes, jumped out of my car and rushed over to pick it up when I discovered several more bills hidden in the grass beneath the tree on my front lawn—enough to pay for a scrumptious lunch. My heart leapt with joy, with the realization that since a looming, inevitable relentless new round of bills and mortgage payments was facing me this month, the fruits of this lucky plant dropped down just at the right moment.

Some time ago I did have my differences with this tree. I'm sorry to say I had objected to its malicious disposition which had culminated in various injuries on my part, as I slipped on wet leaves dropped by the tree on my driveway and fell off a ladder while trying to trim its branches (landing on my tail-bone). Now I realize that trimming any branch or twig off that old tree would only cut into my very own profit because it would also reduce available space for "green", "valuable" fruit. The tree must have known this as well since it had resisted all my previous attempts at pruning its branches with some force in the past.

One lesson I have learned however, since disclosing the secret of the "money tree", is that in the future, I should keep such information to myself (and any other wondrous miracle I again become privy to), because there are more than enough skeptics out there who try their best to dampen your spirits. One of the more severe critics of extraordinary occurrences appears to be my wife who simply pointed at the barren branches of my tree. In her opinion, trees of *any* kind can only produce fruit after a season of blooming and sprouting and being nurtured by months of warm sunshine and certainly not during the time of hibernation in the winter.

I recognize that people who have been employed in the nose-to-grindstone business for some time have a tendency to become extremely cynical. Of course I was aware of the inevitability of nature's cycles but how could you approach such a miraculous event with ordinary logic? It stands to reason that perhaps in this case, a "money tree" might be exempt from the usual run of the mill conventions. Couldn't it be that this was such an exceptionally gifted tree that it yielded cash year-round, particularly whenever I needed it (having allocated several potential bags towards the purchase of obligatory luxury items)? Again, my wife whose belief-system is rooted in the conviction that there is "no free lunch", indicated that the only way to attain a certain amount of affluence is first by working hard, and second by keeping money from escaping via frivolous investments or flying out of your pocket while getting in and out of your car.

Of course I pay no attention to such negativity, and I have developed a habit of rushing to the next garden supply store looking for a healthy supply of tree nutrients. Just barely two months removed from the annual, relentless disappointment of being reminded again and again that there is no Santa Claus, I have no intention of surrendering my belief in the existence of cash-dispensing plant life. Now I have no idea why I was bestowed with such immense luck as a "money-tree" and I'm not about to ask any questions, because I am planning to sit in the shade of that tree, watching everyone else rush out to their nose-to- grindstone businesses while garbs of dollar bills float down from above.

AM I A PROCRASTINATOR?

For weeks now I've been putting off writing on a subject very close to my heart. And now I have managed to write one word to describe the condition afflicting me in a very personal way. That word is: Procrastination.

OK, I think that's enough for now, I'll knock off and continue tomorrow.

Twenty-four hours have passed by since my last sentence, but for some reason I'm still not in the mood to sit down and crank out anything worthwhile. The setting and the circumstances are not conducive for creativity. Perhaps I should make myself a cup of coffee first? There is always tomorrow, and based on history, more than likely this day will be followed by another one, and another one, continuing forever or until the sun burns out (and if things work out the way they usually do, I'm sure that event will probably be postponed as well for some time). So what am I worried about? Besides, if I concentrate on my current task, other projects are likely to be shortchanged. I have a long log of things I need to get done—mowing the lawn, fixing the roof, brushing my teeth and combing my hair, for example. And there is that extensive list my wife left me before she went off to work this morning. I hesitate to look at it. So I think I'll put it aside for now and view it some other time. Gee, isn't it time for lunch already? How quickly time passes—isn't that amazing? More than likely lunch will be a bit heavy and I'm sure I will be a lot more productive if I took a nap afterwards before doing any work.

The interesting thing about procrastination is that no one actually postpones lunch or taking a nap. You rarely catch anyone, when presented with a chance to grab a bite to eat or take a snooze, putting it off till the next day because he is too *lazy*.

This is the moment, I'm sure, when some gung-ho, goody-two-shoes type person out there (the ones who are never late and accomplish any task immediately) will jump at the chance to liberally use pejorative terms such as "lazy" to describe individuals who are merely "promptness-challenged." But actually, probably based on thorough scientific research (unless scientists put it off for someone else to do) procrastination is rooted in the ancient instinct of survival and the urge to protect the family from harm!

For example, per the list my wife handed me today—although I have postponed reading it, I can just tell by the way it *feels* that more than likely it involves using a hammer or a nail-gun somewhere. Now imagine employing those dangerous tools and you can picture how easily one could be placed in a hazardous situation, perhaps leading to lengthy stays in hospitals and convalescence homes, or even worse. And attempting to complete all the items on the wife's long lists will be too much of a burden for any such patient and could lead to further complications.

An unhurried 12-step program might be a more effective way to lead anyone back to promptness. Instead of expecting things done immediately one should, perhaps, be more liberal in terms of setting timeslots? So here's an example for all wives out there—if the color of the wall in the hallway bothers you for example, and you want your husband to paint it, why not allow a more generous time-line for this task to be accomplished? Let's say, a span of a few years might be just perfect to warm up to the project and prevent him from becoming too traumatized?

As a matter of fact, if you really want to help a procrastinator back to recovery, it wouldn't hurt if *you* picked up that tool yourself right now to show the lazy individual just how to do it, perhaps allowing him time to rest after a big lunch. Well, what are you waiting for? Why are you procrastinating?

"CONSPIRACY OF THE REPAIRMEN"

There is a law of nature—fixed and permanent and as inevitable as cows becoming airborne in a tornado—as soon as a used item is bought, the cost of subsequent repairs will equal, or sometimes even surpass its original purchase price. Lately, perhaps due to global warming or the El Nino effect, this law has been adjusted to include new items as well. The Second Law of Nature entails that the price of purchase and repair date are linked so that the more expensive the item is, the faster the need for repairs. Each and every piece of equipment I have ever owned, from cars to washing machines, has obeyed this rule.

An array of "previously owned motor vehicles", as they are now affectionately known, attests to my experience with this cruel and indiscriminate force of nature. Also, being familiar with the subject I learned that, in addition to battling this inevitability, there are also certain other rules of thumb to watch out for that could affect the size of the hole in your bank account even more. In the past, for instance, unsure of automobile technology (I had no idea why a water-pump was necessary in a car, since the car was supposed to run on gas and not propelled by that "big water-wheel under the hood"), taking my car to the workshop, I found that the proprietors of repair-shops are equipped with the necessary keen sixth sense to smoke out your parameters of knowledge, or lack of it, and by and large adjust their bill accordingly. Therefore it is a good idea when dealing with folks in charge of restoring any equipment, to remain pokerfaced and tightlipped or you will have the obligatory—and quite substantial—"dummy surcharge" added to your bill.

This then leads me to the Third Law of Nature, which will come down upon you as inevitably as debris and creatures flying around in the afore-mentioned twister-storm (a bonus quandary, afflicting people in certain areas who are already stretched thin with the usual natural laws). Typically it happens when you actually try to supervise repair procedures, breathing down the neck of the "hapless person" in charge. The repairman will inevitably scratch his head with a "Well, I'll be darned, I have never seen this before" statement. By some coincidence, your problem would never, ever have come up previously, even once, in the annals of repair history and the unfortunate mechanic will be forced to employ his "last resort" in order to save your beloved item—double his fees.

Following these inevitable Laws of Nature, we find for instance, that in many newer homes, major items such as water-heaters (usually tanks filled with lake-sized volumes of water), according to the rules of inevitability are installed, not in places where there would be minor damage should they break, but usually right smack in the middle of the home (most likely hidden in the living room or dining room closet, concealed from scrutiny, quietly buzzing, and completely without safeguards to prevent possible overflows). It seems that the invisible hand of fate guides the architect to design the home with the utmost feasibility and comfort but suddenly punishes him with temporary blindness as he approaches the placement of such items as water heaters. This temporary lapse in judgment may mean that you may be stuck with major repairs if a leaking water heater drenches your floors and walls, in which case, the repairman will then have the ultimate upper hand. A seemingly simple action such as the drying of a carpet or wall could require enormous assortments of blowers and dryers positioned strategically to dry and wither away greenish substance on the floors and in your wallet. With no taximeter to click, you have only the incessant humming of machines to remind you of the fact that you are approaching complete dryness in carpet, walls and bank account. And, according to the service personnel, they will remain there until this is achieved or the cows come home—or fall off the sky.

MY GINGERBREAD HOUSE

The idea of easy living during summer vacations, sun and boozy barbecues usually dissipates as quickly as the moisture on your swimming trunks during the midday heat, as soon as you realize that your life is actually not part of a beer commercial. Instead you discover that responsibilities, like making mortgage payments, are still an integral part of your existence on earth. This notion usually occurs around the end of summer. You also realize that if you want to continue using your home as an ATM device to finance those lavish, carefree, spirit-filled commercial-type vacations next year you need to make certain improvements on your property in order to coax the appraiser into rating the value of your house at top level.

On top of that, the rainy season is about to begin and another realization which hits you like a collapsing building, is that your roof may need to be replaced. This is a giant expenditure (one that could have been used for more essential expenses like more of that pricey microbrewery beer for next year's barbecues). So how do you determine if your roof needs repair? Well, in my case that is what I was told by a professional—someone who actually climbed on top of my house, rummaging around and looking for reasons to further decimate my savings account (actually, come to think of it, using the services of a roofing specialist to find out if your house needs a new roof is akin to employing a goat to find out if your garden is in need of weeding).

The nightmare scenario sketched out by this expert specializing in tops of houses (and who at the same time also seemed to be specially talented in causing disarray to my upstairs—the area between my ears) was one of utter chaos. If nothing was done to my roof, he warned me, bedlam would break loose as soon the rains start. Moisture would weaken the structure, causing it to mold and rot, which in turn would invite vermin of all kinds, as well as crows, vultures and the dark horsemen of doom. The only way that he could see of forestalling this horrendous fate was through an immediate transfer of funds from my bank account into his.

Worried about pestilence and strife, I agreed at once to have my roof invaded by hordes of earnest workmen who had committed their lives to ridding homes of substandard roofs and replacing them with shiny new ones. It would only take, oh, about a day or two, the roof-rep assured me, with the minimum of inconvenience to any member of my family—this, as he showed my wife and I an array of colorful shingles to choose from.

But, as it turned out, our choice of roofing material was completely immaterial, since the taste of the work crew seemed to differ from ours completely and it must have been decided at the highest level—probably next to the chimney—that our house would look "just peachy" with a patchwork of leftovers. With Halloween just around the corner, the roofers turned our place into a colorful gingerbread house—red shingles alternating with white, blue and green ones of different sizes and shapes. I frantically reread the contract looking for the space where I had agreed to seasonal changes expecting the roof would be turned into a Thanksgiving theme after Halloween, perhaps with a gigantic turkey swaying in the wind on top of my house!

The workmen never did finish their job in a mere day or so, as announced beforehand but instead came back day after day, mostly to retrieve a variety of tools, one by one. They also needed considerable time to view a gigantic collection of debris on my lawn and to consult with each other about what to do with it—perhaps how to remove it? This gave me a bit of quality time with the friendly roofing folks, as I tried to question them on my gingerbread house. But so far the only statement I am able to cajole out of them is, "trick or treat."

WHEN DOES CLEANING BECOME A CHORE?

They have "self-cleaning ovens", don't they? *But why stop there?* Why don't they just go one step further and create a self-cleaning house and be done with it? What does it take? All you would have to do is splash the walls with a cleaning liquid, and then heat the house up to 300 degrees and in no time at all you have a place that sparkles like new. It might be a good idea though to remove pets and wayward spouses hiding somewhere, from the premises first.

Of course this kind of solution would be much too easy for most people, especially those who feel compelled to make the cleaning process unnecessarily grueling. I'm different. I like things easy and uncomplicated. Some people would call that "lazy" but since I'm the one writing this column and I am in charge, I will call it anything I like. Therefore I AM NOT LAZY—just different. And if we're lucky, heating the house to 300 degrees, might even remove plants, grandmothers, children of all ages, and any items made of plastic! But I guess the future is not quite here yet and self-cleaning houses do not exist, so I am forced occasionally to hire someone to clean up my mess. I could do it myself but, as you know, *I am different.*

Sometimes though, feeling my wife's probing eyes on my back, I am still forced to do my share of housework to some extent; but it does not mean that I *like* it. When I was in the army I didn't have any choice either but snap to it and clean anything that was not moving. In the military, it is a standard order—if it stands still you clean it first, then paint it. The entire brass in the military seemed to consist of clean-freaks. One of their favorite pastimes apparently was to send us, the recruits, into the dirtiest, muddiest terrain, then order us to "clean up the mess." Afterwards they would come for inspections, probing the bottoms of our boots with needles. A particular drill sergeant relished the idea of discovering the tiniest speck of dirt, which would then justify his calling us all sorts of names, and comparing us to the kind of hygiene-challenged critters that make their living in filthy, soiled surroundings. Apparently the art of "gentle nudging" to get people to do things for you was not available to drill sergeants back then. We were then forced to do pushups until the idea of cleanliness sank through even the most stubborn of thick skulls. Maybe that's why I developed an aversion to housework—because I view it as somehow connected to enormous physical exertion.

So perhaps now is the time to see if that brilliant idea of mine is workable. I think I will crank up the heat a few notches. Not only will I be showered with riches as a result of a genial, new invention but it will also get rid of those filthy critters living in soiled surroundings at the same time.

Oops, it looks like the cat is not moving. I'd better hurry and *paint it.*

CHAPTER SIX

The 1,2,3 Of Buying A New Car And Other Shopping Secrets

Great … I'm impressed! The customers are putty in your hands. Now, how are we going to get a down-payment out of them?

BUYING THAT CAR

I had no idea that the "sticker price" on a vehicle inside any of those car-lots means that you get a nice colorful sticker—but no car. I do appreciate a multihued, vibrant piece of paper with ingeniously arranged numbers and brand-new terms and words proving creativity and imagination. But 25,000 bucks for a sticker is a bit much, wouldn't you think—even if it is prominently and very professionally taped onto the window. I would think that kind of cash should buy you a few shares in the "sticker-company" and perhaps provide you with a bit of clout. You might even persuade them to explain at the car lot (in smaller print if necessary) what exactly is meant by the "sticker price."

But the reaction you receive every time you show an interest in buying a car based on the sticker price is one of puzzlement. By the time you are ready to sign on the dotted line and realize that the cost of the vehicle has multiplied, and you deign to remind the sales-staff of the original price displayed on the car window, your "assigned sales professional" usually looks at you aghast and utters the inevitable, "well, of course, that's *just the sticker price.*" At which time you jerk back, completely embarrassed, "Yes, by Jove—how could I have been so stupid? I knew it all along, this is just the *sticker price.*" After that, you gasp a little, slap your forehead and proceed to sign over most of your paycheck for the next half a dozen years or so.

How exactly does it happen that so many of us, usually competent when purchasing anything from toothpaste to major appliances, become bedazzled when it comes to purchasing a motor vehicle? The problem seems to be the act of stepping onto the turf of a car salesperson in the first place. As soon as this is accomplished the chance for normal human intercourse is forfeited, usually without a shred of realization on our part. The sales representative will introduce himself or herself with the toothiest smile you have ever seen. As a matter of fact, you might be tempted to push back his/her dentures—which you fear might drop out at any minute—with that rolled up Internet printout, proof of your meticulous research on the subject of purchasing that exact car. The car sales person, as a matter of course, always ignores any such paper, even if you stabbed him with it, as well as the fact that you may have come "just to look around a bit." He also ignores your foul mood, perfected to scare off pesky sales staff. Sooner or later, perhaps after you take the car for a test drive, you will be invited in to "crunch some numbers." That is your signal to take the opportunity to jump into your old car and run (perhaps with a little bit of tender care and a lot of oil-changes your trusted friend will sacrifice another 100,000 miles for you).

For some mysterious reason (the secret only available to experienced car-salesmen), numbers cannot be "crunched" out in the open car-lot. Numbers, especially the ones connected to your bank-account, must be mulled over inside a prison-like office. Although one side is usually fashioned with bulletproof glass, open to the public and designed to mislead other patrons who mistake your muffled screams for happy laughter—you have no chance of escaping because half a dozen interrogators are assigned to your case. Pretending that they are on your side fighting against an enigmatic phantom called "the management" whom they periodically consult behind closed doors for hours on end, they finally emerge when you are completely exhausted and close to starvation. It is at this point that they usually tempt you with a free soda, which you gulp down greedily as you blindly sign on any dotted line put in front of you. In exchange for a free soft drink they stick you with the commitment of paying the equivalent of the price of an entire three-bedroom home from just a few decades back. This is the exact moment you finally realize the real meaning of "sticker price."

THE MAN'S WAY TO SHOP

There is an inborn aversion to going shopping in most men. No one knows for sure, but it is probably based on an ancient survival instinct. Men are hunters, women are gatherers (women also take care of the kids, cook, clean the house, do laundry and go to work). So the question is—how long do you think men would survive as a species if in this kind of arrangement they dared to stir up unintended attention, perhaps suddenly demanding exorbitant expenses for flamboyant garments or adorning themselves with all sorts of garish embellishments?

If you want to survive as a successful "hunter", you can't be stupid. You realize quickly that success is mostly based on patience. So you lay low for a long time, patiently waiting for the right time to strike. Then in an unsuspecting moment you—seemingly quite innocently—suggest that now might be the right time to buy that shiny, red sports car that you always wanted. And of course (smiling charmingly, while setting the trap) you indicate how much joy your wife would derive (even more than you) from the uncomfortable, overpriced transportation, and she certainly would not object to the fact that the thing might cost the equivalent of more than a dozen years of your average household budget. But then your wife just laughs out loud and takes you clothes-shopping instead.

It is at this moment you learn the tough lesson that all hunters and predators must discover the hard way—90% of all attempts at seizing the quarry usually end up in failure. Instead of taking down the great big mammoth, you may be forced to manage with a few berries and nuts. You misjudged the situation and tossed the spear too soon and it hit a rock, scaring off the game! Now you will have to start the hunt all over again stalking, tracking but with the disadvantage that the prey at this point has a good idea where you're coming from. That is why you grudgingly grit your teeth, subjecting your incisors to additional strain, as you bide your time while obediently trotting along on the obligatory gathering and grazing ventures. Your objection that you are not physically equipped to survive lengthy outings in shopping malls looking at clothes, falls on deaf ears. And your lifelong research providing evidence that women due to their physiques have no problem at all standing in front of mirrors for hours on end, trying on clothes is seriously ridiculed. From your research, it seems to be a given that men, on the other hand, with their narrow hips, are perfectly equipped to slip in and out of bars quickly and efficiently (although of course, once they have acquired a certain position resting comfortably in front of a large beer they have been known to remain motionlessly this way for hours, waiting patiently for their wives to return).

What a large portion of the population (mostly of the female denomination) doesn't realize is that as long as a substantial part of their bodies is enveloped with an adequate amount of cotton or equivalent fiber, most men seem to be satisfied with the way they look in clothes. Fashion awareness is largely confined to the knowledge that the baseball cap should be worn forwards or backwards during a particular season.

But if the need should arrive to acquire new clothes—perhaps when large holes in pants and t-shirts prevent the patriarch from developing a meaningful relationship with his deathly embarrassed teenage daughter—a man will do so according to his instincts, based on his millennia of hunting experience. Ingrained in his DNA, the male hunter will automatically identify his target, zero in, tear it off the clothing rack and quickly remove himself from the scene before any of his peers has a chance to discover him preening himself in this unnatural habitat.

But usually, tenaciously willing to track down the big game, he will try again for one last shot at the trophy, and argue that his garments could stand several more seasons of wear and tear. So that if the entire clan were also willing to make sacrifices *and not splurge on unnecessary items* (like video games, nasal jewelry, tattoos or window treatments), sooner or later enough funds would be saved up to purchase that bright red shiny new motor vehicle that "everyone" craves for so much. But, sadly (usually after the bout of raucous laughter shaking the walls of his dwelling has died down), the male hunter might realize that he has shot himself in the foot again.

GOOD FURNITURE'S HARD TO FIND

My friend has been my daily companion, as well as my trusted servant for decades now. But he hasn't been himself lately. I wonder if he's sick. Once shiny and full of springy life, he's now old, sagging and battered. He is asking for retirement. He's Mr. Slouch, my couch.

Is there a mandatory retirement age for furniture? Come on, snap out of it, I tell Slouch. A lot of furniture have great second careers as antiques. Don't give up now! I still need you. How difficult is it to be a sofa anyway? It's not rocket science. All you have to do is stand there and have people sit on you. That's it—no agility or special skills required. Is that so hard? Just about anyone equipped with a sturdy back can do it.

I seem to remember that Slouch came to me highly recommended. Should last me "forever", I think the salesman said. In my opinion "forever" should have a very long shelf life, which should at least last as long as "eternity" (another expression I recall the salesman used). Apparently, judging by the way Slouch behaves these days, such terms have an expiration date. The mechanism for one of Slouch's two recliners ceased to work a long time ago. Perhaps it's too much to ask for a device, which lifts up leg support with a lever, to function properly for a while? It's not the space shuttle, for crying out loud!

For quite some time now I've been put in the position, before a night of relaxation in front of the TV, of conjuring up creative ruses and deceptions in order to claim Slouch's lone recliner before my wife gets there. Sometimes I hurry to sit on that spot after my wife vacates it briefly, and then respond with, "Oh, sorry, Honey, are you sitting here?" with as much innocence as I can muster, knowing full well that she had made herself comfortable on the good side of Slouch a few moments before (of course, she's not sitting there now—I am). Sometimes I use all kinds of objects—magazines, books, drinks etc.—to mark my territory like a common dog, to indicate my claim to Slouch's good side. My wife, equipped with eternal patience, naturally would respond that she didn't care where she sat. (See, what you make me do, Slouch? I have introduced deception and fraud into an otherwise splendid relationship. And you call yourself my friend?)

It's time to get rid of this broken-down rotten piece of junk, I think. So now I'm scouring furniture stores all over the place looking for a new couch. I've looked at leather sofas, for example, the kind where you'll find yourself on the floor immediately after attempting to sit on it and then skidding off, like a kid on a slide. Aside from that, even nowadays, I don't think that cows wear coats made from petroleum products, do you? So what exactly is the quality of "leather" being sold? Then there are sofas, nice and sturdy, but only equipped with one recliner, placing me back in the same position as before, where I have to fight for the right spot on the couch. Other sofas I've looked at and tried out, just lack the same feel and comfort I'm used to. Displaying a nice appearance on the outside, I'm suspicious of their quality as well as their exact interpretation of "eternity." Knowing that we would live in very close contact with each other, there has to be a special something, a chemistry binding us together, man and couch, not just the pungent odor of a protective chemical compound. Unfortunately I haven't been able to find it yet.

So okay, Slouch, you can hang on for just a little longer. Maybe you're even one of a kind.

But hold on! What is this; how come this lever isn't working anymore? Piece of junk!

WHAT WOULD THEY BE SELLING US NEXT?

"Wolfgang, try a trial crowfeet and wrinkle eraser," was the first thing I read in my e-mail the other day. I have to admit I was taken aback, not because of a possibility of any creases crisscrossing my countenance but because, first of all, I don't recall introducing myself to anyone connected with the wrinkle-eraser industry lately.

Second, and more important, if indeed my face is marked with such obvious signs of wisdom, evidence of a lifetime of experience, shouldn't I be afforded the respect and reverence of those who make their living bombarding me with inane junk mail? And for this reason, shouldn't anyone daring to spoil my morning refrain from addressing me with vulgar familiarity and forwardness? At the very least the equivalent of a "Dear Sir" alongside a lengthy apology, including admission of guilt and a request for forgiveness should be warranted, wouldn't you think? (I might consider granting clemency if apologies came in the form of two-for-one coupons or a free room in a Las Vegas hotel casino.)

And then, most upsetting of all, how the heck can they tell from where they were sitting that I have crowfeet and wrinkles anyway? How very presumptuous of people, completely unidentified and anonymous to me, to make such an assumption! I can't wait until I find out who they are and then I'll point out their flaws. More than likely I won't bother with their physical imperfections but instead concentrate on their character defects, the kind that assumes that it is perfectly alright to bug people first thing in the morning with conceited comments about presumed shortcomings.

Although I have no intention of "erasing" anything, the least being the markers in my personal historical roadmap, I'd be curious to know though how exactly a wrinkle eraser would erase wrinkles (although not to the point of actually purchasing one). The only eraser I'm familiar with is the one at the end of my pencil. Am I supposed to stand in front of the mirror and start rubbing out my face? After the daily routine effort of brushing my teeth and scraping my chin, I'm pretty much exhausted, reaching the limits of enthusiasm of goggling at myself. Any additional face-time with a mirror would constitute manual labor for which I wouldn't be compensated (a casual crease-count yielding a frightening figure, by the way).

Watching an old Western the other night, I imagined a snake oil-type salesman approaching a tough cowboy in the Old West. Maybe a Clint Eastwood type character in "A Fistful Of Dollars", someone who had spent his life riding amongst cacti and bad guys under the hot desert sun and whose light-sensitive eyes had imposed an eternal squint, thereby forging a network of deep lines in his face. What line of attack could the sales person use to make the Clint character consider purchasing a miraculous elixir that would make it possible to iron out his wrinkles and turn his mug back into the smooth face of an innocent whippersnapper? Taking into account the mileage Clint Eastwood gets out of looking tough, I don't think this anti-wrinkle sales rep would have much of a chance selling anything.

The salesman might have initially assumed he had found a goldmine in them thar hills, overflowing with bad guy mugs with permanent frowns carved into them—heavy nicotine and alcohol use and a bad diet, along with the constant worry of someone shooting you in the back would make anyone's visage look like a battered old suitcase. Aside from that, items like sunglasses that would have alleviated some of the squint were virtually unknown in those days. But if I know bad guys, they'd much rather spend their fistful of dollars on whiskey, woman and gambling, rather than wrinkle cream. More than likely those Westerners would have banded together and handed the pitchman an ancient whole-body treatment, called "Tarred and Feathered"—a potent type of therapy whose time just might have come again.

HOW TO COPE WITH
MALFUNCTIONING PRODUCTS

Recently I came across an article which speculated that half of allegedly "malfunctioning products" returned to stores by consumers are actually in full working order. According to the article, there is usually absolutely nothing wrong with such products, and the only problem lies in the fact that people just can't seem to make them work. The average person who returns the product, tinkers for about 20 minutes trying to make sense of all the buttons, knobs, wires and that *encyclopedia* of an instruction manual, then throws in the towel and returns the item to the store claiming that the thing was the wrong color and wouldn't match the shag carpet.

I've returned many items myself, including things like a hammer (an especially exasperating item). Not only was it the "wrong color", but it came with a substandard instruction manual. No matter how I interpreted it, instead of driving nails into surfaces it caused tremendous damage, pain and injury to various parts of my anatomy—usually my thumbs—which unfortunately, has led to a "prolonged postponement" of various entries on the lengthy to-do list my wife spends considerable time carefully lining up for me.

Other objects, which are hard to master, as for example instruments used for brain-surgery, might take a little more than twenty minutes to set up (which is why before surgery, you should make a habit of always examining the potential surgeon carefully, watching for any signs of trauma to his thumbs, because if he can't handle a simple hammer, should he be handling more complex tools?). But the typical consumer has only patience for less than half an hour before he/she tosses the merchandise back into the box and hauls it right back to the store. There are, however, a few people whose psychological makeup cannot accept the concept of "easy surrender" and they usually sit out the set-up process to the bitter end. I am reminded of the time a friend of mine began to treat me with absolute scorn—the kind usually reserved for contemptible criminals accused of vile, despicable acts and crimes. It puzzled me for some time until I remembered that I had given him a clock as a Christmas present. It was an innocent-looking timepiece which I had initially bought for myself because it supposedly displayed time in a unique way. One of its most striking features was the fact that one could actually observe the hours, days, and months ticking by, while in the process of trying to set the darn clock. I'm sure the poor guy (gnashing his teeth and watching his hair turn white in the reflection of the glass while trying to put the clock together), could think of nothing else but plotting horrendous revenge against the person who caused his life to become worthless.

According to the article I mentioned above, a wave of versatile electronic gadgets has been flooding the market in recent years, ranging from MP3 players and home cinemas to media centers and wireless audio systems, but consumers still find it hard to install and use them. And it probably took a research grant and precious man (woman?) hours to discover that little tidbit? Something I could have told them for half the price! In my careful research around the house I have discovered that very few adults are actually technologically competent enough to even set the alarm clock to wake up in the morning (well, at least 50% of the two adults living in my house). This forces them to come up with feeble excuses at work, as for example that the thickheaded spouse forgot to set the alarm clock, the dog accidentally swallowed it or that, for some unknown reason, a horde of wild Huns targeted the place and stole the blasted thing (perhaps the Huns found it useful for coordinating the conquering and pillaging of surrounding villages, who knows).

There *is* one product remaining "unreturned" in my possession, although I have figured out only a tiny percentage of its gigantic variety of uses (from all indications, it can be applied as a camera, videogame player, photo album and a host of other applications). I utilize this product as a telephone, whereby I open up the little flap and scream, "Hello, is that you?" at the top of my lungs the moment I hear a certain melody playing inside my pocket. For some reason though, lately, I seem to long for the wild hordes of the steppes to return, as I'm secretly hoping for a heist of this item as well, for it appears that my thumbs have healed up enough and I'm ready once again for instructions on the long-forgotten lists of chores.

CHAPTER SEVEN

Why I Hate Cats And Other Critters

"I'm not sold on this new High Protein Diet at all."

WHY I HATE CATS

There is speculation amongst scientists at Colombia University, that cats may cause mental illness in people. This might come as no surprise to you as you may have wondered about this yourself at one time or another, especially when cats drive you crazy munching on filthy rodents from sewers, while refusing to touch the high-priced gourmet cat food you got for them from the supermarket. The Colombia professors assert that cats sometimes carry nasty bugs, transmittable to human beings, causing all kinds of "strange behavior"—such as leaping around the room for no discernible reason or shouting replies to voices in your head (although some people pretend to be talking on their cell-phones).

Some folks think cats are mysterious and enigmatic but maybe they are—just plain and simply—"nuts." Which other type of animal typically struts on high fences and roofs without a care in the world and then, out of the blue, is stuck by a sudden bout of vertigo and refuses to move down from a tree? As anyone working in close proximity with unstable people knows, unpredictability makes them more precarious than facing any bruising bully.

Here is an example from my own frightening experience—I once stayed overnight at a friend's house, and waking up slowly the next morning from a nightmare filled with a brooding sense of doom, I opened my eyes and was instantly paralyzed with fright, for I was staring directly into a set of menacing eyeballs—a pair of cold calculating alien eyes focused on me, at a distance of a mere inch or so removed from my eyes. Who knew how long the cat had been sitting on my chest patiently waiting for me to wake up in order to sink its razor-sharp claws into the apple of my eye? I stopped breathing at once, trying hard not to display any signs of life. As far as I knew (and I was hoping frantically that my information was correct) finicky felines feed on fresh food and are not generally interested in humans struck by rigor mortis. After some time, perhaps bored by my fantasies of horror about facing life without my eyesight, the cat jumped down from my chest and disappeared. It had probably decided that it would have much more fun searching for a mouse to torment than waiting out a large immovable object such as myself.

Nobody has been able to explain to me what fascinated that cat so much about me that it spent half the night stretched out on my upper torso just to get a glimpse of my terror-stricken eyes in the morning. Call me crazy but that's pretty strange behavior in my book. I wonder if we have straight-jackets for cats. But what really strikes fear into my heart is the possibility of that cat having transmitted the "crazy-bug" to me during our slumber-party. As a matter of fact, I do feel a bit queasy right now. On the other hand, isn't there a chance that I might have infected the cat instead? What happens if the Colombia professors got it all wrong and infections are the other way around—we humans drive the poor cats insane? This actually makes more sense (even to a reality-impaired human), but how can I be sure, since I'm suddenly not certain what is real and what is crazy? From a cat's point of view, it doesn't really show much sense when we lock a predatory, carnivorous animal inside a house, dress it up with pink bows (and sometimes additional clothing), feed it tuna from cans, require that it goes to the bathroom in a sandbox and otherwise expect it to conduct itself "normally" per human standards of behavior. Maybe I (that large human laying lazily on his back) presented a complete puzzle to the cat. Besides, who in the feline world, would want to waste the prime hours of the night sleeping? That is the time when cats get busy checking out dark corners, nooks and crannies, and if they are lucky, possibly hunting down a rodent or two for a great midnight snack.

Come to think of it, that thought alone might trigger the return of those nightmares tonight, or am I simply going nuts?

BIRD ATTACKS

Lately it seems that birds are targeting me—twice during the last month alone! I remember I was once trying to sketch a seagull at Monterey's Fisherman's Wharf and was just in the process of completing the rendition, a fine drawing of what I had assumed was my feathered friend, when one of the seagulls (some of which had been expressing their disapproval with ear-shattering squawks around me all afternoon) flew up right above my easel in order to make sure I got the message of his distaste in my artistic creation. With the skill of an assassin, right smack-dab in the middle of my drawing, he deposited what are quaintly called "droppings." But if you think about it (and due to lingering psychological trauma I'm trying hard not to), these droppings are actually the result of rotting fish, worms and similar garbage making their way through a seagull's digestive system. Although it happened quite a few years ago the experience is still seared into my memory. I don't think there is a word in the English language that expresses critique of my artwork with greater clarity than this act. To this day I refuse to draw any critters in public, especially with a member of the particular species within the vicinity. Just try to imagine the result of painful criticism if I somehow should misinterpret the jaw line and the canine teeth of a Doberman, for example.

Lately, I was simply minding my own business walking through the financial district in San Francisco (not harming or insulting anyone or drawing exaggerated caricatures of birds, no, I was just walking) when out of nowhere I was attacked from above. This time it wasn't just the result of digested foodstuff that hit me, but actual beak and claws! If it had just occurred one time only, I could have interpreted it as an avian error, a misread flight plan, perhaps. Although the ability to fly had supposedly been perfected by millions of years of evolutionary progression, one still learns about the occasional bird smashing into windows and mirrors. But a few days later it happened again! This time

I caught a glimpse of my assailant. It was the gray flash of a pigeon or some other flying goon of that color.

Why did they select me out as a target of airborne anger? I meant them no harm. I have no idea where they hide their eggs, so it cannot be that they seek the need to protect their offspring. And I have no interest in climbing any trees or high-rises to find them either. They should know that if I wanted an omelet, I would find my eggs at the grocery store, conveniently stocked a dozen per container. Later, the solution hit me. Color. My own personal evolutionary progression has forced a change in the color of my hair. Over the years it has transformed from a dark brown into some kind of streaked slate gray for some reason. I have no idea why. Maybe evolution demands that at an advancing age one should blend into the background more.

But with careful detective work, meticulously piecing together evidence, I am led to the following conclusion—clear as day: What for most, is understood to be the color of camouflage, the same kind of gray, arouses incredible ire in birds. I know that some species of birds mate for life. Maybe some bird saw me as a potential rival, a taller competitor with more striking plumage parading in front of someone's love interest perched somewhere above. I undoubtedly was a victim of avian jealousy.

How can I make it clear to such a stupid bird that I'm already happily married?

BIRD LANGUAGE

Birds know how to distinguish between languages, a team of scientists in Japan found out recently. They exposed sparrows to reading from novels; one version was in Chinese, the other in English. I guess they weren't interested so much in editorial opinions of birds as to see if the birds could tell one language from the other. The way they did this was to withhold food in one version and provide it in the other and in no time they raised language experts. About 75% of the birds were adequately motivated by this stimulus. This is something almost every international traveler becomes familiar with in a short time—you either learn to order something from the local menu or you starve. Assuming the percentage is about the same in humans, I suppose the "less adaptable" other 25% end up boiling shoelaces in their hotel rooms for food.

Fortunately, in the case of birds, the list of culinary options is limited to either seeds or worms or a combination of both, hemming in their gastronomic choices enormously. For migratory birds escaping the harsh winter conditions in Canada and ending up in Mexico, it seems only a few choice expressions in local lingo can get them the best a maggot-rich cuisine has to offer.

What appeared to fascinate the Tokyo scientists was that bird-brains are able to distinguish between languages of another species—us. That raises them heads and shoulders above any human in linguistic talents. I doubt that any of us can tell the difference between languages of an animal species (and that includes sign language, like the baring of saber-like fangs of the larger more ferocious beasts, for example). The message conveyed looks and sounds exactly the same to us anywhere. You either respond to the "fight" or "flight" mode of your more primitive past (the "flight" portion is highly recommended) or the "I'll rip out your throat", the carnivores seem to indicate. I suppose faint nuances have no place in inter-specie communication.

Growing up I had personal knowledge of how birds pick up languages. At least it seemed that way, since the parakeet in our family learned a whole range of words and phrases, including its name and address. This was, of course completely useless knowledge because no one would have ever trusted that parakeet with the key to the front door anyway. The reason for this was that the bird already had troubles with the concept of a window, which it ran into headfirst on many occasions. It did seem a bit subdued after those experiences and perhaps that was the reason the parakeet never made it to college.

But its linguistic ability was something to admire because, no matter how hard I'd try I could never make sense of the parakeet's chirping or screeching, much less imitate parakeet sounds. Human languages were tough enough. In school I found that out the hard way, especially when my teacher at that time communicated to me (both verbally and nonverbally—consisting mostly of glaring) that the correct use of grammar is regarded as the highest expression in human sophistication and culture. Well, how about learning to dance the tango? I bet no bird could ever master that.

Since the use of animal labor went by the wayside in modern society due to improved technology, maybe some of these critters could start earning their keep again, instead of just lazily squawking and demanding tons of seed. Maybe birds could take a lesson from dogs, which, as the last remaining dedicated beasts of burden, are still toiling day and night to protect and rescue people. Perhaps they could start working at the UN straightening out some of the misunderstandings between languages and peoples, for example.

They will have to be extremely careful though; there are a lot of windows in those buildings.

YOU JUST CAN'T WIN WITH ANTS

I do like animals. But the ones that have the biggest chance of endearing themselves to me are the ones you can watch on TV. There they are—cute, charming, even ferocious and dangerous but there is never an occasion where they bother you by smelling bad, running up and down all over you or biting, stabbing and pestering you. Wildlife needs to remain *wild*, in my opinion, as well as *in* the wild. If you're thinking about domesticating a wild animal—just look at how long it took to turn a wolf into a dog—it will probably take a few millennia for successful domestication of a new species. So don't undertake such an endeavor, unless you have time.

Canines and felines shouldn't get too cozy either. We've been spoiling these critters for much too long, allowing them to mooch off us and our hard work. Send them out to get a job, if they want to live in civilized society! A lot of animals are trained (or should be) in the security or pest control fields. I'm sure there are ample openings waiting to be filled. The same goes for partially domesticated species, like high school football players.

I had a recent experience when wildlife decided to move in with me. Although how a creature which stays indoors all day can be called 'wildlife', I don't know. The only thing wild around my home is the way I look right after dragging myself out of bed in the morning—unshaven and unkempt and bumping into walls. Nonetheless, the other day, just as I was enjoying a quiet evening at home watching television, I experienced a strange, disturbing sensation. Previously I only experienced something close to that in nightmares—insects crawling all over my body. Now, completely awake, I suffered something even worse—insects crawling all over me in *real life*! In no time at all the wildlife indoors had managed to drive me—the domesticated kind—outdoors to the porch. I was dancing under the stars with ants in my pants.

My friends had always compared the way I danced at clubs and parties to someone in the process of ferociously stomping on ants. So, I do have some experience in that field but even that skill is of little value if those pests brazenly make the audacious decision to invade your person. There I was flailing and cursing on the dimly lit patio with my wife enjoying my quite entertaining jig immensely (mostly due to the fact that there was nothing much on TV because "Shark-Week", featuring flailing and cursing victims had already passed). Then while in the process of fighting the ants, I felt burning, hungry eyes of further wildlife staring at me from murky, dark corners in my backyard. I felt they were waiting for me to collapse in exhaustion from my dance marathon, before pouncing on me to finish off whatever piece of carcass was left over after the ferocious ants had their fill. That is the law of the jungle—survival of the fittest, and as I grudgingly have to admit, I wasn't fit enough to dance—either with or under the stars (I can imagine the judges on "Dancing with the Stars" would have thrown me to the wolves).

Down for the count but not out, I picked myself up again, and getting back indoors, I decided to test that law of the jungle to see how "fit" the ants really were. Would they survive a can of pure poison which the fittest species on earth has developed in its very capable laboratories? Of course not! Now there they were, completely finished off after I had soaked them.

But wait a minute—was that me or was that an ant moving on my arm?

CONVERSATIONS WITH A SPIDER

Stepping into the shower the other morning, I was just about to soap up, when by changing the direction of the shower jet I flushed out a *spider*. As I watched it racing towards the drain I thought I heard something scream. I realized suddenly that instead of the terrifying shrieks my wife usually elicits when coming across such a critter, it was actually the spider who yelled.

"What are you doing, you moron!" he shouted angrily, desperately holding on to the grid of the drain hole. "Are you trying to kill me?"

"Well, sorreee," I replied a little perplexed. "I didn't see you. What were you doing hiding behind the shampoo bottle?"

"Are you a sadist, getting your kicks out of picking on someone smaller than you?" the creature hissed.

"Come on, you're just an insignificant bug," I scoffed.

"Oh, am I? We have been here longer than you. Maybe you're not as important as you think you are."

"I've been living here for over four years and I don't think I've seen you before. Although I might have flushed a few of your relatives down the drain", I replied.

"See how stupid you are," the spider said sarcastically. "Of course I didn't mean you personally but your species. We've been here much longer than you dumb humans."

"You sure are a big talker for such a small insect," I said redirecting the showerhead, eliciting another angry scream from the bug on the drain. "My wife doesn't care for your kind, by the way. She gets the creeps whenever she sees a spider. Come to think of it, *your* wife doesn't seem to care for you that much either, does she?"

"What are you talking about?" asked the creature.

"Well isn't it a custom amongst spiders that the wife uses the husband for a wedding feast right after consummation of marriage?"

"You're talking about some of my cousins, not me", the spider sneered.

"Well, actually maybe she does care for you quite a bit, depending on what you *taste* like," I mused unperturbed, laughing out loud.

"I told you, that's my cousins!" the spider protested. "We are a highly developed species, just look at the sophisticated nets that I crafted in your corners. You might realize they are beautiful as well as functional, with unbelievable tough yet incredibly light material. This is something you bipedal creatures just dream of producing. You could never do that with any of your fancy machines in a million years."

"If it means having to eat ants, I think we could do without it," I replied flippantly.

"It's no use," the bug said. "I knew I couldn't have an intelligent conversation with someone like you."

"What's going on?" my wife suddenly popped her head around the bathroom door. "Whom are you talking to?"

"I'm talking to a very intelligent bug," I replied.

"What? Intelligent . . . bugs? Oh no, he's completely gone off the edge now," she mumbled, as she slammed the door shut. Apparently she was having trouble hearing me through the shower curtain. "Now he thinks he is some kind of secret agent."

"See what I mean?" I said turning back to the bug. But he had disappeared. "Just wait until my wife gets a hold of you, Mr. Spider!" Then I added with a loud chuckle, "Or, better yet, just wait till YOUR wife gets a hold of you!"

"If I told you once, I told you a thousand times, we don't eat each other in my family. That's my cousin!" the spider yelled angrily, as his head reappeared from underneath the drain.

Well, sorry, but you shouldn't have done that, I thought while aiming the shower stream at the bug. Insisting on having the last word is sometimes not very smart, Mr. Spider. I learned that from my wife.

WHAT DO YOU DO WHEN YOUR NEIGHBORS' DOGS TURN ROGUE?

There are some frightening things out there—sharks, tigers, mother-in-laws, IRS agents etc. But even those aren't as menacing as a vicious pack of ferocious, feral animals—dogs, in my case.

As it happens, the neighborhood canines decided to turn rogue where I live. I assume they timed the idea of morphing into anti-social creatures (at least where living with human neighbors is concerned), as soon as they detected that adult supervision had ceased because everyone next door had gone to work. The transformation from cuddly, endearing little charming pets and companions for the children into a pack of vicious beasts was sudden.

At first the dogs just ganged up by the fence the moment I dared to venture into that vicinity on the other side—my side. Probably the mere idea of *anyone* living next-door drove them close to insanity, a notion so unacceptable that they barked themselves hoarse and banged into the fence for hours. Then one day, as I was sitting in the shade, quietly reading my book on the back patio, the dogs suddenly appeared in my yard. Apparently they hadn't noticed me, as they frolicked all over my property sniffing, yapping and happily leaving their scent marks where they could be certain their human neighbors walked around barefoot.

It's a fact, that in the dog world it is completely unnecessary to put down a deposit and sign a deed if you have your eye on a certain piece of real estate. Since printed material is only known in the form of a rolled-up newspaper, an unpleasant instrument that may have been utilized to terrorize the canine during its formative years, as a dog you need some other system if you want to stake a claim on some property. To accomplish that, in the world of dogs, all you need is a full bladder. Then you can leave deposits all over the territory. Apparently that is equivalent to making mortgage payments in human terms.

Of course I objected loudly. I didn't see why the fact of my wife and I working hard all month to make payments should be on an equal footing with gulping down gallons of water and then leaving the product of an overactive canine digestive system all over my place. I decided to stand up and face this gang. There I was staring them down, about half a dozen dogs the size of—well, OK—rabbits. They immediately went into overdrive with eye-popping fury, growling, barking, snarling, and yapping, beside themselves with anger as to how I, a mere human, would dare to enter their territory that they had worked so hard all morning to mark as their own. Outweighing them by hundreds of pounds I was confident that I could put some fear into them and drive them back though the hole they had dug underneath my fence by acting in a similar mental state—I went bananas. Screaming and yelling and crazily dancing up and down, while at the same time hoping that neighbors, worrying about my inner health, wouldn't attempt to calm me down by perhaps, shooting me with a medicated dart, I succeeded in chasing the dogs back through their hole, into their own yard—except for one. This one refused to budge, instead it jumped forward, barking and growling and displaying its terrifying teeth, reminding me of undersized chewing gum chiclets.

That's when I shouted, "Sit"! Now this command seemed to put the animal into a tremendous mental conundrum. Should it follow its ancient animalistic instincts of defending its territory or should it obey the incessant brainwashing sessions inflicted upon it by its human masters? Alternately sitting down and defiantly barking, it finally thought it best to slink back into the hole as well before suffering a total mental collapse. Brimming with confidence as the conqueror of beasts, I rolled a heavy rock in front of that hole, one of many dug by the neighborhood dogs, despite my frequent protests to their human parents.

I only hope this bunch isn't connected to something like a Doberman gang.

CHAPTER EIGHT

Don't Let The Extended Family Get The Better Of You

Mere words from her mouth falling on deaf ears, Mrs. Wilson utilized her nose to give that son-in-law of hers a piece of her mind.

WHAT TO DO WHEN YOUR
MOTHER-IN-LAW VISITS

What is stress? Imagine walking high up on a tightrope with snarling carnivorous beasts licking their chops in anticipation down below, while a bad guy is feverishly sawing at the rope. Perhaps that might be considered a very taxing situation. Or maybe, seen from <u>another point of view</u>, stress is fearing your dinner is walking on the said tightrope but is *able* to escape before the bad guy cuts the rope, or worse—having your dinner fall down on your head knocking you out and escaping, leaving you without nourishment but with a sizable bill from the *vet*. In still another situation, stress may mean trying to secure a tightrope-walker's faulty footing, while he assumes that you are attempting to harm him, as he (calling you a "bad guy"), tries to knock you off with his lengthy tightrope-pole into the claws of several hungry monsters below.

All these scenarios, while very stressful, pale in comparison with trying to make a good impression on your mother-in-law when she comes for a visit (which means giving her a chance to observe you in your own habitat around the clock). Starting out, she might for example, wonder aloud about the significance of colorful tattoos covering quite a substantial area on your torso or question the need for jewelry piercing sensitive areas on your body. Once she begins casting disapproving sideway glances at her daughter you will find yourself in a stressful situation. She may also want to see the entire collection of diplomas and certificates that you had been bragging about, featuring you as a successful brain-surgeon and showcasing your accomplishment in the area of rocket science. Then she may express her great disappointment in the fact that just around the time of her visit the piano was in the shop for repairs, since she had looked forward so very much to listening to your masterful rendering of the great works in baroque music. Seizing this opportunity, you may volunteer to find out why it would take the repair person the exact span of time of a mother-in-law's visit to make the instrument concert-worthy. Full of anxiety you dive into the next bar for a soothing drink, laden with reading material on how to become a brain-surgeon, rocket-scientist and concert pianist in five easy steps. Realizing that even these five easy steps would require much more time than anticipated, you instead begin heeding the information and advice around you stemming from patrons who are experts in the art of excuses, justifications and plausible deniability.

Filled with useful advice on how to sidestep and circumvent scrutiny, and overflowing with barrels of inebriating liquids, you finally sneak back, just after everyone's bedtime (when you are sure they have finally given up waiting for you, anticipating news of the ailing piano). Instead of sleeping in the next morning, and recovering from the draining effects of poisonous liquids ingested the night before, you get up and again steal yourself off to work. But, consumed with worry and the latent fog of dubious liquid substances, you are unable to concentrate fully at work, leading to a greater number of errors than usual. Your boss somehow faults you for taking your taxi-fares to the wrong addresses and fires you. Now you wander the streets aimlessly and only occasionally call home to let your loved ones know that, although you would love to spend time with your beloved mother-in-law, a "caseload of ailing brains" has been overwhelming while at the same time malfunctioning rockets need your careful attention. Your wife, unwilling to empathize with you in such a vital matter, sketches out a scenario of damage to your own frontal lobes if you don't return immediately since the rent is due.

Finally you break down and, after a tearful return, confess that it had all been a lie. But the reaction of your mother-in-law confuses you, because she tells you that she had known all along about your employment as a cabdriver and your proclivity for embellishment (since she left the area of baroque music untouched, you promise a full-fledged concert on her next visit).

The stress is subsiding and you finally recover your bearings until the phone rings and Aunt Mary—the gossipy one—announces her visit.

HAPPY MOTHER'S DAY, MOM

Imagine living completely rent free, in a nice warm cocoon, totally protected, without worry for nine months? Then, through no fault of your landlady, just because you got too fat and started thrashing around and making a nuisance of yourself, you leave her with no choice but to kick you out. It would be quite understandable if, after the way you behaved, she simply dumped you to make it on your own but instead, she continues to worry about you, taking care of you without demanding one single penny in return. She actually pampers you 24/7, tending to your every whim immediately without too much complaint. And how do you pay her back? By producing eardrum-bursting shrieks at all hours of the day and night and stinking up the place.

And then you really let her have it. First you provide her with a serious case of heart palpitations by falling off bikes and trees, and then you draw her into drawn-out battles about cosmetic adornments, ranging from fuchsia Mohawks, to facial tattoos, to piercing steel rods through soft tissue. And soon after, while you waste your time "finding yourself" by trying to join rock bands or bands of gypsies, she quietly finds a job for you at an accounting firm.

That's your mother. And how do you compensate her for all that? You and your siblings, once a year on Mother's Day, schlep in a box of candy costing a couple of bucks and maybe a bunch of flowers hacked off at the stem, expecting her to turn cartwheels marveling at your incredible feat of thoughtfulness. And what else do you do? After years of listening to all of your complaints about problem bosses and obnoxious coworkers at your workplace, where she supported you and tirelessly encouraged you to make it to the top and you now make more money per year than she made in her entire life—you suggest, on her special day, to take her out to a coffee shop where you can get all-day breakfast for 2.99.

And then although it is her day, she patiently listens to all of you complaining about your lives. Maybe now you don't make a lot of money because you quit that job your mom got for you, leaving you completely broke and forcing you to borrow the 2.99 from her. Or, your sister Anne, instead of marrying that nice fellow with the taped-up glasses and ink-stained shirts, as your mother had suggested, who by the way is working on his second billion, hooked up with that daredevil dude who now sits in jail, having spent all his money on tattoos instead of paying her alimony. And your brother Sam never paid attention, at your mom's urging, to that quiet pretty girl from church, who by the way, got married to that high powered attorney. Instead his multiple divorces from a variety of flimflam floozies has resulted in his being bled hefty sums for alimony.

But it's all-okay with your mom, and naturally she'll pretend to believe you when you say you'll pay her back as soon as you get back on your feet. All she wants is to spend some time with her children, even if it means she has to continue listening to all of you whining and moaning about the meaning of life. She may even encourage the youngest, Shannon, at 25, to give American Idol a try. "Folks made it there with a lot less talent than you," she'll say, even though she noticed paint peeling off the wall the last time Shannon sang shrilly off-key for her in her kitchen. She'll even suggest springing for a guitar, which for her would mean having to sacrifice her bingo nights or going to the beauty parlor for a few months. All she wants is for you all to be happy. That's your mom.

Happy Mother's Day, Mom!

IT'S MOTHER'S DAY!

After living off another human being for months at a time, mooching her food, making her sick and subjecting her to enormous weight-gain, don't you think you, at least, owe that person a call of thanks for all you've put her through?

That's right, today is *Mother's Day* and you'd better have planned to take Mom to a nice place for dinner and start showing some appreciation for all the times she fed and clothed you without complaining once. Well, maybe she did complain once or twice, for example when the toilet backed up, with the phone ringing at the same time, and dinner burning on the stove and you stood in the middle of the living room screaming that you had soiled your pants. Those "hoity-toity" folks in college didn't teach you how to clean your behind. Guess who did? What do they teach you at college anyway—how to get smart with your Mom? Now wash your hands before you sit down for dinner!

And how about all the times you were crying, feeling bad because you fell off your bike or because you caught your boyfriend smooching with your best friend, wasn't Mom there to dry your tears? Not only that, but she had that bike fixed in no time and presented you with an elaborate plan of revenge for that wayward boyfriend. When alternative plans were rejected because the expense of paying for a hit-man would have overstretched the household budget, didn't mother comfort you by predicting that "that heel would end up in jail for sure anyway"? And then didn't she have the good sense to hide all the newspaper accounts showing the ex-boyfriend as a captain of industry alongside that bimbo of a wife, when you came home crying again because those big shots in Hollywood were too stupid to realize that they had another Oscar-winner at hand?

That's your Mom, slaving and working her fingers to the bone for you. And what do you *kids* do instead—fighting and feuding all the time! Why can't you get along? Why does "Johnny" always have to tear the heads off his sister's dolls? You're thirty years old now, for crying out loud, shouldn't you have worked out your anger issues by now? And don't give me that "blaming your mother" nonsense. Even if she did dress you into your teens (and still does sometimes), what does that have to do with your not getting a job? You haven't "found yourself"? You better do that quickly or find yourself another mother. I doubt you can find one who makes your favorite cream pie the way she does. Your mother was able to "find herself", wasn't she? And also found herself with a bunch of kids who depended on her day and night. Did she quit motherhood one day to travel with the circus? No she didn't. Perhaps she should have, maybe caring for a bunch of monkeys would have been much more rewarding than looking after you kids. And don't talk with your mouth full!

I know what you are going to say, that she wasn't always there for you. She missed some of your recitals and didn't know how much pain and suffering you went through because she neglected to understand that covering yourself from head to toe with tattoos was an important statement to make. Now suck it up and walk it off! You think your mother wouldn't have liked to get some tattoos herself? But she refrained from it because clients don't trust real estate agents with skulls and crossbones on their necks as much as property professionals without them. You also have no idea that she was not just a "mother" but also a real person with desires of her own. Maybe she really did want to join the circus or go to Hollywood or ride off with that handsome, young daredevil. But she didn't—why? Because of you, of course.

Now quit slouching so much! And if you make that face again it will get stuck!

FATHER KNOWS BEST

There comes a time in every child's life when the realization hits that his or her parent is a mere human being. This sudden discovery is usually the very first great disappointment in life. In fact, as one grows older it becomes abundantly clear that it's just the first one in a never-ending series of disappointments and disillusionments. But luckily most of these shortfalls can easily be blamed on one's parents because they should have prepared us for such shocks a long time before, or tried harder in their lackluster attempts to become Superman or Superwoman. Other folks do it. I think just about every one of us can point to a friend from the neighborhood whose dad had been busy splitting the atom, while doing his real job as a secret agent on the side, as well as winning the Super Bowl in his spare time. It's true because our friend (someone who will take the place of our parents for reliable information from then on) has sworn that it is. Why couldn't our parents be more like that other dad?

From the vantage point of a grownup, one understands now that there actually is a gradual breakdown process in trust that begins with the realization that there is no Santa Claus, although I like to believe that there might be an exception in my case and that's why I continue playing the lottery. Usually vicious playground vigilantes sooner or later identify and expose anyone still clinging to such infantile notions as the existence of Santa Claus and treat such babies to never-ending ridicule. That is the moment when you realize that the parents you had, thus far assumed to be infallible and beyond reproach, were lying to you. Clearly, they probably didn't care for you as much as they pretended. Why, otherwise, would they have put you into a situation of such derision and ridicule? Many of us from that moment on plan a sinister plot of retaliation, which often culminated in refusing to set the clock on our parents' VCRs a few years back, or looking the other way today while they fumble trying to get on the Internet to download Bing Crosby tunes.

But the real silver lining in the dark cloud occurred when we realized that we knew everything better than our parents, a fact we weren't shy to let those ignorant folks know at every turn.

My moment of truth—the fact that my dad was not all-knowing—came when I was playing cowboys and Indians in my native Germany. This game required that one spoke essential and important phrases in a certain lingo, known as English. Apparently, when certain parties such as cowboys and Indians approached each other in this mysterious "country" called, the Wild West, it was of utmost importance to utter the phrase "hands up!" Heeding the advice of the linguistic genius I had assumed my dad was, I pronounced it "hands oop", something causing enormous hilarity amongst my more enlightened fellow cowboys. And after numerous bloody noses during playground cowboy barroom fights, defending my father's linguistic integrity, I finally had to grudgingly admit that it was indeed not pronounced "hands oop" but rather more like "hands ahpp." What a shock.

Now after spending decades speaking and writing in this language of cowboys, I think I've become fairly proficient in it. But this is not a fact easily conceded by my father in the old country who actually has not progressed very much from a few words, like "hands up." I had no idea that our linguistic dispute still raged when, on a recent visit, my father dragged me in front of the TV displaying someone from Great Britain. "Is this man's native language English, or is it not?" my father demanded. It was, I guessed, a gentleman from Liverpool who, pointing upwards and engaging his dialect, was—lo and behold—pronouncing a very familiar word loud and clear—"OOP!"

See, father knows best after all.

CHAPTER NINE

The Working Life

"I understand that this is a transitional stage until management finds a better use for us."

GOING TO WORK IN THE MORNING

Yesterday, I thought the unpleasant first chore of the day, plunging from the coziness of sleep into cold, harsh reality, had already been achieved—it was my belief that I got up swiftly, took a shower and greeted the day with burgeoning enthusiasm. But something was not quite right—why then was I still lying in bed? Instead of frolicking through the hallway, I found myself snuggling into the comfort of my warm pillows.

Then I realized the disappointing dilemma. My subconscious mind, ever so protective of my fragile disposition, had tried to shield me from my usual brutal morning upheaval and had presented me with a charade. I had dreamt that I had already breached the toughest of obstacles, got out of my cozy bed and jumped into the dark chilliness of a humdrum weekday morning. But instead, there I was, rolled up in my cocoon, faced with the enormous challenge of crossing from fantasy into reality as the digits on my alarm clock pulsated menacingly like the flashing lights on a police cruiser.

Fighting for each and every morsel of the tiniest of chances, I reasoned that perhaps, since my mind was capable of such trickery, it may also have deceived me into believing this morning to be a workday while it really was a weekend—*the scoundrel*—after a good laugh, I thought, I would turn around and go back to the restful sleep I craved. As I held on to this flimsiest of illusions for as long as I could, like a drowning man on a sinking lifeboat, the sudden screeching blare of the alarm clock obliterated this image, tearing it to a thousand pieces.

I had one more chance left, I thought at that moment. If I could just get up and stumble to the dresser, I could dig through my wallet and find my 'lotto' ticket. Why shouldn't I be the one to win the overnight jackpot? Someone always does. Then not only could I sleep as long as I wanted but I could meander to work one last time (much later of course) and, with great relish give the boss a piece of my mind. This image caused me to smile and in no time, placed me back into peaceful slumber for a few more minutes until it slowly dawned on me that verification of such a windfall would involve getting out of bed and therefore defeating the whole purpose of wanting to complete my lengthy sleep-cycle. What would happen if, by chance I had not been showered by the golden yield of divine intervention? I would stand there shivering and embarrassed without the benefit of a few more desperate moments of restful sleep.

Then it hit me—of course—today was a holiday. How lucky I was to recognize this before I was completely awake. It must be—there was no other explanation for it. As I drifted back into the comforts of the unconscious, my mind began to mull over the possibility of such fortunate circumstances. What kind of holiday could it possibly be? The major ones glimmered too afar in the horizon to be a possibility, and most of the others, I was not eligible for anyway, since I had neglected making the smart job-choices with a bank or the government. A wave of anger almost *did* jolt me completely awake, as I realized that even that possibility was suddenly slammed shut.

Suddenly I felt a slight tingle in my throat. Could it be that I had a touch of the flu? Or maybe I had eaten the wrong food yesterday and I had somehow become ill with that mysterious ailment commonly known as "stomach-flu"? After additional contemplation, my body obliged me and suddenly I felt under-the-weather. The more I considered this possibility, the more my concern increased, not only for myself but also for everyone else at work. Of course, I would under no circumstances, risk limping to work in such a condition and perhaps infecting my co-workers with this illness, risk shutting down the entire operation. It was obvious to me that my boss would thank me on his knees for such selfless thinking and more than likely will reward me with additional days off. I might as well take advantage of this future generous offer and use my additional days off straight away. With that, I turned over and dozed off again.

The second blast of the alarm clock almost jerked me into an upright position. I had no sick-days coming to me anymore, I realized as a jolt of pure terror jarred through my entire body. They had already been used up at the last round of the flu season, at which time my boss had also suggested that I should investigate the possibility of "making my home under a bridge", since lack of employment might be an option.

Somehow, suddenly, the act of getting out of bed and racing to work seemed a cinch.

IT'S TIME WE TOOK A LITTLE REST

Perhaps you have found yourself in this situation? Due to no fault of yours, the wicked Masters of Evil decide to descend upon you with such sudden force as to render you sick and exhausted, virtually unable to answer the call of duty, which slams into your consciousness in the form of another force from hell—the shrieking alarm clock. Fully aware of the immense quandary of having work piling sky-high—perhaps due to recent layoffs at your place of employment and your boss' desire for a leaner, *meaner* workplace—these depraved ghouls from the deep dark bowls of evil wantonness never seem to be able to satisfy their sadistic cravings as they watch you struggling out of bed and schlepping yourself to work.

To make a long story short, what happens when you're sicker than a dog and still have to haul yourself to work anyway? You're not alone if you decide to go to work while ill, as institutions like the Harvard School of Public Health and the Kaiser Family Foundation have discovered in recent polls. But the question is *why* would anyone voluntarily drag himself or herself to work under the influence of influenza or after being knocked down by thuggish bugs? Dedication, devotion, undying commitment to one's work—is that the reason many of us sit in our cubicles, shivering, sneezing and coughing, while watching inquisitive vultures commencing lazy circles underneath the neon light tubes? Not according to the abovementioned survey. It seems that instead of dedication, what most people lack is medication—the proper kind prescribed by doctors, as well as bed rest under the care of healthcare professionals. But this seems to be something we readily surrender. Why? *Fear!* The simple reason is that we are afraid that we will lose our jobs if we stay at home nursing our ailments.

Because of the following graphic depiction of objectionable workplace goings-on, parental guidance might be advised from this point. The most strident example, which illustrates the hazards of this disturbing trend (i.e. ignoring illness in favor of struggling with never-ending, overwhelming work), surfaced in a recent news item. A 45-year old Japanese man actually literally worked himself to death in Toyota City, Japan recently. Apparently he had logged in more than 80 hours of overtime per month regularly until his heart simply gave out. While undying dedication may indeed be immortal, the physical body might not be so sturdy and robust, and may give in to the temptation to take a rest, sometimes terminally.

I remember during the heady times of yuppies starting "startups", almost everyone seemed to agree that sleep was an unnecessary interruption of important work and should be done, if at all, on the sly in front of a buzzing computer. Most of the startups came to a screeching halt, belly-up, but it makes one wonder whether the idea of startups was nothing but a setup to get us comfortable with the notion that working nonstop is the future standard and rest is not a normal condition of the human experience.

Let's take a page from wildlife. I understand that predatory animals, like lions and tigers, work only three hours a day, at the very most and they usually clock that in at night because it is too hot during the day (must be nice to call your own shots). Their prey, gazelles and wildebeests, on the other hand don't have that choice and do work all day long as well as at night, just as we do, grazing, constantly wearily looking over their shoulders, afraid someone might be breathing down their necks. They also never call in sick. As a matter of fact, being sick, old and feeble is a death sentence. It's a jungle out there.

Well, I've seen some exotic plant life growing inside cubicles in offices all over but the question is, do we really want to invite jungle conditions into our workplaces?

THE SUMMER HOLIDAYS ARE HERE

The sun was shining in the vast blue sky above us. Balmy weather soothing our weary bones and a calm breeze was blowing to remind us that we shouldn't pine away in stuffy, windowless offices all week long. Instead we should be on a vacation; someplace where we can while away amongst pine trees or palm trees. A little sand, surf and some Pena Colada wouldn't hurt either. Imagine a tropical beach and yourself floating on gentle, warm waves, slowly drifting back towards the shoreline expecting to be served a scrumptious lunch in your equally sumptuous hotel. That's the life that you deserve!

My wife and I were in complete agreement on this issue, we definitely deserved everything that life has to offer and so we decided to embark on a trip. But instead of choosing the abovementioned tropical island, a likely place for refreshing and soothing the battered body and mind, I don't know what possessed us to settle on a whirlwind tour across Northern Europe to visit relatives amongst all the other European relics. Perhaps we got carried away; the can-do, go-getter spirit of my wife's superiors at work might have egged us on. Because in no time at all, as soon as they got wind of the fact that she intended to go on a journey, they decided to heap double and triple amounts of work upon her. Of course she can do it with enough can-do spirit they reasoned, besides, she would have ample time to relax once she found herself on vacation (Ambitious notions of get-up-and-go and getting the impossible done, do sound grand, especially if you are able to pile the workload onto the shoulders of others). Unfortunately to their chagrin, there was a moratorium on overtime pay. So naturally pretty much, time and energy spent burning the midnight oil would have to be charged to her own dime. Well, my wife did not complain, as she kept in mind the picture that it would all be worth it, once she stepped onto the plane on her way out of that bleak place responsible for much of human misery, called the office.

Everything went fine, as she suffered in silence laboring through mountains of files and documents, until, a couple of weeks before the start of our vacation, my wife drew my attention to her upper lip. She has the most perfectly sculpted mouth I have ever seen and it took her several times to have me look closer, until I recognized a tiny pimple.

"This has never happened before," she whispered with terror in her voice. "What are your relatives in Germany going to say if I show up with this ugly growth on my lip?"

No matter how I tried to calm her, telling her that no one would even notice, in her mind the tiny imperfection took on the dimensions of a small planet. And indeed, perhaps malicious spirits in her office envying her vacation playing a wicked sort of voodoo magic, her blemish seemed to balloon as quickly as her workload during the next few days. But anyone who has ever suffered with blemishes during adolescence, that habitually pop up exactly at the most inopportune of times knows that there are potions on the market designed to clear these things up in a hurry. At least that's what commercials lure us into believing. The next week, instead of planning our vacation strategy, time was spent at drugstores amongst angst-ridden teenagers, hyperventilating about prom nights shattered by the ominous enemy, called acne.

My innocent remark about drawing a face on the thing, choosing an appropriate name and treating it like a Siamese twin, earned me an angry welt on my arm. Now we were both damaged goods. But fortunately I can hide my imperfection under my shirt. I shouldn't have said that either. Excuse me—I have to duck. A load of heavyweight files, filled with documents has become airborne suddenly, being somehow hurled towards the direction of my lip. Next week—airport blues.

B.A.R.T

Our domestic transport system, BART (an acronym for "Be Aware—Rare Tropical diseases"), was built some thirty years ago for two main purposes: one, to entice motorists out of their cars into cars on rails, and two, to provide a safe haven for unemployed, hollow-eyed Hollywood horror movie creatures. I recognized one from a horror flick on my recent BART trip. He was the one who had been featured gnawing on a leg of businessman, one who had been busy reading the Wall Street Journal, aghast that his transit stocks had been dropping like flies. The fact that normal folks going to work sit quietly and stare stoically ahead, trying their best to ignore the nuts sitting next to them reminds me of the Haunted House ride in Disneyland. Towards the last part of the joyride, nasty-looking crazed ghouls, grinning happily, suddenly place themselves right next to each visitor. But due to the fact that they've been created by laser-technology they are largely odorless, a desirable condition our very own hygiene-challenged BART-banshees should learn from.

One of the most important rules of riding the rails is—do not, under any circumstances, touch anything whatsoever, even if it means you're being hurled through the air in one of the many unscheduled stops; unless, of course you are encased in one of those protective suits used to clean up toxic, radioactive spills. The reason being—not only are tropical diseases to be found in abundance there, but also a large variety of known and unknown germs and viruses thriving in the Northern hemisphere. Some of the more notorious viruses had been busy a few centuries ago, wiping out half the population of Europe. That is why you see each and every one of the commuters starting to cough, sneeze and wheeze as soon as they step across the threshold of the train-netherworld.

Of course no train station should be without a public address system, broadcasting important announcements, such as "something . . . something . . . do not roar." At least that's what it sounded like to someone with normal hearing when I was traveling. While the first part was completely unintelligible, the last part seemed to be clear enough but was totally ignored by several passengers who immediately began roaring, howling and carrying on, probably due to the fact that they were unable to hear their own voices because they had large headphones clamped to their ears.

The warning for things to come is at the very beginning of the journey, as it is extremely difficult to find a gate that is in working order and allows you to pass after inserting the ticket. Anxiously dancing up and down because your train is about to leave the station you finally manage to make it past the gate entrance doors, shaped like gigantic teeth that snap shut immediately and force you to leave a good part of your luggage behind. I assume that the contents are sold on flea markets all over the county, in order to make payroll for the attendants who sit in glass-booths staring at you vacantly. Their purpose, if you should have the time, is to provide you with needed information, which is rendered through thick windows: "something . . . something . . . do not roar."

Once you make it inside the train it is imperative to stay clear of the doors, which constantly tease you by opening and closing for no apparent reason. You might be tempted to step out again. Of course at that very moment the jaws snap shut at once yet again and you will be stuck, your luggage will be sold and most of your body will end up as feed for the ghouls. But the rest of your journey should be trouble free, perhaps only occasionally interrupted by the haunted wailing of lost ghost-children and adults late for work. Have a safe journey.

CHAPTER TEN

It's Holiday Season Again

After living without oxygen for a record of 33 days, Walter Bungle, instead of filling his lungs with air, made the fatal mistake of ordering a beer first.

MAKING YOUR NEW YEAR'S RESOLUTION

There should be a law against New Year's resolutions or at the very least New Year's resolutions should be heavily regulated to fit within the parameters of reality. Maybe we should each be outfitted with some kind of collar designed to deliver a mild electrical shock whenever any middle-aged man or woman announces the ambitious goal of being married to Brad Pitt or Jennifer Lopez or frolicking—rail-thin—through Hollywood mansions, all to be accomplished within the span of a mere calendar year, and right after having digested any and all works of world literature, that is, besides having achieved a mastery of several major tongues. The severity of the electrical shock could be adjusted according to the expanse in the flight of fancy.

Most New Year's resolutions follow this trend: Lose weight, get in shape, make a million bucks and still have time for lunch the next day. Many people also add finding and marrying their soul-mate (preferably one who has already lost weight, is in top-shape and worth millions), reading a few of the 800-page classics in literature and learning a foreign language or two. If at all possible, folks usually like to get this out of the way by early spring in order to take the summer off. Reality hits hard when we realize, perhaps around the second week of January that due to unavoidable sessions with certain merry necessities during the festive season (which happen to contain colossal calorie counts), that our weight has quadrupled. After the initial grueling bout with a variety of treadmills, which results in a swift plummeting off of the holiday frame of mind, the subject is revisited on the way to the gym the next day. Sometimes we find that the substantial protective shield of eggnog and Christmas candy is still useful when warding off winter chills, making our postponement of regular workout sessions entirely plausible.

Hardly anything can be compared to the shock of realization, after the humdrum of normalcy has set in, that the days of the get-rich-quick billion dollar "startups" are part of nostalgic fantasies of the last century and that instead, we might have to rely again on the random luck of the lottery or the hope that a rich relative might decide to abandon earthly pastures right after signing over substantial funds to the favorite offspring. This sad and hard-earned awareness has the effect of killing off another one of our important promises to ourselves.

Finally, after comprehending that we might be condemned to slough away forever in the tediousness of mediocrity, another idea might also begin to sink in when spending some "quality time" with that new-found beau—that just because another person shares your bad habits, does not exactly mean that he or she is soothing for your soul. This realization usually obliterates the myth of the magical mate.

While for some individuals the shock of these insights might crop up a few weeks into the new calendar, for most people it happens right after the fog of the New Year's party begins to clear. Then the questions begin, "What was I thinking?" "How am I going to lose 40 pounds and the ravages of two or three decades?" Just around this time the memory of your New Year's resolution begins to dim and is soon forgotten. Or perhaps it isn't completely forgotten but just pushed back into the outer corners of your mind where it takes every opportunity of sniping away at you at the most inopportune of times throughout the year.

Promises to yourself should be limited to realistic goals. For most of us that means creeping up the ladder within the increments of minimum-wage laws, for example. That doesn't mean though that we cannot hope for a windfall or two—just don't announce them to everyone. And don't tell anyone the real reason you're sending all that unhealthy candy to your wealthy relative.

HAPPY NEW YEAR

Have you ever wondered why there are no peas in peanuts? Or why kidney beans which have absolutely no relation with kidneys, are called that only because they are shaped like kidneys? If so, then this automatically leads to the next question, why then are some swimming-pools which are shaped like kidneys not also called "kidney-pools"? And why shouldn't they be shaped like the liver instead, to elevate that organ to its rightful, all-important place since it worked overtime processing the lake-sized merry bubbly that many of us consumed at last night's New Year's party?

But most of all I wonder why another one of my vital organs, my brain, is working overtime, inundating me with inquiries about all sorts of useless trivialities this morning? Wait a minute—morning? What am I talking about, isn't it way past noon? Should I perhaps have used a bit more prudence in celebrating kicking the champagne bucket of another wasted year, and stayed away from beverages causing havoc with that delicate chemistry in my brain? (see it's doing it again—another question) Now, instead of welcoming the New Year with enthusiasm and gusto, I feel like the old, worn-out 2005 year in the last wee hours of December; and I'm only a few hours into the fresh one.

More than likely you are aware that we are breaking into the sixth year of this new, hardly used century. But the foolish people we are, instead of taking care of the mint-condition we find it in, we don't waste any time at all abusing it (and it is already looking quite battered and worn-out around the fringes). Mother would be appalled, since she always tried to infuse in us the idea of taking care of things as a matter of extreme importance. You might remember her fury, for example, when you managed to remove the wheels of that new toy only a few hours after you had unwrapped your Christmas presents, don't you?

As you might have guessed, the deadline for making your New Year's resolutions is approaching quickly. You might as well hanker down and commit to it, especially because you are facing months of bleak, cold weather without the single interruption of a revitalizing holiday. This is the tiny window of opportunity left ajar to make promises to ourselves—in between the exuberance of indulgent gluttony during the holidays and the prospect of facing a nose worn off by the ever-churning grindstone—who would want to risk posing any challenges to oneself while shivering in the rain and darkness?

The first resolution (its importance I discovered the hard way)—don't tamper with things and leave the wheels alone. Let professionals handle repairs and upkeep. Now, lucky for me, that should give me some leeway with the running toilet. Although I mentioned to my wife that I would take a look at it, I cannot violate the covenant of my sacred pledge now—sorry.

The next vow, since cold weather, rain and the banalities of everyday living don't hold too much interest for me and I would rather live a life of luxury and extravagance in a tropical setting, I would need to bump up my current standard of living. A big casino jackpot or two or a win in the lottery should do the trick. Therefore a greater investment into lottery tickets will be necessary. That, in turn, would also automatically take care of the first resolution, since shelling out big bucks for experts in home-repair would be no skin of my nose. Come to think of it, no skin of my nose would be sacrificed to that grindstone either anymore. The effort of bringing tedious toil to a grinding halt would have been my next resolution anyway. See how quickly you can achieve anything you want, if you just put your mind to it? Most resolutions have already been achieved and the "baby New Year" has not even had a chance to dirty its diapers yet. In that case I will have ample time now to wonder, why they left out the "peas" in "peanuts."

WHY NEW YEAR'S RESOLUTIONS RARELY WORK

What's the use of making New Year's resolutions every year? Haven't those ten or twenty pounds you vowed to lose on December 31st each year returned with regularity the following year, time and time again? More than likely you actually acquired brand-new pounds in addition to the old ones. So why fight the pounds, especially since they will help keep the winter chill off your bones?

People go through the motion each New Year's Eve of pledging to "improve" themselves by perhaps, learning a new language. Why bother? What's wrong with the old one? Most languages require that you talk through your nose or twist your tongue into pretzels anyway. Why not use your tongue for something more useful, such as eating some *real* pretzels to keep winter away? Then there are people who want to improve relationships, or who promise to be nicer to others around them. Why would anyone do that? Isn't it reasonable to assume that those people you are nice to will then take advantage of you, probably stealing those pretzels and leaving you to freeze to death?

I rarely make New Year's resolutions. In my opinion, if you can't make a promise to yourself on *any* date, say May 17th, what makes you think that you'll keep your pledge just because the number changes behind the 2 and a couple of zeroes in the middle of winter? My beliefs are rooted in the old school of making resolutions on birthdays. That's why I exclaimed one day, during my foolish twenties, that I would be a billionaire by the time I was thirty. Little did I realize that one actually had to do something constructive to achieve that, such as creating one single item that everyone would want and use. A gadget in all households for example, that would take a tremendous amount of unpleasant chores off our hands, such as doing math and keeping track of recipes, while also providing entertainment and supplying the news. Unfortunately as it appears, someone else already had the same idea, and that person actually produced the item before I had a chance to work out the details of my plan.

So over the years, I promised myself that I would do a lot more reading, and I devoured titles like *Think and Grow Rich*. But after some time I came to the conclusion that in order to do more thinking I had to stop reading, and that's about the point where I am right now. So it seems that I'm due for a New Year's resolution this year after all—I have resolved that I will develop new software to inform people about the fallibility of New Year's resolutions, and finesse the art of demolishing everyone's spirit right before the real bleakness of winter begins and the blues and hangovers set in! I would show people charts and graphic interpretations proving how small the actual chances are of realizing their dreams for the following year. This could be a huge hit at New Year's parties. Imagine what would happen for instance if I could prove to you that you have no chance whatsoever of succeeding in show business, and that you should instead, follow your mother's advice and stick with that paralegal job of yours? In all probability, according to the ironclad mathematical logic of computer calculations, you'd be kicked out of Hollywood and will end up asking to move back home again. Wouldn't I spare you a whole lot of embarrassment with my new invention?

In actual fact the "hit" at the party may be more like a smashed lamp across my skull and blame for spoiling the festivities as a "killjoy." But it would bear out my prediction as correct after all—that most resolutions won't work out anyway.

But don't listen to me, I was the guy you talked to at the party last night . . . remember the one who wore a lampshade on his head?

PLANNING ANY UNUSUAL GIFTS
FOR THE HOLIDAYS?

Have you ever noticed that there is an abundance of holiday gift items available today which were previously "unattainable" or "off-limits" to gift givers only just a few years ago? Earrings for men, for example? Of course if you were brave enough, you could have offered some shiny ear adornments to your cantankerous ole Uncle Al a few decades ago, say—during the period when beehive hairdos and cigarette packs rolled-up in t-shirt sleeves were all the rage. But don't bet on a pleasant, enjoyable rest of a Christmas evening following the ritual of gift giving, especially after the eggnog has been flowing abundantly for a while. Past Christmas gift lists would also not have included a gift-coupon to a session at the local tattoo parlor. Until just a few years ago the thought of offering your skin as canvas to fledgling artists skilled in the art of rendering skulls, dragons and red roses was frowned upon. There were exceptions of course, but they mostly involved a few bold sailors whiling away their off-days in foreign harbors during the holidays, some of whom had gigantic sailing ships tattooed on their chests, the bright idea for such gifts occurring right after the bored and lonely fellows had warmed themselves up on rum or similar spirits.

Nowadays, instead of going through the trouble of packaging a boring shirt to place under the family Christmas tree (one that gets damaged after only a few cycles in the laundry), you can pay to have one actually tattooed directly onto someone's body. It might cost a bit more but it will be permanent and the colors won't fade as quickly either. To make things really *festive*, you could ask the artist to perhaps, drop in a Santa theme—one featuring a cheerful reindeer with a bright red nose. Just make sure no names are included in the artwork, especially not the name of the subject's wife or girlfriend. More than likely he may have to change the name pretty quickly anyway, probably right after he shows off his newly acquired Christmas present.

Another available present for the creative gift-giver today is exotic animals. In the past, the only kinds of critters one could purchase that might have been considered "exotic" (aside from weird-looking mutts), were brightly colored fish. But such fish have the unusual and perplexing habit of refusing fish food, and swimming upside down after just a few days in your tank.

These days it is possible to purchase the most exotic animals imaginable from faraway lands. Anything goes—from iguanas to gigantic snakes, like pythons and boas. The good news is, you only have to feed them once a month or so. It might be a good idea in between meals though, to keep them out of the way of any of your weird-looking mutts.

So this year if you plan to give any unusual gifts such as exotic critters, tattoos or items like ankle bracelets, nose-rings and studs piercing the eyebrows etc., don't forget your Uncle Al. You might recall that Aunt Martha usually complains about his ever-increasing, protruding beer-belly. Now imagine this, his most prominent feature, adorned with a bright, shiny belly-button ring—how happy he would be. You might want to remember at the same time, that if you do decide to present him with such a gift, you must keep the eggnog out of his reach for a while.

HALLOWEEN IS HERE AGAIN

Time has come once again to suit up, put on a mask and shake down the neighborhood. Halloween is upon us. Anyone knows that to be successful in this "extortion racket" your most powerful weapons are cute little costumes and adorable smiles and giggles. What kind of defense is there for the rest of us against tiny tykes ringing our doorbells and staring at us with big longing eyes while shaking empty bags? I for one, am totally helpless and have no choice but to give up vast amounts of candy. That's why it is a racket, because the rules are completely stacked against you as an adult. You just have to hand over the sweet loot by the bucketsful. If we had an equal weapon at our disposal to level the playing field, I wouldn't complain so much about giving up the booty. But there is no protection against "cuteness" for us grownups.

Who would want to call a grumpy, middle-aged guy "cute and adorable"? Well, maybe my wife used to. But she buys her own candy now, which leaves me without a reasonably priced item for bribery (more than likely I now would have to dig deeper into my pocket to present something harder than mere candy, and a lot shinier, in order to extract sweet nothings from her). I used to have an acquaintance, a married man, who, after having overstayed his curfew at the bar, wearily announced that he desperately needed to buy some "dragon fodder." After noticing my confusion, he explained that it was "flowers and candy." You can guess who the "dragon" was. Probably recognizing himself that he was completely deprived and disadvantaged in terms of "cute and adorable" he needed to produce something capable of deflating the enormous ire of his spouse when he arrived at home. In his case a variety of a dozen colorful plants, hacked off at the stem, along with some sugary foodstuff seemed to help him appease his fire-breathing spouse.

Just as an experiment, let me try to open the door this Halloween, after the bell rings, and offer nothing but a big smile, while sheepishly displaying the yawning emptiness of my own large container. You think I would end the night with a ton of candy in return? More than likely my house would be pelted with raw eggs and my tree decorated with toilet paper, while my teeth would remain un-rotted and my stomach un-aching. How unfair!

So, there is no alternative to waiting for the doorbell to ring with a ton of obesity-causing candy at the ready? Yes, there is! And I have a plan! Instead of gut-rotting jawbreakers, fireballs and gummy-bears, I'll toss some sweet oranges into the bag and some apples, maybe some carrots as well. How about some of that tasty spinach, something healthy for children? But guess what would happen then? I would be known as the Halloween equivalent of Ebenezer Scrooge. What a nightmare. Perhaps this might just initiate the sudden appearance of very angry Ghosts of Halloween (more than likely sponsored by the candy industry). Halloween, more than Christmas actually, naturally would lend itself to the emergences of all kinds of nasty spirits and phantoms. Maybe some ghoulish, dentally challenged Jack-o-lantern type could be my Ghost of Halloween Past. He would take me by the hand and time-travel to my childhood in order to show me . . . Ha—Gotcha, you nasty ghost! There would be nothing to show in my case. Why?—Because there was no Halloween during my youth in Europe. No stores blanketed in orange, no grocery clerks dressed in pirate outfits, and no one walking around knocking on doors expecting to be fed with pounds of candy. I would break into loud, ghoulish laughter at the historical and geographical ignorance of Halloween ghosts.

If spirits are dim-witted, I could claim Halloween-custom ignorance also, couldn't I? So, prepare yourself, children, this year it'll be broccoli and cauliflower for sure!

WATCH OUT FOR THAT HALLOWEEN COSTUME

When would be a good time not to wear your Halloween costume? At the Bank for one! I remember standing in line at a bank last Halloween, watching customers and employees alike going about their business dressed in costumes, and thinking—what if someone actually dressed up as a robber and then went ahead to rob the bank for real? Would that not be the perfect crime? Bank employees watching the security tape later would not exactly claim that they weren't forewarned, since the robber would have stood in line wearing a mask and carrying a bag prominently inscribed with the letters "LOOT."

When I told the teller about my idea, her reaction was a frown. Perhaps you're not supposed to talk about robberies in a bank for the same reason you should avoid mentioning hijacking or bombs at the airport. Or maybe the reason for her dour demeanor and display of an upside down smile was because she was dressed as a sad clown, which actually cut her ability to display emotions down to a minimum.

Although I've never myself gone through an entire day conducting business wearing unusual, elaborate garb, I find the custom of sporting costumes at businesses on Halloween fascinating. I do remember though dressing up as an old-time circus strongman, complete with leopard-spotted garb and handlebar mustache, quite a few years ago and stepping into a store before going to a party. My date at the time was dressed as "the bearded lady", overdoing her circus-freak act a little, in my opinion, by adding extra arms and legs. The cashier happened to be clad as a "blond bimbo" who began to admire the overabundance of papier-mâché muscles under my skin-color turtleneck shirt in a loud high-pitched voice. This earned her an immediate slap, courtesy of my circus-freak companion's third hand. This event was, I'm sad to report, the only occasion I'm aware of when females felt the need to fight over me, even though they only consisted of an IQ-challenged empty head and a bearded lady with three arms.

I think the practice of pretending to be someone else started during medieval times, when the biggest fool in the realm became king for a day (although, to the detriment of the ruled, the standard of foolishness was often already surpassed by that ruler himself on many occasions throughout the year). But the fool was permitted on that day to hold up a mirror to the monarch and people in power.

In that spirit, a fun idea has just occurred to me. Why don't we all, from now on, dress up as characters reflecting the way other people see us? I'm sure everyone around would inundate us with an avalanche of suggestions! You might be shocked to see how quickly the Superman of yesteryear suddenly turns into a doofus with a giant wallet and car keys, as seen by your teenagers.

As another example—lawyers, as well as some members of a certain government revenue-producing agency, could easily turn into bloodsucking vampires. Doctors could log around stomach pumps, directly connected to bank accounts. Ex-wives, donning pointy black hats, would be identified as evil witches, a very useful costume by the way, that could be employed to easily avoid commuter traffic by utilizing supercharged brooms. Ex-husbands would almost get a free ride due to the fact that many naturally already own the costume of a lazy lay-about, no-good bum.

Politicians might pose a problem because the bloodsucking vampire and the no-good bum costumes are already spoken for. Obviously they could dress as slowwitted Asses or as giant lumbering beasts of the wild but we should insist in encouraging their creativity.

The only problem I see arising would be, if someone actually came up with the idea of dressing up as a dictator (a Stalin perhaps), and then decided to take over a country. Looking at tapes later and watching the mustachioed, goose-stepping dictator giving fiery, inflammatory speeches, we couldn't claim that we weren't forewarned.

HOW CRAZY IS IT TO BUY GIFTS
THE DAY AFTER CHRISTMAS?

There are some people out there, some really smart ones (actually the kind who know everything better) who tell you that it's foolish to buy presents *before* Christmas. Why? Because, according to them, everything drops down to at least half price the day *after* Christmas. There they will be, smug and self-satisfied showing off their newest gadgets, which they supposedly get for pennies on the dollar the instant the Christmas holiday is declared over, while you end up maxing out your credit cards paying top dollar for your gifts. I would hate to be in their house on Christmas Day though, when everyone opens their packages in great anticipation and, instead of playing with shiny new toys, trucks, and dolls, find nothing but IOUs inside otherwise empty boxes.

The wrath of the wronged will weigh on you, as war will be waged henceforth forever. In other words, if you dared to be that penny-pinching, your actions will live in infamy. Try as you might but you will be unable to live down the fact that you were too stingy to buy that nice diamond necklace for your wife, for example (the one she was dropping hints about all season long). Your excuse that you'd rather look into crying, disappointed eyes on Christmas Day, than helplessly observing famished faces in the coming year (when you must make the minimum on your credit cards, instead of buying food), will ring hollow during the time of cheerfully ringing bells.

But even if you're tempted to commit such acts, especially during the current dubious economic climate, which is not conducive to expensive spending sprees, do not, under any circumstance, listen to those folks when considering buying a Christmas tree! What happens is, you may indeed get $30 trees for a buck a piece but they usually are unsightly shrubs that nobody wanted. And, I'll let you in on a little secret, the day after Christmas means—Christmas is over! Even if you did manage to find the most excellent of specimens amongst the picked-over sad wallflowers, something that would have netted you a chorus of you oohs and ahs from everyone *before* Christmas, will mean absolutely nothing the day after it. In fact, people might just wonder about your sanity, and wonder what motivated you to get the strange fir tree, chopped off at the trunk, withering away in the corner (good thing you don't have any malnourished members of your family also meandering around, thanks to your frugal holiday shopping habit, or I'm sure certain authorities would want to keep a closer eye on you).

For your sake I do hope, you've got all of your shopping done beforehand and are now ready to hand over adequate gifts, designed to put smiles onto expectant faces on Christmas morning. The reason—have you ever dared to walk into stores after Christmas? Let me tell you, I did it once and I'm still trying to recuperate from a massive post-season purchasing trauma. The first thing you encounter is a sea of humanity standing in line to return gifts. Anything, from Uncle Al's smoked salami, to toy trucks (that supposedly came without wheels), is free game and ready to be exchanged for diamond necklaces.

The next thing you wonder about is that you must have missed a recent hurricane, a natural disaster of enormous proportions that hit that particular shopping mall and caused tremendous havoc. At first you may feel the urge to congratulate yourself on having had the good sense of waiting until *after* Christmas to shop, a decision that may have saved your life (and therefore elevated your standing in the family due to your continued gift-giving prowess). But then you realize that not only are the shelves almost empty but also anything that did survive is smashed and broken (including toy trucks with missing wheels). Frantically you end up grabbing anything halfway decent.

Good luck being the last one in line during the "Christmas gift return season."

THE DAY AFTER THANKSGIVING

After indulging in the culinary delights of a certain kind of fowl—the kind unfortunate enough to have been lurking around when Indians and Pilgrims invited each other for a party, and which was from then on conscripted to serve as a symbol for Thanksgiving (the kind that weighs you down especially when served with heavy sauces, and causes you to become droopy even while watching an exciting game of football), well, overloaded with such bulky poultry, what do we do the day after Thanksgiving? *We go shopping*!

In addition to the very heavy responsibility of feeding millions, the poor turkey's job does not end at Thanksgiving. No, instead it is recruited to serve as another symbol, or better stated, as a *warning*. As soon as you have put away the remnants of what was once a proud bird, turning it into leftovers for the next couple of eternities, you suddenly realize that your days are numbered too—the days left to go shopping for Christmas gifts. This shocking fact then leads to a hectic state of frenzy, as the Friday after Thanksgiving Thursday traditionally turns into some kind of "Valentine's Day Massacre", a free-for-all mêlée fit only for tough, hardened veteran shoppers.

If you are unfortunate enough to be caught in this fracas, as I have been many times, better pray for rescue from above, this time not from an airborne turkey but perhaps in the form of a sturdy flying machine, like a helicopter. Frankly, if you should be unlucky enough to be entangled in shoppers' gridlock you might not even *get* to the mall at all. You will most likely languish in traffic, whiling away the rest of your days watching "turkey buzzards" circling above in hungry lazy loops, the shopping mall appearing in the distance, a faint, unreachable mirage. But at least you will be allowed to rest somewhat safely in your car, a steely cocoon. Your complaints of starving half to death inside your vehicle will ring hollow to anyone who manages to make it to the stores and is exposed to the ferocious hordes of desperate shoppers and in danger of being trampled flat.

All this right after the "exciting" family day of stuffing turkeys, stuffing yourself and getting the stuffing beaten out of you by your infantile brother, as a payback from last year's thumping. The human body and mind can only take so much. Especially when your in-law, the banker wants to show off his investment portfolio to everyone, the kind where certain financial instruments greatly expanded his bottom line, whereas the only expanding line you have to show spans around your waist and the only instruments you managed to employ were a limited array of silverware.

And talking about "being employed" (a sore subject that everyone seems to enjoy harking in on during Thanksgiving dinner, as soon as the topic of conversation focuses on you), what, in heaven's name does "gainfully" mean anyway? Why does that word always need to be connected with the word "employed?" Just wait until you put out your first CD, and then those "gainfully employed" will eat more words than turkey, I'll promise you that! Or maybe you will show off that book that you started a few years ago and have finally finished. It will be featured on bestseller lists all over the country, as the "Great American Novel" of course. Just wait until next Thanksgiving—they have no idea whom they're dealing with.

In the meantime, the day after Thanksgiving you're supposed to pick out a nice gift for all those who tormented you the day before? That is why I propose a total shopping moratorium on that day. You should not shop while under the influence of hatred against anything and anybody carrying your family name, as well as the ones they married, engaged, adopted, made friends with, pets, anything they touched with their grubby little greasy fingers . . .

Now calm down! No law requires you to go shopping for them now. Just wait until the day before Christmas.

LET'S CELEBRATE OKTOBERFEST

We are around this time of year inexplicably drawn together by a mysterious ritual called Oktoberfest which has its origins in Germany, where grown men are condemned to the sad fate of wearing short pants made of tough leather, called "lederhosen"—we are bound by its oath to quaff vast amounts of hop products and are condemned to eating and drinking outdoors from simple, unadorned paper plates, while harshly exposed to the elements. And finding ourselves at the mercy of this ancient rite, another dark power called "weather", has suddenly changed the usually pleasant California autumn into a gloomy period as a warning for more unpleasant things to come.

I own up to the fact that I once wore lederhosen, those short leather pants that many Americans think Germans are born in. I was an innocent, impressionable youngster when I wore lederhosen in my native Germany, coerced into squeezing myself into them by the "fashion police" of the time. I finally gave up on lederhosen and turned to blue jeans instead, which as you know must not only be worn-out, washed-out and shiny, but should also feature an adequate number of holes in them. Now you see how the pressures of fashion can make you turn to drink?

But who needs an excuse to drink during the Oktoberfest? As you can see, some Germans have cleverly sequestered and reserved, not merely a day or two, but an entire *month* for party time by simply changing the "c" into a "k" in October.

Oktoberfest is the period when someone like me, clad in the above mentioned super-cool lederhosen, is supposed to jump up at the first note of Polka music, grab hold of a gigantic mug of beer and slap whoever is standing near silly while loudly crooning drinking songs. I never really have figured out why, but I always seem to happily oblige, although I tend to go lighter on the crooning part these days and I carefully pick out someone smaller than me to stand next to before the music starts.

More than likely the tradition of merrily partying during this fall month started in the rural areas after the hard work of harvesting crops was done and the peasants were able to unwind, eat gigantic knockwursts and knock back enormous amounts of beer. Who could blame them? Have you ever tried bending down and picking up potatoes with stiff leather pants holding you back? Just accomplishing this task without major injury to vital organs should have made everyone happy, I'm sure.

For myself, it is important to celebrate Oktoberfest early because I have stoically accepted the ominous fate awaiting me on the horizon this fall, as inevitable. I am aware that all "the dark forces" overwhelming the end of summer will culminate in one unpleasant finale at the end of the month, as the waning of happy, sunny days will be wickedly celebrated by repugnant masks, ghosts and goblins demanding "treats" and threatening "tricks" in case of noncompliance.

In my case, the preordained scenario at Halloween usually plays itself out this way: The doorbell rings, I drop things and bump my head as I frantically look for candy. Then to my dismay I realize that *ants* have invaded the sweets-dish. I run to the door and slip in the rain outside, as my dinner burns on the stove.

Although helplessly submitting to the inevitability of my fate, you can see why I feebly lament the beginning of winter. At this time "all the evil forces" habitually and unmercifully always work against me! But at least I don't have to wear lederhosen anymore.

SANTA MAY BE BUSY THIS CHRISTMAS

Imagine you could have anything in the world you desired. The only prerequisite being that you provide proof that you remained "good" the entire previous year, and that the goods you request be able to fit through a chimney. Well, as any lawyer would advise you, the definition of "good" can always be argued in a court of law (or during arbitration later on). For the time being it is safe to assume that you indeed have been good all year long. In that case, what would you *wish* for?

You might think that many things are too large for easy transportation but most items nowadays are taken apart at the plant anyway and require assembly after shipment. That is why you could wish for just about anything and the red-suited delivery service can slide it in neat packages down the narrow passageway right into your fireplace. It might be prudent to request fireproof packaging though.

I am reminded of the popular story featuring a genie that grants some folks, stranded somewhere, *three* wishes. Usually the hapless protagonists find themselves back on the same desert island they came from because they wasted their wishes on foolishness. But one smart one uses his last wish asking to be granted three brand-new wishes! Now I have no idea if such a scheme would actually be considered a legitimate maneuver in the wish-industry. You might want to have an attorney take a look at the language of "wish regulations."

Being able to wish for things and actually getting them seems mostly restricted to a particular time in one's life anyway—say early to mid-childhood. That is why from the standpoint of an adult, one realizes that most of those wishes back then had been foolish ones, to say the least. If I had a chance to do it all over again, instead of opting for a single toy car, I naturally would have been much smarter and would have wished for the six correct numbers on a lotto ticket, after which I could easily have purchased the entire inventory of the toy store.

This might be the exact reason why mostly only *children* are allowed access to wish granting. Adults would certainly be tempted to abuse the privilege. Just picture your buddies in a wish-fest. Not only would they want more than you but they would also only opt for the biggest, the greatest, the best and the most. And as soon as those wishes are granted everyone would immediately want to top them and wish for even more. Santa's Helpers would have to work overtime and may eventually go on strike because they wish for better working conditions. The entire operation would grind to a halt, while superfluous items would pollute landfills all over the place.

To prevent chaos, Santa's only option it seems would be to deny your wishes and he can only do so by questioning your claim that you have been good all year long. Your lawyers, of course, would immediately challenge the legal definition of "good" and threaten to tie up the case in court for years. Eventually Santa might be forced to settle out of court. Bankruptcy might follow and in a desperate move he may turn things over to the Easter Bunny, a dubious outfit that is only experienced in handling smaller, more delicate merchandize.

You probably understand now why strict age restrictions have to be placed on the granting of wishes. Only children, not yet touched by adult greed and gluttony, will get what they want. And sadly therefore all anyone like you or me can hope for this year may be a colorful tie and a pair of warm socks.

CHAPTER ELEVEN

I Hear Voices In My Head

Suddenly the voices came over demanding to be heard.

MICROBES TALK TO ME

Microbes talk to me. It's very confusing sometimes though, because as soon as I start to get a hang of their broad Southern dialect, they suddenly switch to a nasal New York accent. Happens to me all the time. Maybe that's why I have a hard time identifying what ails me at a certain moment.

See, just now some microorganism informs me that I shouldn't talk to you about this subject or I might face serious repercussions, maybe an illness down the line, one that will make my tongue fall off. I just couldn't figure out that accent though. Sounds like Spanish to me, you know, the kind where they roll their "R's" and enunciate their vowels very clearly. Well, I've got the message. No talking to you.

That's why I switched to writing. See, now I can tell you all about those darn multi-lingual bugs. They won't be able to figure out what I type. How can they? It's all just black marks and incomprehensible gobbledygook for them; symbols from the alphabet that we humans devised to communicate with one another. They're probably wondering why I'm not talking anymore but instead my fingers are moving all over this keyboard. Gotcha, darn microbes! We're smarter after all.

Anyway, here it is: I'm able to listen to their conversations. Sometimes they want me to hear it but most of the time they don't. That's why I think they switch to other dialects or even languages. But what I understand is this: they are planning something very big, very serious, maybe even another Medieval-type plague! They've had it up to here with antibiotics. I'm here to warn you. I guess that is my mission now. I have to help humanity to survive. I'm not charging a penny for it either. I'm about to save mankind without being compensated for it—it boggles the mind. That's how patriotic I am.

James Bond at least had fun spying for the Queen, with glamorous women at his side, at exotic places, gambling at Monte Carlo for example, quaffing mysterious beverages that, for some reason, need to be shaken not stirred. However even Bond is reduced to nothing but a number, and the Queen is prepared to deny acknowledgement of his existence if captured by the enemy. But then that is the fate of anyone daring to go undercover. In my case, instead of exotic people and places, I deal with mysterious bacteria (unfortunately, you can't choose your assignments). Like 007, I would need state-of-the-art spy equipment. Fight fire with fire—fight bugs with bugs, I say! I would need the most advanced listening devices, as well as the most up-to-date translating service (can't understand one word as soon as they decide to switch to teen-talk, for example—very frustrating).

Hold on, there seems to be some talk about the subject of bacteria actually being necessary for human survival—turning milk into cheese, helping digestion inside the stomach, that sort of thing. *Sounds like diversionary tactics to me.* Maybe they're on to me? Isn't that a virus? There can be no case where bacteria and viruses can be good for you, can there? This assignment is becoming very dangerous . . . excuse me a second . . .

Guess what has happened now? I just threw up all over my laptop. I guess they figured me out . . . my typing. I'm doomed! My mission is finished.

"What did you say?" I didn't understand what it said—some tough bug from Brooklyn—if I could only make sense of this mumbo-jumbo . . . I think they have me now. Save yourself—make sure you wash your hands all the time! And stay away from birds and rodents! Don't eat raw food, bad peanut butter and . . . ahhrrgh

"PARANOIA" IS A LADY ON TV
WHO TALKS TO YOU

Paranoia, expressed is the fear that someone might be pursuing me, and has finally caught up with me. What ultimately convinced me that I was being followed, day and night, was the time I recently walked by a giant flat-screen monitor fastened to the wall in a posh hotel in the Silicon Valley recently. As I glanced at what I had inadvertently assumed was the face of an anchorperson reading the news on TV, I couldn't help but think that her smile was directed at me. As a matter of fact, her eyes actually seemed to follow my every move as I passed by. Instead of causing me to smile back, a chill went down my spine. It was an eerie feeling, like the eyes in a painting pursuing the frightened protagonist in a scary movie. Dumbfounded I stopped and scratched my head, something I shouldn't have done because it made the phantom on television wave at me, saying hello. It was a friendly phantom for sure but as a veteran of numerous horror and science-fiction flicks I was also aware that once you get suckered in, all kinds of unpleasant events start to happen all of a sudden. For example cheery, kind faces such as hers suddenly change into ghoulish masks equipped with spider-like fingers that drag you inside and expose you to questionable behavior of evil, goateed psychiatrists in insane asylums.

After watching the phantom intently for a while, I finally figured it out—what I thought was a television screen was really a "concierge station", and the phantom watching me so closely was actually a hotel employee teleconferencing with any patrons who stopped by. Why she would chat with guests via video camera, while hiding in an office somewhere, instead of out in the lobby behind a desk, I have no idea. Maybe management was trying to squeeze out as much work as it could from employees, because aside from answering questions, I observed her hands quickly moving up and down on the screen. It seemed as though she was plucking chickens and talking at the same time—perhaps helping the kitchen staff get ready for lunch? On the other hand, she could also have been typing on a computer. *Maybe she sent an e-mail to hotel security alerting them about me?* Because as I stared at her for a while trying to figure out if she was real, and as she stared back eyebrows raised, a man in a very loud Hawaiian shirt suddenly came around and began to strike up a conversation with me. I had watched the man for some time as he circled, grinning at me in an embarrassed manner when I locked eyes with him. Naturally I assumed that he was an undercover agent, someone who doubled as some kind of 007 (who else would show up in a Hawaiian shirt in the middle of winter?). I asked the fellow if he liked his Hawaiian Punch "shaken not stirred."

Of course he acted confused. Instead he asked me quite "nonchalantly" why I had been sitting in that particular chair for hours staring at the poor phantom on TV. As I told him that I was doing some important investigative work involving people being followed, shadowed and tailed, he informed me that whatever I was doing was most unsettling to the virtual person on TV, causing her to develop serious symptoms of paranoia. I then asked just as nonchalantly (*the art of nonchalance seems to be a prerequisite in undercover assignments*) why a normal, everyday hotel guest, dressed nonchalantly in a Hawaiian shirt would know so much about the well-being of clerks on monitors?

This inquiry seemed to unsettle the gentleman enormously.

"Why would you want to question that I am not a normal, everyday hotel guest?" he asked in return—a bit too anxiously in my opinion. "Have you been following me?"

Now, why would anyone be so paranoid?

FRITZ

Sometimes I talk to my refrigerator, usually late at night when I can't sleep and come down for a glass of water. There it stands in the corner of the kitchen, jet-black and very cool looking, making humming sounds. It's a rhythmic kind of a noise, which could—and actually should—be interpreted as nothing more than the racket that everyday, ordinary refrigerators make to cool things down on the inside. But once I settle down and listen for a while that noise sounds awfully like,

"Get that piece of pie . . . get that piece of pie . . ."

Now I'm not much of a pie eater. I do enjoy a piece of an exciting culinary creation fashioned by the talented hands of a baker every once in a while but I can go for weeks, even months without having a single morsel. But dark chocolate is a different story, or cookies, so are cheese and ham, sausages, salami, pizza, bread and mayonnaise. Now these things I must have. And of course I have to wash them down with a bottle of beer or two.

"So, why are you trying to talk me into a piece of pie, knowing that my wife put me on a diet after the holidays?" I ask Fritz, a suitable name for a fridge I think.

"I'm just worried about the expiration date on things," Fritz insists. "That's my job. I can't have anything spoiling inside of me. That would give me indigestion and, to be honest, would be horrible for my reputation as the guardian for safe and edible foods."

"Don't you have anything besides pie? That's probably my wife's anyway."

Fritz, the fridge yawns widely, opening the door to show me his treasures. Racks and racks filled with scrumptious stuff. But wouldn't you know it—many of these goodies are indeed outfitted with looming expiration dates, and if not consumed immediately much of it would go to waste. What a shame, I think.

"Wasn't it appropriate that I warned you?" Fritz asks.

"You're completely right and I'm proud of you," I reply. "I must remedy the situation immediately."

The reputable talents of Dagwood, the cartoon-husband of Blondie, whose sandwich-making skills are legendary, pale against my handiwork following this conversation. My chest fills up with pride at the same rate as my stomach fills up with food. Fritz who cheers me on at every turn of the knife and fork urges me to ascend to even greater, unprecedented heights. In him I have a comrade in the fight against the threat of approaching expiration dates, as well as against unreasonable approaches to diets (unfairly decreed by wives not totally familiar with sustainable dietary requirements for husbands).

"I heard voices," my wife says sleepily when I return to bed. "Were you talking to someone?"

"I was talking to Fritz," I reply.

"Huh? Who is Fritz? Does he work in a bar? You smell like beer . . . and onions too."

"I'm doing my part in fighting the good fight against food spoilage," I proudly proclaim.

"Huh? What are you going on about—food spoilage?" my wife asks groggily. "Are you drunk?"

The poor thing, I muse as my head hits the pillow, has no idea how close she came to disaster. Fritz and I, more than likely, saved her from the ravages of food poisoning, a nasty kind of illness that is fatal in some cases or may cause brain damage and organ failure in others. I do feel like a hero.

"Don't tell me you went downstairs in the middle of the night and raided the fridge," my wife asks me, suddenly completely awake. "You're supposed to be on a diet!"

"Fritz, the fridge made me do it," I meekly offer as a defense.

"You'd better not have eaten my piece of pie!"

UH-OH.

LEARNING TO SPEAK "AMERICAN"

I was struck by the beauty of a lovely foreigner a long time ago, and that was the first time I realized how important a common language was. There I stood forlorn, a teenager smitten by love at first sight, beset not only by the common afflictions of teen-awkwardness, as my tongue seemed permanently attached to the roof of my mouth, but realizing also that even if I were able to utter one word, she would not have understood me. My on-the-spot sign-language skills were limited to a goofy grin and clumsy hand-signals, which were likely to be misinterpreted by her father who stood nearby and eyed me with suspicious sideward glances. Who knows how many fights and skirmishes have been started throughout history because of misinterpretations and misunderstandings? Since I lacked the necessary vocabulary to explain to the man that I had nothing but honorable intentions towards his daughter, I relented in my quest to find love, as I had no intention of becoming another statistic.

Misconceptions, false impressions and misunderstandings, seem to be a common occurrence when people who learn a foreign language try to communicate with the natives. Native speakers tend to have little tolerance for linguistic faux pas, and they soon lose patience with foreigners who don't comprehend the basics. A friend of mine, for example, who had been quite accomplished in his native country came to America and started work as a cook in a diner some years back. He told me that he had been puzzled when waitresses began plunking down platters of pastries on his counter with the demand to "eat it." Not wanting to offend anyone, and overwhelmed by common American friendliness, he obediently munched down scores of calorie-laden sweets until it dawned on him that the waitresses had not wanted him to "eat" the pastries but instead to "heat" them for their customers.

I remember, as a newcomer myself speaking German, that language obstacles seemed sometimes insurmountable. I did have a rudimentary knowledge of English (having studied it in school), but as soon as I hit these shores everything I had ever learned seemed swallowed inside a black linguistic hole. I remember forever confusing "truck" with "trunk" and "altitude" with "attitude" (this would have been a fatal fallacy for a pilot, for example, since no matter what your attitude is towards life, it will be cut short quickly if the altitude is incorrect—good thing I wasn't a pilot). It also took some effort to explain to people that the drawn-out pauses I needed in order to answer their questions were not because I was on drugs but due to the fact that I needed time to translate their comments into German first and then prepare an appropriate response using the same method.

Thinking back, I must have come across as an insensitive klutz myself, probably on more than one occasion. As a young man newly arrived from Germany I remember hitch-hiking across the country, and being picked up by a nice man needing company and a conversation partner on the expansive stretches of highways. Not being completely conversant in English, especially swiftly worded "American" (my English teacher back home had spoken slowly with a tedious German accent), I had adopted what I thought at the time was a clever technique to help me across awkward pauses when I really had no idea what people were saying to me.

"Oh, really . . . ?" I would cheerfully exclaim when I sensed someone anticipating a response, and then I would add the inevitable, "Well, that's great!"

Everything seemed to go on splendidly until that particular driver asked me and my traveling companion (who was dozing in the back), to leave the car much sooner than I had expected. While I was puzzled, my friend, an American, was in great pain stifling chuckles.

"You can't blame him for throwing us out," he informed me later, "what do you expect when you very happily told him, 'oh really—that's great'—right after he told you that his mother-in-law had passed on."

If you read this, dearest driver, I have improved my comprehension skills considerably and can now identify with your grief and I am still very sorry.

WHO SAYS YOU CAN'T SING?

I used to sing in the shower. It was utterly enjoyable for me to belt out anything I could think of, mostly mere fragments of popular songs I remembered from listening to the radio. The shower walls greatly reverberated the sounds of my voice, encouraging me to ascend to greater and greater heights, usually culminating in a crescendo that combined the musical intensity of opera, rock and pop alike. Great care was also given to amplifying decibels and volume. I imagined myself in front of an audience filled with swooning groupies who urged me on to attempt all sorts of vocal experimentations.

Then the show came to a screeching halt. It was years ago when I lived in an apartment complex. Someone banged against the wall next door yelling, "Stop beating that dog!" Well, you guessed it—I didn't have a dog. Apartment regulations prohibited possession of any pets. And even if I had owned one, I'm not a person driven to violent acts against a defenseless animal, especially the kind that would elicit singsong sounds from a dog.

Needless to say, quite embarrassed, I avoided that particular neighbor for quite some time and reduced my shower show to mere humming from then on. Now I only sing when I'm sure no one can hear me, for instance in the car. Due to modern technology I don't even have to pretend that I'm chiding a small child in the backseat, if someone happens to catch me moving my lips, now I just act as if I'm in deep conversation on my cell phone. More than likely, anyone curious enough to watch me, won't want to observe my antics for too long, since it now looks as if I'm giving someone a piece of my mind in a very angry manner. You'd better be careful with someone who, with a sneer on his lips, is "all shook up" belting out Elvis tunes.

Being now somewhat painfully familiar with the mental anguish that exposed failed musical aspirations provides for you, I have nothing but admiration for folks who bare their very souls on shows like, American Idol, and are told by callous judges that they should contemplate pursuing other talents, like parking cars.

There are incredible musical talents who regrettably are shot down by the judges sometimes but the vast majority of the people who try out at these contests are usually less than gifted. As a matter of fact, many of them seem to be completely tone-deaf but try their hardest to impress the judges and the audience. The more sensitive amongst us die a thousand deaths on their behalf, painfully cringing at every embarrassing sound coming from those earnest, completely un-embarrassed faces, as they mimic the soulful expressions of their idols, adding to already considerable humiliation. Don't they know when to stop, one wonders. Perhaps they suffer from comparable symptoms of folks who never stop eating because their stomach is lacking the threshold that makes them feel full. And even after the most acidy, sarcastic, scathing and derisive critique of the judges, some of them seem to be completely unfazed.

Good for them, I think. I wouldn't have the guts. And who are those judges anyway? Although some of them are entertainers, others are merely connected to the music business in some form and, I would bet, wouldn't have the courage to go on stage exposing themselves to ridicule either. And, come to think of it, who is to say that singing off key couldn't just be a new form of avant-garde interpretation? It just takes an expert to explain the significance and importance of a new art form to the world. Remember Vincent van Gogh? In the vanguard of impressionism, he rarely sold a painting to his contemporaries who were accustomed to the realistic portrayals of the old masters. Now his paintings are worth millions. Maybe I could start a new trend with the sounds of mournful canines.

LEARNING MUSIC THE HARD WAY

I can't play any musical instruments. My only ability at eliciting musical sounds from any type of contraption is restricted to fiddling with the radio. But even that seems to be a prohibitive endeavor nowadays. Have you taken a look at all the knobs, buttons and gauges on these things lately? It's truly frightening. That's why I leave the dial of the radio in my car alone, resting solidly on one channel of a station I trust. This causes me to maneuver carefully around bumps and potholes, since I haven't been able to figure out how to preset the radio to desired stations and I am terrified of the possibility that it might jump to another station and I would have to listen to hellish sounds created by tattooed band members whose idea of music involves recreating shrieks of wounded animals and car crashes.

I do though earnestly envy anyone who is able to make music utilizing an instrument of any kind, no matter what the sound. The last time I tried learning to play an instrument was a long time ago as a youngster. Before then, I had no idea that your very own fingers could be your worst enemy, sabotaging you at every turn. I had naturally assumed that one's physical appendages would largely be in agreement with the rest of one's body, mostly harmoniously coordinating all kinds of endeavors with the brain. So if I wanted to play the guitar or the piano, I thought that the process of learning perhaps, might be a bit slow in the beginning (a few missteps here an there), but on the whole, that in no time at all I could perform in a concert in a matter of *months*. It did look pretty easy watching musicians stroking their fiddles and plucking at their guitars. All they seemed to do after all was look intense and sincere and possibly close their eyes to demonstrate a genuine effort, or distort their faces into woeful grimaces at certain moments when a particular soulful passage demanded it.

I did manage quite a few distortions, but my physical memory, instead of guiding my fingers to hit the correct notes, seemed to be plagued by bouts of amnesia. Some kind of forgetfulness also seemed to affect my music teacher as well because he almost "forgot himself", and nearly smashed the musical instrument I was torturing (a mandolin as I recall) across my skull. Luckily for me he held back, as he appeared to remember just in time that he was the educator charged with the task of teaching an unfortunate reluctant beginner the secret of coaxing musical notes from an inanimate object. Therefore, instead of pounding a rhythmic beat into my head with the instrument (which probably was too fragile and expensive to use for this purpose anyway), he brutally *pried* my little tender pupil fingers apart, and told me instead that I needed to press down much harder on those strings of steel that cut into my flesh like knives. So much for the assumption that musicians are gentle, soft types because, as I discovered soon afterwards, not only did I develop calluses on my fingers but also a lot of tough buildup around my ego.

Then, as an older child, I became fascinated by another instrument—the trumpet, an instrument that I actually really wanted to learn to play. To me, it seemed perfect for a boy aspiring to prove his masculinity since one needed extraordinary lungpower to extract such enormously loud sounds and intense decibels. But my mother convinced me that, due to its "metallic consistency", I would develop even more calluses on my lips which would be a detriment to romantic intentions later on, and aside from that it could become a much too expensive hobby. She actually convinced me that I would be much better off with a wooden flute-type thing that she just happened to have laying around somewhere. Little did she realize that an instrument requiring a soft puff and light touch was a much greater detriment to amorous pursuits than leathery lips—at least in my pre-puberty boys' world.

So, now unfortunately as a victim of the rough and tumble macho world of music, I'm simply reduced to playing the radio.

CHAPTER TWELVE

Crime Doesn't Pay

"I needed a creative outlet."

DO CRIMINALS WATCH REALITY TELEVISION?

Because we spend endless hours watching crime-shows on television, most of us have become "skilled experts" in the field of law-enforcement. This is especially so today with the introduction of "reality shows" which allow us to tag along with investigators tracking criminals. We are privy to the minutest detail of every particular crime, becoming at the same time, educated on how to solve it. That is why it is a mystery to me that criminals are still getting caught. Are they not watching the same shows as we are? Perhaps the only time criminals get interested in such programs is when their faces are splashed all over the screen as the central characters of the series specializing in mopping up fugitives. More than likely, bathing in their fifteen minutes of fame with enthusiasm, they will call up acquaintances to remind them that—yes—it was indeed their visage portrayed prominently on television right that moment. Those same associates would then waste not a minute of time advising the authorities on the exact location of their "good friends" in order to claim the hefty reward.

After the culprits are caught, it surprises me once again that after a little time spent in the interrogation room they usually seem ready to make a confession. Don't they realize that the reason the detectives berate them for hours is because they have absolutely no clue as to who committed the crime and need a confession? All of us watching understand that without a confession the police would have to release the suspect for lack of evidence. Although we despise them we are tempted to warn the perpetrators the same way we try to alert a hapless victim in a horror movie not to wander into that dark room where we know the monster is lurking. The reality is that with a little nudging by the friendly detective counseling them on how "relieved they would feel" with an admission of guilt, the delinquents usually break down and confess almost immediately. This fact alone seals their fate—spending the next decade or so inside a room, the size of a walk-in closet. Maybe they fall into the trap so easily because they had spent their loot on illegal substances instead of on the smart investment of a television—something that could have helped them keep up with the newest in law-enforcement techniques? Maybe they actually planned their dirty deeds in order to purchase a television later (since everyone else seems much better versed about criminal activities and subsequent police action, especially when it comes to conducting themselves in the interrogation room). Or perhaps the only time *bad boys* get to enjoy the "square box" is when so-called friends throw a party for them to celebrate their fame, while secretly planning how to spend the reward money.

Taking a chance of revealing valuable information favorable to criminals, we should advise them that had they been able to examine crime shows along with the rest of us, they would not do anything in the interrogation room but utter four little words, "I want my lawyer." Although in a catch-22 conundrum when they realize how much lawyers get paid by the hour they might have to put the slated television set on the backburner after any subsequent heist in order to make enough money to pay the lawyer (therefore extending this seemingly never-ending cycle of crime, and keeping us glued to reality crime television).

This makes me wonder if we should not—in addition to prohibiting felons from voting and owning guns—add the ban of television ownership or at least access to cable or dish networks.

JURY DUTY

One of your civic duties as an American includes being called upon to sit in judgment of one of your peers. It is called jury duty and *sitting* is exactly what you do all day long. First, while your ability to serve on a particular jury is determined, you sit on the most uncomfortable chairs imaginable in a waiting room while a grainy ancient romantic comedy is put on view on an equally ancient TV. Of course they wouldn't dare to show The Sopranos or another crime show, I assume probably for the same reason airliners don't show airplane disaster movies on the airplane. A flick showing fiery airborne passenger planes hurling to the ground while one is crossing ragged mountain ranges, might turn one against air travel (especially at the moment when overpriced lunches are served). In the same vein, showing a movie of despicable criminals might prejudice the juror, clouding his judgment and probably contributing to his decision to condemn the accused to the chair (one at least as hard as the one I was sitting on for hours on end while waiting to hear if I had been chosen to serve).

When I received my summons to appear I wondered what kind of peer I would be sitting in judgment of. I definitely would not include an ax-murderer as one of my peers. Perhaps such an individual would be better served being judged by some of his ax-murderer peers on death row? But that was my first mistake, as I learned later, when the judge informed us that everyone is innocent until proven guilty—even ax murderers. That means that even such a vile person would be considered one of your peers until smart detectives discover his fingerprints all over a handy instrument used for bludgeoning victims and a jury of his peers finds him guilty. After that you are free to ax him from your circle of peers and pals.

Following the long wait in the waiting room—in my estimation about equal to a sentence for armed robbery—we finally filed into a courtroom. Facing the crowd of potential jurors were the

County Prosecutor, the defense counsel, and the dejected-looking ax murderer. Soon a jovial, buoyant judged trotted in, in a good mood, I assumed, because he might have already sentenced someone to hard labor for a few lifetimes. He told us that nine individuals out of the roomful of people would be chosen, as well as some alternates. As American citizens we had many rights but also quite a few duties, he informed us. Many of us hoped that these rights would include one that permitted us an excuse to get out of jury duty.

Next the County Prosecutor and the defense counsel made their case about what they expected from a jury. The defense counsel, especially, was adamant about that, although the defendant *looked* like an ax murderer we should not automatically assume that he was one. And as it turned out, the "ax murderer" was only being charged with having a few over the limit—i.e. several alcoholic beverages, as well as several miles. Of course many of us had already made up our minds that this was a capital offense, at least these individuals who took this as their best chance to be excused from jury duty. Although the judge implored them to look into their hearts to see if it weren't at all possible to divorce themselves from any bad experiences with sharp instruments and/or drunk drivers and perhaps somehow achieve objectivity, few relented. Most of them confessed that they were still too traumatized by the bad breath of alcoholic drivers to make a fair decision. That is why it took the rest of the day to find a few courageous individuals untouched by the scourge of drunk drivers and bestowed with the important gift of having enough time to sit through lengthy court proceedings. Regretfully, I was not among the chosen ones.

I probably couldn't have been objective either, my mind being occupied throughout the trial about an ax in the defendant's trunk.

SPYWARE

Spies invading the sanctuary of the home, viruses spreading infection, worms infesting the corpse of what once were thriving intellects—sounds like a tale from the war and pestilence-torn medieval times, doesn't it? But actually this is what is happening right now in our homes. That little square box sitting on your desk, called the "computer", is under constant, relentless attack and with it any and all of our intellectual properties, like Aunt Mary's casserole recipe for example, which we store on our hard-drives. And all we have to defend ourselves with is a tiny little mouse.

And where exactly is this newfangled "cyberspace" located that is causing all these nasty new diseases? If we knew, perhaps we could send in volunteers armed with gallons of powerful solutions capable of disinfecting and cleaning out the place.

I once saw a documentary about the micro world of dust-mites. Somehow the filmmakers were able to magnify the landscape of these tiny beings a thousand times and feature monsters more frightening than any Godzilla ever created in Hollywood. There was a whole world in existence where creatures fed on human skin-flakes, competing with each other, and also viciously attacking and devouring one another—right under our eyes, literarily on top of our noses—and yet we have no idea that it is happening. I have to admit that I could have lived without that knowledge for quite some time longer, since it generated ghoulish nightmares of alien organisms eating my brain afterwards, but it did supply me with some kind of metaphor for this brand new concept of spies in cyberspace.

We are completely oblivious to the possibility that there are powerful entities in existence, operating beyond our control, which we cannot see, feel, hear or touch (well, maybe sometimes we can smell them if we spill a bit of the morning coffee unto the keyboard). Therefore we have no idea that right next to us is a "parallel universe." Even more mind-boggling, as proponents of the "String Theory" tell us, there are more than ten different dimensions present in our world, and if we are smart enough, and susceptible to other dimensions, we can reach through and cross into some other sphere (I must have tried this tactic quite a few times myself as a teenager on a date, but suffered immediate consequences of physical trauma caused by the powerful velocity of wrath originating from several dimensions beyond my peripheral vision).

Another way to look at it is, we are like the ants that are busy with seemingly insignificant, unremarkable tasks of constructing ant-hill homes, climbing out to find food for the queen and attempting to defending same against rival ants. These ants are completely unaware of the fact that probably close by, are highways cramped with cars leading to cities where people build high-rises, computers, space shuttles, and mull over the best ways to get rid of ants.

Now if common mortals such as ourselves, are unable to grasp the full concept of this new spy-enigma, who then is generating all the trouble? Who out there is capable of perpetuating this mysterious conundrum? Well, anyone who knew all the answers in math class and used scotch-tape to fix his/her glasses in school is suspect. It seems that the only way to comprehend this alien world of spies, is to understand the universal, common language, accessible only to a certain segment of society—math. There are some of us who are unable to comprehend mathematics beyond employing fingers and toes in the counting process, and as a result now have to suffer for it, as our computers are seized and controlled by newer and better versions of spyware. In the ultimate "revenge of the nerds", we are now helplessly beholden to the same geeks who create the spies in the first place, to purge our systems of brand new and more aggressive worms.

Looking at my computer last night, I finally relented. The spies had won. They could go ahead and destroy my files, eat my brain if they must, but I begged them not to touch Aunt Mary's casserole recipe.

IDENTITY THEFT—HOW DO YOU AVOID IT?

Instead of physically appropriating items of value from you directly, such as your car, TV, jewels or that nifty lava lamp, devious individuals have devised a much more effective way of getting their hands on your riches these days; they just steal *you*—or, more precisely, your identity. This way they cleverly avoid a potentially perilous face to face encounter with an enraged homeowner who might be willing to train the volatile section of a firearm at vulnerable spots on their bodies. Cunning as they are, they usually get whatever they wish by ordering things directly from the store and—most ingeniously—having *you* pay for it. It is a very convenient scenario for them since they not only get their goods brand-new (no more bothersome scratches or dents from careless former owners) but this new approach to the art of getting something for nothing also cuts down tremendously on awkward, bothersome theft-equipment, like bulky ladders and clanking break-in-tools.

Pretending to be you is getting a lot easier today, according to the reports—identity thieves don't have to mimic any of your facial tics or nervous scratching habits. All that is required is your most private information, something so sacred to you, that you would never hand it over to your closest friends or relatives (especially not to that bothersome brother-in-law of yours) but which you, curiously, regularly give to anyone who asks for it over the telephone, acting officious. And you are even more generous handing out the keys to your life and soul when they convince you to sign up for that fantastic *something-for-nothing* deal on the internet.

Even the most careful person may become a victim of identity theft. Even if, for some reason, you had been reluctant in the past to divulge information to strangers, distrusting promises of instant wealth by individuals who profess to have only your well-being in mind, those same individuals have sometimes been known to obtain such information directly by digging through your garbage. More than likely any hardy individual, robust enough to compete with rodents, raccoons and all kinds of night-critters will find a mother lode of information on you that could help transform him from a crusty, tattoo-laden, villainous criminal into a nice, hardworking person such a yourself. All he would need is a few of your secret numbers, which are usually plastered quite prominently all over papers that frequently end up in your trash.

This is the reason why I have recently, rather hastily obtained a shredder. Now, day and night, I pass each and every paper within reach through the busy knives of this slicing-machine. You should try it yourself. It is very effective as it is fun watching documents and all kinds of other paper sliced into pieces. The only danger is that you might get carried away and some of the pictures of your brother-in-law or any of the others close to your spouse's heart might find their way into the roving blades as well. Next thing you know your marriage certificate might be threatened with a similar fate.

But, as we are finding out, all our precautions and safety measures protecting us and shielding our vital information from evildoers might be futile when our trusted institutions "lose" documents by the millions or sell our most confidential records to the highest bidders who then bombard us with "great deals" on potency pills, depressed real estate or expanded collections of velvet Elvis paintings. Not only that, but our most private information is susceptible to exploitation by an untold number of criminals who would like our identity, but without the responsibility of having to pick up the kids from school, cook dinner, make it through the gridlock to work every day or pay the mortgage.

Come to think of it, this might be the perfect deterrent—anyone who gets caught impersonating you and running up your bills should be required, not only to pay you back but to do all your menial chores for the next dozen years or so. And that should include cleaning the bathroom, doing the laundry and yard work, as well as other family obligations expected from you—like loaning that brother-in-law some money to finally get his business off the ground.

CHAPTER THIRTEEN

All You Can Eat And More

"This is the gentleman who registered the complaint. Apparently his steak is too rare."

OUR "BUFFET-STYLE" CULTURE

It must have been the Swedes who first came up with the notion of buffet-style restaurants, with their idea of the "smorgasbord." Maybe their ancestors, the Vikings, ancient seafaring warriors, started it, because after a day of swinging heavy swords and shields and rowing boats across rough seas they, more than likely, were in need of an above average caloric food intake. *The Scourge of Europe*, as the Vikings were affectionately known in some parts, were not about to be satisfied with smidgens here and morsels there of the finest that Europe had to offer in culinary achievements, even if garnished with parsley. They needed the entire cow on a spit, roasting and ready to be chopped to pieces by the starving men of war. The finer points of gastronomy were naturally completely lost on such patrons, as their appreciation of food was anchored more in volume than value. This seems to be the idea behind many of the "all-you-can-eat" restaurants we see around today. Although not a few do offer scrumptious dinners, who really makes a fuss about quality, as long as quantity is taken care of?

Our reason for frequenting these places of plenty usually hovers around the fact that they are reasonably priced, and we can harbor the illusion that we are just sampling all the many different dishes, a feature not offered in the conventional restaurants. But once confronted with the vastness and variety of dishes, any resemblance of civilized behavior is suddenly conquered by ancient animal instincts of survival—"Perhaps this is the last day you will have a chance to feed for months", the subconscious mind suggests, "better stock up, winter is long." So instead of sampling tiny tidbits here and there, we inevitably return to the buffet line time and time again until our breathing becomes labored. In one sitting, we can consume the equivalent of three or four meals before we stumble outside, causing serious damage to the sidewalk, but finally completely satisfied that we have indeed eaten "all that we can possibly eat." That same evening, we may actually find ourselves in some gym for a routine guilt-workout, before yet another binge of buffet the following day. The unfortunate consequence of this has been a steady increase in our girth, compared to our counterparts some ten or twenty years ago.

Since Vikings lacked automatons to help them get through the day, and since they completely relied upon their bodily strength (with the possible assistance of a beast of burden every once in a while), excess calories usually burned up quickly after large meals, leaving the Vikings lean and well-muscled (although still covered with scraggly red beards). No doubt, they would have questioned our practice of utilizing machinery to alleviate physical labor, sitting down to eat the equivalent of four meals at once, and then afterwards, spending endless hours in front of mirrors lifting weights up and down for no "apparent reason." They probably would have allocated that wasted time to more useful purposes, like chasing fair maidens around the campfire. It is obvious that getting exercise by doing things naturally (for example jogging to the battlefield, or escaping same chased by cantankerous townsfolk, unwilling to part with their precious foodstuff) is much less complicated than squeezing into your car after a buffet dinner, and maneuvering through commuter traffic to the gym during a downpour.

It seems that the "good old days", when people could eat all they wanted and still remain in tiptop form (although the term "losing weight" might then have meant getting a vital limb or two chopped off during a battle), is over. Since we cannot benefit from daylong brawls nowadays, the next best thing to do is to cut down on those mountain-high plates on the buffet-line. And as for exercise, chasing around your fair maiden may not be such a bad idea either.

I CAN'T COOK AND I'M PROUD OF IT!

It appears that Penn State University chemists have found a way to burn saltwater with a radio-frequency generator they have developed. This recent headline does not impress me at all. Had they asked me I could have shown them how to "burn water" without all that *scientific rigmarole*, those doodads and thingamajigs with wires sticking out. All you need is a medium-to-large-sized pot, a liberal amount of water and <u>no idea how to cook</u> even the most basic forms of edible edibles and—*voila*—you have a kitchen bursting into flames in no time at all! I've been trying to inform everyone of this rare talent of mine for years, especially people who just never give up trying to convert me into a cooking fanatic. But of course no one pays any attention. Spurred on by TV reality shows that feature "iron chefs" in epic "battles" with each other, which are promoted and hyped like championship fights, as well as cooking shows that have animated folks operating a dozen blistering pots and pans in blazing speed while quipping one-liners, my friends and relatives see no reason why I too shouldn't be able to find enormous pleasure sweating in front of a hot stove whipping up batches of lasagna. That such a place is filled with an array of very dangerous cutting utensils—which, if used improperly, could result in painful consequences, like disembowelment of unfortunate kitchen staff—does nothing to deter these cooking extremists. They just slap me on the shoulder, lead me towards a GIGANTIC library of cookbooks and tell me that I too would soon *love* hacking living things into bite-sized cubes or smashing them into powdery substances. All I have to do is read how legions of people just like me have done just that for ages now and I would learn to love these activities as well.

Those folks have obviously never heard of *restaurants*—a wonderful place to be for people who don't believe that chopping onions equals some kind of spiritual awakening.

Apparently the Penn State University chemists mentioned above achieved the burning of saltwater by using radio frequencies, which act to weaken the bond between elements that make up saltwater, releasing hydrogen. Once ignited, the hydrogen will burn as long as it is exposed to the frequencies, the researchers report. Well, for me this is only good news as long as they can perfect this system by next Sunday when I need a safe and efficient fuel source for my barbecue. This somewhat primeval procedure, I have decided, might go a long way to finally showcasing my dinner-making prowess. I have used coal for this purpose in the past but I have been informed that this form of energy is highly inefficient, dirtying up the atmosphere, which in turn will eventually cause icecaps to melt and drown Florida as well as New York. Since I have friends in both places, I do hope this unfortunate act of nature does not happen by next Sunday because I'm not sure I have perfected my barbecuing procedures well enough with so many guests coming.

I'm never certain, for example, when exactly the coals are burnt and white enough for them to be ready to do their job of cooking the meat on the grill. I'm usually either too impatient and toss the burgers onto the grill too soon, ensuring their fate of being immediately engulfed in flames and burned into nice, black crisps or I wait too long resulting in half-cooked meat. In this case I am tempted to add more coal on top and soak it with lighter fluid, which, I'm told, can result in an interesting but very painful, almost surefire method to commit suicide.

I could hope for seawater to rise and douse the flames but now the possibility of burning seawater might just completely spoil my cooking endeavors! So now do you agree that maybe I should let someone else do the cooking?

BEER & WINE

It was reported recently that wine has overtaken beer as the favorite alcoholic beverage for the first time in America. Products from hop and malt are being replaced by fermented juices made from grapes in the race for the number one spot on the booze chart. The difference between the two is, one kind you are supposed to sip in small, dainty doses, while the other beverage you are allowed to swill in larger quantities, washing down peanuts and pizzas.

It appears that lately the small-sip wine crowd has been indulging at an incredible rate (probably while the beer guys were napping, exhausted from lifting large mugs), guzzling down enormous quantities of good stuff and making their beverage the premier choice in the country. Nevertheless, both kinds of drink are aiming at the same result—fogging up your thinking apparatus and putting you into a cheerful mood, which in turn encourages you to toss down more of the same stuff (now that's a really clever way to obtain customer loyalty). Few other products have this built-in device assuring that the customer buys more of the same over and over again, even though the very first consuming experience (as well as perhaps, subsequent ones) might have resulted in violent physical rejection of the merchandise.

That is why as a child I always wondered about the mysterious allure that made adults drink the horrible stuff. As any curious youngster, I did try a few times to sneak a taste of beer from my father's glass at one time or another and when I succeeded, I thought it tasted disgustingly bitter and hideous. It baffled me then, why any sane human being would ever drink gallons of "it" (as I often watched adults do). Little did I realize at the time that as a young adult I would find out how miraculously one could "transform" oneself from a shy, insecure youngster into a confident, self-assured man-about-town with a mere glass or two of the stuff. You may need to keep refilling the glass though, in order to restore any possible sagging in buoyancy. In this state, even the disapproving stares of strangers only fuels alcohol-induced merriment, invigorating the life of the party, and encouraging one to prance around with lampshades on one's head. On the other side of the dance floor those disparaging attitudes soon would be tampered with similar spirits and the formerly obnoxious "jerk" would astoundingly be transformed into a witty, handsome daredevil capable of fulfilling one's life's dream.

However, the fairytale of handsome and beautiful hotshots, steeped in success, sophistication and wealth, finding their soul mates while quaffing indiscriminate amounts of alcohol unfortunately only exists in TV commercials. This fantasy usually dissipates as quickly as a bottle of booze on skid row when reality hits as hard as the inevitable hangover the next day.

Of course there are the ones who claim the reason they drink wine, for example, is because their refined taste—finely tuned by the advantage of superior breeding—elevates them to the heights of epicurean sophistication inaccessible to normal folks. I knew a guy once who declared that he had attained such expertise in the art of wine-tasting that he was able to ascertain the origin of grapes in each bottle of wine, when they were grown and when they were harvested. Perhaps he could even tell the name of the man who stacked the bottles. It appears to me that this kind of proficiency can only be accomplished by years of experimentation with vast quantities of alcoholic beverage, which seems to put him and likeminded connoisseurs on par with drinkers of rivaling intoxicating liquids, facing DUI charges and debilitating liver damage.

Perhaps I am a bit biased, since my own grandfather in Germany belonged to the brotherhood of men who hitched teams of gigantic horses together hauling huge vats of beer to the local pubs. Beer was favored as "liquid bread" and to this day, due to the German "beer purity law", is hailed as the only remaining foodstuff untainted by anything but ancient ingredients.

It remains to be seen how long wine will occupy the number one spot of favorite alcoholic beverages in this country. Maybe a few commercials featuring highbrow intellectuals savoring a bottle of ale or a lager with snooty expressions will change things around. Or maybe not . . . we will see. Until then—cheers.

IS CHOCOLATE GOOD FOR US?

No matter how the "powers-that-be" struggle against it, trying their selfish best to keep the information secret, the facts finally have to be revealed after all—chocolate is good for you. After trying to convince us for years that anything and everything bringing joy to the palate, as well as to the soul is "bad for you", they have finally relented and reluctantly admitted that—yes—chocolate, the dark and bitter kind, is actually a health boon.

Hesitant to completely let go of their strings of authority, they naturally place strict stipulations upon this announcement, couching it in the caveat of limited approval by narrowing the parameters of hue and taste. But who is really fooled by the solemn-faced insistence that it has to be the "dark and bitter chocolate" only? It surely smells like a ploy—giving the bitter-tasting stuff to us and keeping the rest for *themselves*. I always wondered anyway who exactly these "powers-that-be" are. I imagine them to be easy-to-spot bureaucrats, hunched over, shifty-eyed with large chocolate stains on their fingers and on their guiltily grinning visages. More than likely, they are operating right next door to the ones who were forced to announce, just as reluctantly, that red wine is also healthy. While we were dropping like flies from clogged arteries, due to fast food consumed every once in a while, the French and Italians seemed to be gorging themselves on multi-course feasts of cheese, salami and pasta with sauces so rich they could grease the moving parts of entire tank divisions, as well as sumptuous desserts, dripping with toppings that had to be supplied with warning labels screaming in red ink: "very bad cholesterol." As we pounded our treadmills, panting and soaking wet—hoping to at least make it a day past retirement—Europeans were dancing in the streets, tipsy and happy from too much "nectar of the vine", probably smoking cigars, and celebrating their one hundred and second birthdays.

After observing this shameless display of "vigor-though-wine" for some time, it seemed that we whipped our authorities into shape, threatening that unless they found a way out of the clogged artery business, their wine supply would be cut (and not only to save their lab-rats from alcoholism). Then, wouldn't you know, in no time at all, after clanking a few laboratory beakers and pretending that certain difficulties (for example, lack of suitable assortment of excellent wines) had delayed this scientific project, they declared null and void entire volumes of previous health recommendations. Red wine taken in certain quantities was now deemed good for us. As they feigned prudence and concern, we were told that the ingredients of red wine (rather than the alcohol) are healthy, and we are advised to stick to one little glass per day. But in the millennia-long history of the Mediterranean region, I doubt that there had ever been a case of anyone just sipping one tiny glass of wine, satisfied that it had to last from sunup to sundown. More than likely, the bottle was uncorked, old friends were invited, and everyone feasted and drank, toasting each other in expectation of yet another century of life.

Now our "powers-that-be" seem to catch on. Knowing what is good for them, they are increasingly starting to release more useful information. Perhaps in no time at all we will find out—something many of us already knew—that resting cozily on a comfy couch watching a game on the tube is extremely healthy and very beneficial to our well-being. And while we glance outside, feeling sorry for the joggers in the rain, with boxes of chocolate and cases of wine stacked in front of us, we contently offer a toast of thanks to our "powers-that-be" for finally putting an end to the age of "no pain—no gain."

COPING WITH REAL FOOD

A friend of mine, returning from a trip to China, reported that although she had enjoyed Chinese food in the past, now after experiencing the real thing over a lengthy period, she is not as keen on it anymore. One thing she found most objectionable was the custom of routinely garnishing her dinner plate not only with various parts of the animal she was accustomed to eating but also with things that actually reminded her that she, in fact, was eating an animal—the head, for example. She just could not get used to the idea of chomping down on the breast of a succulent duck, while disapproving poultry eyes would stare at her.

My wife once almost spat out the soup called "Isi Ewu" at an exotic restaurant once she found out that it was made of goat brains and that the bit of meat she was chomping on at the time was the tongue, and the round balls floating around were an eye or two.

I guess over here we're not used to being reminded that the slice of turkey or ham we're munching on was formerly fastened to a creature that was happily frolicking through the countryside not too long ago.

Perhaps the eyes in the bowl serve the same role as mothers in this country who not so long ago encouraged children to finish everything on their plates because, as they were reminded over and over again, kids in India have nothing to eat. That argument never made a lot of sense to me—if you are concerned about someone not getting his or her share, shouldn't you eat less in order to leave something behind for that person? But, then again, maybe folks were worried about waste and were trying to teach children the value of food? I don't think the message got through, though.

So, I have come up with the brilliant idea of requiring every hamburger joint to supply each table with the head of the particular cow patrons are about to devour. It could also come with a taped message along the lines of, "Moo, look at me! Remember, buddy, I gave up the ghost just for you! So, you'd better value what you eat! And don't talk with your mouth full!"

Vegetarians don't have the problem of food items looking at them, making them feel guilty. Although lettuce and cabbage do come in the form of heads, they're not equipped with eyes, disapproving or otherwise. But that could be easily remedied by having the cow's head on the neighbor's table make disparaging comments about them as well, "Well, look at you over there! Yes, you the vegetarian! You're taking the food right out of my kid's mouth—you know that? So, you better shape up and eat everything on your plate or else!"

But even that may be a waste of time because children nowadays don't make the connection between what they eat and where it actually comes from, no matter what. In a TV show the other day, children were asked to identify various vegetables. They were at a complete loss because they had no names for tomatoes and potatoes, probably viewing them as alien creatures from outer space. In contrast, they had no problems at all immediately recognizing ketchup and french-fries.

I think it's time to slowly educate our kids to let them know where their favorite foods actually come from. How about candy? Maybe candy containers should be required to depict a picture of that nice chemical plant that makes their artificial flavors? Pizza? No problem. It comes from Italy, doesn't it? Show a world map with an arrow pointing at the boot of Italy. It'll turn your kids into geographical whizzes, while learning about food. Donuts? I have no idea where donuts come from, but how about a lovely picture of a donut tree in full bloom?

See, in the newspaper business we're already way ahead of restaurants in this country. You can clearly see the head of wherever the abovementioned ideas come from.

FOOD, FOOD OR JUST FOOD?

The average person supposedly makes over 200 food decisions every day, according to a report I read recently. Perhaps there are so many choices in dishes available nowadays that concerns about nutrition, flavor and caloric intake makes one waffle back and forth. *I'm* different—I only make one decision. If it's in front of me on a plate, smells pretty good and doesn't wiggle anymore, I'll stab it with a fork and eat it.

My wife is the total opposite. She doesn't just make 200 decisions per day; she burns that number up merely looking at the menu in a restaurant. Little does she know that you need to be vigilant in a restaurant if you want to get fed. Timing is of extreme importance because there is only a certain special precarious moment available, which I call the "golden opportunity", to place your order with the waiter. Once this "golden opportunity" is missed, the service professional will curtly, with chilling deference, inform you that he will schedule another appearance later on. But what it actually means is that you will have lost him for an eternity and he will refuse to return even if you end up writhing on the floor, tormented by pangs of hunger.

Of course I'm prepared for such a situation, having a cunning plan at the ready, which involves a lengthy list of tasks for the waiter to accomplish before he can take our order; for example, sending him on some wild goose chase to fetch drinks, cleaner silverware or more water, hoping that this will keep him occupied long enough to prevent him from demanding our immediate verdict. My wife, in the meantime is usually completely oblivious to these goings-on, as she works herself through the first several dozen decisions on the menu.

It goes without saying that one needs the skills of a seasoned diplomat in order to maintain a delicate balance between sustaining a good rapport with the waiter (who needs to be kept in the dark about your scheme of stretching the "golden opportunity" time span), while at the same time encouraging your wife to cut her vast array of possible options in half. Missing just one point in any of these sensitive areas can spell a miserable extended period of famine. It will mean a despondent time, sitting forlorn in a restaurant booth, interspersed only with hopeful moments as one locates the waiter in the distance every once in a while, and longingly and enviously pursues him with hungry eyes while he serves hot plates to happy patrons at some other table in the corner. And don't even think about trying to bribe the waiter with tips by placing a few dollar bills inconspicuously, yet prominently next to the silverware. He will merely assume that the previous guests had left them on the table as reward for his prompt and efficient service and will unceremoniously and swiftly swipe them off the table while pretending to rearrange the condiment containers.

Suddenly, "the golden opportunity" returns. The waiter places himself next to your table, feet slightly apart, pen poised, waiting for you to make a move, like a gunslinger before a shootout. When this happens, I am aware that with the smallest blunder on our part, we will end up rotting away for another eternity. And then it happens—my wife, completely innocent in the rough and tumble world of meal ordering, dares to open her mouth to pose a question about a certain dish. And the waiter gleefully uses this as an excuse to leave the table at once, supposedly in order to make inquiries in the kitchen. Finally, totally mentally exhausted, eons later, I joylessly munch on my dinner when it finally does arrive.

Lucky for me the holidays are here, a time which I hope, translates into a tremendous reduction in food decision-making. How many food decisions can you make facing leftover turkey anyway?

CHAPTER FOURTEEN

Science And Technology
Resolve All Problems

This is Prof. Blueback who is conducting experiments with gravity and the Big Bang Theory.

LET'S TALK ABOUT HARRIET

Harriet, the 175-year-old tortoise died recently in Australia. It just happened that I celebrated yet another birthday around the same time. Now I'm wondering if that means that the title of the world's oldest living creature has now been passed on to me? My speed does seem to be more of a slow crawl these days and (although I would like to think of it as a masculine weathered look) my visage seems to be wrinkling at an alarming rate.

Harriet was long reputed to have been one of the three tortoises taken from the Galapagos Islands by Charles Darwin on his historic 1835 voyage aboard HMS Beagle, although that has been disputed. DNA tests have proved her age but she came from an island that Darwin never visited, handing her the title of not only having been the world's oldest critter but also the world's oldest fraud. At least she never lied about her age, something I'm always tempted to do now. Why would she have to? She looked exactly the same in her younger days, which was more than a century and a half ago, as she did right before her demise. The only thing that changed was—she gained in size. She went from a tiny hand-held version to a gigantic rock of a tortoise with a middle so thick you could sit on it and ride around.

So if increasing girth is a prerequisite for longevity, it seems that I will definitely make it past the century-mark myself as I have no problem at all increasing my dimensions. Just tell me what the "goal" is and I can easily tailor my dining habits accordingly. You need 20, 30, 50 pounds? No problem, I am the "can-do" type of person who will take care of this task with the appropriate amounts of peanuts, cheeseburgers, pizzas and a variety of creative eating techniques to accommodate whatever goal you have in mind in order to make it to the ripest of old ages possible. Good ole Harriet though, allegedly became gigantic without ever chomping on a single piece of cheesecake. Instead she supposedly only fed on veggie-type health food. I have no idea how that can be done. Who here today can testify about what she consumed one hundred years ago anyway? She outlived them all and more than likely, being the smart cookie she was, she ate up all records that showed her cheating on her diet.

Harriet never seemed to worry about wrinkles (I wonder if this feat alone, worrying about wrinkles, will produce just that—more wrinkles). Besides, spending most of your day submerged in seawater will make you look like a prune, whether you worry about it or not. And it seems that those who might have been bothered by Harriet's looks were not around long enough for Harriet to fret about what they were thinking. Living in the fast lane, also didn't seem to bother Harriet much since she seemed to saunter through life in slow motion. I wonder if she ever kept a diary. How interesting it would be to hear firsthand experiences from someone living almost through the entire duration of modern history.

Maybe it would read like this: That Thomas Edison was a decent fellow. Too bad he didn't stick around for very long, he could have been a movie star . . . World War One was a terrible experience. It took me that entire period to make my way from the kitchen to the living room . . . Today the computer crashed. What was the name of that blacksmith who outfitted President Lincoln's horse with excellent shoes? I'm sure he could fashion a sturdier one . . .

Even if she didn't keep a diary, there are quite a few things she could teach us. For one thing, it seems to be of extreme importance to call a comfy home your own, even if it means, as in Harriet's case, that you carry it on your back. Then, most importantly, no matter how frantic everyone gets around you, all you have to do is grow a thick skin and *outwait* them.

STUPID CREATURES MAY LIVE LONGER, SWISS STUDY FINDS

I recently came across a study conducted at the University of Lausanne in Switzerland, which found that stupid flies live longer than smart ones. Now with all the other news items about the threat of climate change, escalating oil prices, nuclear proliferation, wars etc, they're scaring us with something like that. How devastating—dumb beings live longer than smart ones. One naturally would assume it to be the other way around. Is it time to toss that college degree into the trash with the rest of the creepy-crawlies? It stands to reason that the very subjects of this study would not care one way or the other, mostly because they're too dumb to comprehend the results anyway. So why conduct the test—who else would care? Maybe it has something to do with smart researchers finding clever ways to get research grants. Although with the results of the Human Genome Project now available, telling us that we're not as far removed from insects as we had hoped, perhaps parallels could be drawn. Anyway, the result of this study was that the Einsteins in the fly-world cut their lifespan short by about one third just by the virtue of being intelligent. Now how smart is that? The researchers speculated this is most probably because the increase in neural activity weakens the fly's life-support systems.

Devising an IQ test for mentally challenged insects should not really demand great genius either. In Switzerland (that's where all the money is, isn't it?) someone can obviously afford to finance such a test, although one would assume that the lower life forms in the university hierarchy could have come up with a cheap and workable way to test flies. Anyone in possession of a barbecue can do it pretty quickly, actually, in my opinion.

But just picture yourself as a fly. How horrible—as soon as you realize you're more intelligent than the others, it suddenly hits you with a vengeance that your days are numbered. No wonder there are always flies hanging around the beer kegs at outdoor parties. They're probably trying to drink themselves into a stupor, in the attempt to extend their lives.

That's the same reason people drink on airplanes I think. Smart people know humans are not made to fly. These gigantic machines—how are they supposed to remain airborne? See, a few shots of liquor at the airport lounge and on the plane, and you're too stupid to care, leaving you with more energy to increase the workings of your life-support system by loudly demanding extra nuts and pretzels from the flight crew.

In addition to that, in my experience, watching onboard movies will definitely deflate any chance of increasing neural activity as well, a free service that might add decades to your life. I can vouch for that from my last trip, a ten-hour overseas flight. My intelligence was definitely reduced by multiple IQ points, watching airline movies. I can't even remember the titles of the flicks now. One was a sitcom, something involving people flailing with arms and screaming at each other, while laughter was piped in from somewhere to cleverly alert us when something was supposed to be funny (I've been trying for years to get a laugh track inserted into my humor column but the editors just keep laughing at me). I don't remember any plots or funny dialogues, I just know that these movies were so mind-numbingly predictable that the anger-produced increased heart rate probably nullified any of the age-enhancing benefits that declining intelligence promised. Now, if this Swiss study is a guide, I'm probably facing the challenges of decreased intelligence with a shortened life to look forward to. Not very smart, is it? In that case I think I might have to leave flying to the flies. I just hope they're not watching any movies. We surely don't need any more elderly flies, do we?

FINDING OUR WAY BACK HOME

The Swedes are coming and they might find us.

A recent study determined that the average American student is unable to locate his country on a world map. Just scoring in the low twenties, while the Swedes, Germans and Italians approached the forties out of a possible fifty-six-point questionnaire, it seemed that Americans were more stymied by geography than others.

Although it proves that our kids are becoming less and less informed, the study also found that the entire world youth population seems generally below par when it comes to choosing a destination for the next vacation. So, who knows, we might have Brits or Danes looking forward to a sunny vacation in the South Seas and ending up in Alaska instead, digging for coconuts under icy glaciers.

But unless riddled with Ritalin, I am completely rattled about the fact that a student can possibly miss a landmass the size of North America. Perhaps it poses a challenge for someone unaccustomed to the mysterious symbols and renderings of map-making. One could easily mistake Italy's boot for a sock or the American continent for a pizza.

Even so, the two Americas cover a pretty large portion on the globe, hardly to be mistaken for a coffee-stain. Chances are, that spinning the globe around really quickly and then stopping it, you'd put your finger right on top of one of the two Dakotas. Only one of them would suffice to claim our home, although most of us live in California. If we can't find the expansive living space of more than a quarter billion people, how much slack do we have to cut the guys in Luxembourg?

Now I try my hardest to refrain from saying that things back then were much better and people a lot smarter, and that you would meet dogs in the streets that had to muster the equivalent of today's PhD just to pass the "roll-over" test in obedience school. The reason I swore I'd never put down younger generations was because I remember my parents comparing the *Rolling Stones* to the squeal of unlucky farm animals, about to be converted into succulent sausages. That is why I quietly suffered through heads being bitten off defenseless bats by crazed, rocking mascara-smeared madmen, just to prove my affinity to the then current youth-culture and now nod my head to the rhythmic earthquake of rap, exploding a dozen cars behind me at an excruciating long traffic light.

In order to empathize with today's busy youth, I wonder how my own geographical knowledge held up when I was a student? It must have been sufficient enough for me to have made it back home for supper every day, that's for sure.

In my opinion, it is fruitless to compare today's generation to ours way back then, when we had to slough to school for miles, barefoot, through waist-high snow, sometimes in 100 degree Fahrenheit. Nowadays we have computers, for crying out loud, which at the very least could aid the student in finding affordable footwear for appropriate weather conditions.

So why in this great information age we are so ill-informed? Perhaps because back then we had to go through the effort of actually learning how to read and write words, comprised of the alphabet and our only spell-check was the red-hot pen of a very irate teacher.

Therefore with all the very important phenomena of youth-culture, from biting off bat-heads to music that sounds like squealing pigs to more mature ears, and all the exiting, innovations in technology, we are stuck with an old-fashion item—learning. No matter how much knowledge and information there is out there in cyberspace, we need to have some of it in here, internalized inside our brains. Or, one of these days, we might not find our way back home.

HOW VITAL IS THE APPENDIX?

I knew it! Just as I had always suspected—the much-maligned appendix is good for something. It was always believed that the appendix was nothing but an evolutionary leftover, as useless as the tailbone. Well, let me stop right there! Who says even the tailbone is useless? Those smarty-pants, hoity-toity scientists don't know everything, do they? Who can say for sure that we don't need our tailbone in order to grow a tail in the future? If the current global warming trend continues, with the icecaps melting and floods imminent, sooner or later we just might need to grow a tail in a hurry, so we can quickly climb back up trees again—before the sharks get us. An extra extremity like a tail could prove very useful for escaping famished, marauding fish (or the inevitable used-boat salesmen).

Lucky for us, medical professionals don't usually cut out our tailbone as enthusiastically as they do our appendixes (although I have to confess there were many times I wished they had done just that, especially when I slip on oil slicks or banana peels and land on my behind). Come to think of it, many a silent movie star's career depended on their tailbones, since extreme trauma afflicting their tailbones seemed to miraculously elicit extraordinary amusement and laughter from the audience. The lowly appendix, though, never enjoyed such prominence.

It was recently discovered by scientists that our appendix does serve an important function as a vital "safe-house" where good bacteria could lie in wait until they were needed to repopulate the gut after a nasty case of diarrhea. It was also found that the appendix can help make, direct and train white blood cells. How it might accomplish such training, I have no idea. Maybe they do it like old-time circus animal trainers, with a chair in one hand and a whip in the other, motivating the white blood cells forward by subjecting their tailbones to a bit of trauma.

Naturally I was not informed about this vital function when my own appendix was removed. Actually I was not informed of much of anything during that time. Being five years old, adults didn't seem to be too concerned about consulting me or asking my opinion about too many things at all. There I was complaining about a stomachache one minute, and next thing I knew, I was lying on a hospital bed, a team of white-masked strangers hovering over me, while someone put an evil looking contraption on my face. Then one friendly lady asked me how far I could count. Seizing the opportunity to finally prove the vastness of my knowledge to the adult world, I was prepared to go to at least 10 million, although perhaps not in sequence. I apparently had not anticipated how labor-intensive and exhausting such an activity was, as I fell asleep almost immediately. When I woke up, I am now told that I was apologetic about my miserable mathematical failure but no one seemed to be too bothered at that time. Everyone though seemed extremely exuberant about having saved me from the dire consequences of appendicitis, with a procedure that included a violent intrusion into my abdomen cutting out the offending part and leaving me with a gigantic scar across my belly.

What no one was aware of at the time (according to scientists today), was that a potentially deadly inflammation of the appendix may not have been due to a faulty appendix at all, but may have been due to cultural changes associated with the industrialized society and improved sanitation. Good thing that we might now again face a life in the trees without all that complicated plumbing. We might finally get a chance to give our immune system a decent workout.

But in my case, with no appendix, I find myself without the vital appendage to fight off diarrhea—not a pleasant thought when hanging upside-down from a tree.

SNOOKI MAY NOT NEED THAT TAN

I understand that in 2009 the world suffered one of the hottest years on record, and it's not getting any better. Snooki may not need to pay for that tan after all.

I remember growing up in Germany, whenever the thermometer passed the 30 degrees Centigrade mark for several days in a row, schools would close down. 30 degrees Centigrade, that's not even 80 degrees Fahrenheit, a normal, quite pleasant summer day around California today. However in northern Europe then, it was considered unbearable heat, welcomed only by us kids who got the day off to go swimming. I also read an article where someone once had found an amusing headline in England proclaiming that London was suffering under the intolerable conditions of "Scorching Seventies." Folks in northern climes were just not prepared for hot weather, as air-conditioning was unheard of. Even a simple fan was an uncommon sight.

As a kid, I had actually only seen a fan in old movies scenes, like one featuring Humphrey Bogart in Malta drinking gin, as giant blades above his head cooled things down. He could also have taken off his jacket to make himself even more comfortable, but apparently etiquette current at the time must have prohibited that. Only the "natives" were allowed the freedom to walk around in their traditional clothing, which, rooted in millennia of experience, was based on the principle of deductive reasoning—the greater the layers of clothing, the more you sweat. Maybe that's how the phrase "only mad dogs and Englishmen . . ." was coined. The indigenous population watched in amazement, as crazed canines and early colonialists ventured out in the blazing midday sun and, in the case of Englishmen, more than likely, dressed in full regalia. While dogs had the excuse of possible brain ravaging disease, the natives wondered what exactly possessed the strange foreigners to undertake such foolishness.

Looking at the dizzying heights the thermometer has reached this summer the 2009 record might be broken again, although in some places, like the San Francisco Bay Area, the opposite is true. In our coastal areas the fog tends to hang around longer than usual and that has cooled things down considerably. In northern Europe however, the temperature went up into the nineties, something completely unheard of before. If things continue, before we know it, they'll be able to grow coconuts in Scandinavia! Here on our continent, things weren't much better, as the Northeast suffered under extreme unusual heat.

My wife, who seems to have developed an incredible tolerance for watching dim-witted folks doing silly things on reality TV shows, reports that the participants of some popular reality shows not only lie in the sun on the beach, but also regularly visit tanning salons and then top their bronzed bodies off with vigorous doses of tanning spray from some kind of paint can. As the icecaps melt, and polar bears and penguins disappear, reality TV folks, in the forefront of fashion, are determined to demonstrate that the "pale look" is dead. And not a minute too soon for my wife who stems from the equatorial region in Africa and had therefore been provided with a natural tan from birth, a privilege saving her a fortune in tanning material.

Perhaps in the future, as we will need to cope with extra doses of sunrays, evolution might just endow everyone with necessary darker shades, therefore wiping out any form of bias based on skin color? But knowing humanity, as I know it, I'm sure we will find other ways to discriminate against each other. Perhaps nature will provide folks in coastal regions, who need to cope with the rising tide of melting icecaps, with the necessary equipment to deal with such conditions. More than likely they then will be confronted with signs like, "People with WEBBED FEET keep out!"

DARK MATTER

NASA says it has found proof of the existence of dark matter, as a report recently stated. Big deal, I say. Had they asked me, I would have informed them of such matter years ago. The first time I had a chance to personally witness the existence of such dark matter was when I bought a used car as an impressionable, naive youngster from some shady character. I seem to remember the presence of pure, dark evil when I drove it off the car lot. Normally this wouldn't have mattered much but as soon as I got on the freeway all kinds of unpredictable occurrences began to happen, starting with the lock on the hood coming undone.

They say that inside of a Black Hole, gravity is so strong that nothing escapes, not even light. But my case seemed to top all scientific predictions because inside the black hole that my car turned into suddenly there was no light coming from either direction. The reason being that the hood had flown up with a bang, blocking my windshield and any chance of the slightest rays of light creeping in, while at the same time all at once, all light-generating sources inside the vehicle quit functioning. Lucky for me, I was in the slow lane and managed, while completely blind, to pull my jalopy over onto the shoulder without getting hit by either cars or comets.

Since my unfortunate incident happened during the Dark Ages of technology when the idea of cell-phones was not even a flickering spark on the panorama of cyberspace, I languished in the vacant, vast emptiness of space that separated me from a public telephone for some time. I realized that I needed to call a tow service because the "power" that had forced open the hood had also bent the hinges, preventing me from closing the darn thing again. Even my scheme of letting gravity do its work in conjunction with an asteroid-sized piece of concrete which I had found on the side of the road, worked against me, as the rock slipped off and dropped on my foot instead of aiding me in closing the problematic hood.

Although NASA may not have been talking about the kind of evil darkness that lurks within malicious vehicles and their sales staff, and may instead have been focusing on the stuff that holds the universe together—presumably some other kind of "matter" besides hot gas and galaxies, and although astronomers have long suspected that some substance holds together galaxy clusters, other than gravity of visible stars, which would not be strong enough to keep them from flying apart, whatever this "dark matter" is that holds together the universe, it can't possibly be as dark as my mood on the day my car fell apart.

I plotted terrible revenge on the evil car salesman who sold me the jalopy, and I began to come apart at the hinges as I walked the long distance between my broken-down car on the freeway and a telephone, reflecting on the darkest of matters in the universe. Then as the rays of the afternoon sun brightened up my mood, I forgot about dark matter altogether. That is until the relentless darkness caught up with me again a few days later, necessitating a major engine job on the car. After shedding more green matter from my wallet I tried to locate the evil salesman I bought my car from, but it turned out that he had dissipated into thin air.

Now that NASA has finally found the source of the "dark matter", which may have been the cause of many of my troubles; perhaps they can now also help me get some of my green matter back?

CHAPTER FIFTEEN

I Finally Found The Cure
For Writer's Block

Although he had shown early promise excelling in a janitorial career, Max decided to devote his life teaching Latin to ordinary farm animals. A thankless task, as he soon found out.

I FINALLY FOUND THE CURE FOR WRITER'S BLOCK

Sooner or later almost every writer will collide with the gigantic, immovable, impenetrable obstacle called "writer's block." It is a monstrous slab measuring more than 10 x 10, consisting of pure granite, intimidating any person of words into becoming a puddle of quivering jelly. No amount of begging, wailing and pleading will cause it to budge an inch. There are many who try to soften it up with alcohol or even more dubious chemical matter but with little avail. More than likely they typically slam even harder into this massive lump than before.

Normally one starts out with a blank screen or white page, which becomes blanker and whiter the longer one stares at it. As a matter of fact, after sitting in front of it for some time the bile of pure hatred against anything so pristine and immaculate will well up with such violence that the protagonist needs every fiber in his body to restrain himself in order not to soil it with the most foul, putrid substances imaginable. After a few vicious but impotent outbursts of cursing and screaming, one gets up to make a cup of coffee. That is when the writer finds that doing something else such as checking "important items" in a magazine, TV or the wanted ads in the paper will need to be attended to right at that very moment. After a few more glances back at the "white, blank page", more than likely he or she will turn away from it and head directly to the employment office and on to a glorious career as a high-powered attorney, taxi driver or "greeter" in a large department store.

But soon after immersion in the drudgery of making a living by mere repetition of absurdly menial tasks long enough, the pain of crashing into the "writers block" and facing the "blank page" is forgotten, especially when the failed writer learns about others winning Pulitzer and Nobel Prizes or making billions writing about an inane little teen wizard.

That's when the whole "story" starts again (someone should write a book about it). Sometimes a novel is attempted.

Usually the writer begins with great enthusiasm and joy. The characters are fleshed out, the tale develops greatly. The baron and his mistress are off hurrying from adventure to adventure. Or the good guy is closing in on the bad guy while sweeping local beauties off their feet. Life is great for the writer. Making widgets day in, day out suddenly is not such drudgery anymore. Until one day when the ominous edges of writer's block come into view again. Just at the moment when the humble waitress is about to marry the billionaire, doubts might develop about the reason why the limousine had pulled up to her drive-thru window and the billionaire had chosen her instead of all the beautiful debutants he knew. Or how could the heroine possibly have a doctorate in nuclear physics, speak a dozen languages (including several Bedouin dialects), adorn herself with the darkest shades of a black belt in a variety of martial arts and be able to operate any and all aircrafts while barely out of her teens?

The nagging doubts about one's ability to tie up all the loose ends might hit home as hard as a block of concrete.

But, of course, there is an easy solution. Just when everything fails there is a simple plot-device, designed to rescue each and every novel and, as a result, toss the writer into a privileged life of fame and fortune. It's the secret weapon capable of annihilating even the toughest of writer's block and available to talented and mediocre authors alike.

When writer's block occurs, end all stories like this:

"Suddenly, out of nowhere, a gargantuan, green snake appears and eats the whole town."

See, that was easy. No reason to explain why the butler could not possibly have been at several places at once doing his dirty deeds and still maintain a spick and span residence. Everyone just ends up inside the "giant snake." Each book could be rescued by such blessed serpent and in the spirit of variety the color could be changed from green to blue or yellow each time.

And in case someone offers some snide critique harboring doubts about why they all should die tragically and so suddenly as a result of the unexpected appearance of that menacing reptile, the person could be silenced quickly with the reminder that one does not speak ill of the deceased.

HOW CAN TV WATCHING BE BAD FOR YOU?

Let's talk about your TV-watching habit. What sort of couch potato are you? Apparently your character and personality can be assessed by how much of your life you are willing to sacrifice to keep commercials alive and advertisers thriving. If it ranges around 19 hours per week, you're supposed to be a normal, happy, socially active person. That's what a recent survey concludes. That means your tendency of gawking 2 to 3 hours each day into that rectangle box supposedly squares you as a well-adjusted individual. But not all is happy if you decide to spend just 30% more of your time on the couch surrounded by your trusted companions—pizza, peanuts and beer—taking in the soon to be fully digitalized airwaves by the bushel-full on that big screen TV. For some reason, this additional time flushes you out as a lonely person, unhappy and without a friend in the world. I wonder though, even as supposedly average happy people wasting "only" a couple of hours of TV time a day, *in addition to going to work, with all the chores piling up, and surfing the Net*—exactly what time we have to be social?

I would advise these scientists not to conduct such studies in my house. My input would completely spoil their findings because my TV habit last week might erroneously have recorded 12 to 24 hours of watching TV daily and would have blacklisted me as the loneliest of lonesome recluses. Why? Well, I imagine in my effort to be a part of the well-adjusted, happy crowd, I was required to put in my two to three hours of TV-watching time, wasn't I? But since I also had to be socially active and do all of the other things asked of me I definitely had to cut off at least a dozen or so of my forty winks at night, didn't I? Well, guess what happened after that? I placed myself in front of the tube in the evening for my required TV watching time but next thing I know, I was suddenly yanked out of my deep slumber to the blaring of "Good Morning, America" or some other morning show the next day because I had dozed off. Then, dazed, I ran out of the house to get a jump on the day and naturally forget to turn off the TV. This error alone will then incorrectly put me down as some kind of lone-nut TV addict (I think the Nielson Family probably would want to disavow their kinship with me and vote me off the island instantly with this kind of terrible behavior).

With the depressing economy, the tube has become our only entertainment lately! Less people are going out to the movies and social events, and more people are spending their time in front of the TV. To compound issues, another scientific study conducted by the University of Toronto has found that "social isolation" actually makes individuals cold, literally. The study found that when people are happy and interacting with others they actually feel warm and cozy, while people who are cut off from others experience unpleasant chills. Does this mean that with our TV time increasing, we may have to pay more for heating? I can imagine people socially interacting in an average household, feeling warm and cozy, until some lonely nut decides to sneak away from the dinner table, to watch the game on TV *all by himself*! More than likely the temperature will suddenly plunge south, unless, of course his team is winning. In that case the scenario quickly develops into a happy social activity again, when everyone joins him, high-fiving, whooping and cheering and then getting really hot under the collar.

So this is what I believe would finally solve our energy problem—in the winter, get together with family and friends to celebrate the holidays with that warm and cuddly feeling, and during the summer heat, make sure you clock in at least 25 to 30 hours a week in front of the TV to get the chills and cool down. Just make sure you're rooting for a losing team to stop yourself from heating up again.

TELEPHONE REPAIR

Can you imagine a world without the telephone? As in the past when uninvited guests dropped in to surprise you on Sunday mornings as you lounged in your pajamas concentrating on important things like reading the funnies? The telephone, a unique tool that has revolutionized human communication, makes it possible to gauge the mood of potential surprise guests, while communicating your own mood of not being able to receive them. But for me, this unique communication device has been breaking down lately, and more than once, during my ordeal, I contemplated introducing it to another valuable tool, one that revolutionized construction—the hammer.

I suspect that excessive moisture is not compatible with effective communication, as you might have found out yourself talking to people who have a habit of spattering spittle (especially while drinking your coffee Sunday mornings). The reason for this assumption is that every time it rains my phone blocks out voices and instead exposes me to exotic sounds of the ocean, leaving this tool completely ineffective as a communication device (although I still might have been able to use it as a hammer). I do enjoy the sounds of the ocean, especially the mysterious music whales produce to attract potential mates, but since my business is largely with human beings, I have no need to communicate with sea creatures, and I doubt that they have any interest in someone as scrawny as me.

In order to get a human being to communicate with me, I finally decided to call up my phone company to complain, using my cell phone. I was directed to a machine, which turned out to be a device equipped with quite a pleasant disposition. In a calm, amiable voice the machine suggested to me that under no circumstances should I have a repairman coming to my house unless absolutely necessary. It then proceeded to instruct me on alternative ways of making the repairs myself—and then it hung up on me. "Good bye" it said quite abruptly without waiting for my response. Apparently they had neglected to program the machine in other areas of telephone courtesy, leaving me to crave attention from whales again.

What the machine had instructed me to do, before it had so brusquely cut me off, was to check out some kind of peculiar box which was supposedly attached to my house somewhere on the outside. I must confess that I passed this spot numerous times each and every day but I had never been conscious of the fact that this box existed (does it surprise you now that some people keenly claim that we are being studied by aliens ogling us from the insides of weirdly shaped spaceships, right outside our windows? Perhaps there is one sitting right next to you on the sofa and you are not even aware that you are being observed).

As it turned out, on the inside of the box was a spaghetti-plate of colored wires and connectors, prompting me to poke at it with my screwdriver a few times. Satisfied that I had done my job I called up the alien machine again, appealing to its mark of distinction as a fellow mechanical device, which inner workings were far too complex for a normal mortal to comprehend. I called several times, punching alternative numbers for solutions, and then quite reluctantly and warning me about excessive repair costs the automaton promised to send a repairman, presumably a member from the human family.

The window of appearance for the repairman was scheduled on a Sunday and actually grew into a yawning gate, covering an eternity from dawn till the cows came home. Being reminded of Sundays in the distant past when phones were a rarity and visitors just surprised you without warning, my wife and I sacrificed precious morning hours waiting tensely for the moment of the stranger's appearance. He turned out to be a pleasant fellow, much like his boss, the machine. And immediately upon arrival, he proceeded to open "the box" and heartily probe the wires with his screwdriver a few times (apparently I am a natural when it comes to telephone repair, as I did the same thing). Then I realized, all I had needed was a few more stabs and I could have saved myself a fortune. Now we are back in the business of communicating with fellow human beings, although every once in a while I still seem to hear creatures from the ocean squawking. Or are they perhaps alien visitors waiting to surprise us on Sundays?

DO YOU NEED HELP WITH YOUR MEMORY?
TRY COLORS!

How good is your memory? Do you remember exactly when and what you ate for dinner last Wednesday?

The tiny hummingbird is said to remember exactly where it last dined and what time that occasion took place (although I'm sure their notorious tipping habits do not make them stand out amongst the service personnel). I have no idea how scientists discovered this information. Did they provide the birds with tiny, little watches and notebooks? And what happens when it rains—won't the notes get smudged, perhaps rendering the entire research findings useless? More than likely scientists did the hard work themselves, straining *their* brains to recall where the little birds feasted last, in order to observe them and record the events. What is astounding is that hummingbirds do all this without any effort at all, although their brains are 7,000 times smaller than ours.

Because our brains are 7,000 times larger than the hummingbird's, we should be able to recall not only where we ate, but also what we ate, the color of the waitress' eyes, and also which commercial on TV coerced us into stuffing ourselves full of unhealthy junk food!

I once bought some books on the subject of memory—I forget how many—*and I wish I could remember where the heck I put them*. But if I had one in front of me I could demonstrate to you how important colors are in memory (I seem to hazily remember that part). Just like hummingbirds which remember the brightest flowers, you can also make things stick by involving color when trying to memorize events. For example, that clown with the purple hair and red nose stands out in your memory much more than even that pale little girl or boy whose birthday party you were invited to as a youngster, doesn't he? This happened probably mostly because the clown scared you half to death with that giant bright flower that squirted some nasty liquid in your face. This technique with colors is called mnemonics. I urge you just to remember that word, instead of trying to pronounce it—or else people might think you're prone to mumbling or that you are a bit slow on the uptake, and might possibly dismiss you as having less than stellar memory.

It all comes back to me now because one of the great features of this technique is that it helps you to remember names as well (a tool that could prove very useful for politicians, for example, as they routinely emotionally blackmail constituents into shaking loose donation dollars, by memorizing everyone's moniker). Mnemonics techniques teach that you should try to use colors as well as your imagination to make abstract words and ideas tangible. For example, if you want to remember someone's name—a person called John Smith, for example—all you have to do is to picture a john and a blacksmith. Can you see it? This works great, doesn't it? So go right ahead and try it out on someone. Next time you see this guy you can say, "Hello Mr. Outhouse have you put any shoes on some hoofs lately?" And sure enough, you will receive a great big wallop on the nose. Of course, memory will be *painful* and you can sue the heck out of this guy, which will go a long way to help you definitely recall his name. This method might be a bit cumbersome at first but if you forget his name again, it is always helpful to re-read the court papers.

Lucky for the politicians that we (perhaps enthralled by their ability to recall everyone's name) regularly forget the promises they make during their campaigns. Maybe we should forget about "remembering" and mark those promises down instead in color to take to the voting booth next time?

But no matter how many problems you have with your memory, be sure to tip the waitress after your lunch because she is equipped with an excellent memory and will definitely remember you on your next visit.

CHAPTER SIXTEEN

How To Deal With Back Seat Drivers And Other Similar Pests

"NO, NO, NO… Listen! Forget about Left-Right for a minute. This is UP and this is DOWN!"

BACKSEAT DRIVING

"Backseat driving" is a very popular activity which avails itself to anyone sitting on any seat inside the car except of course on the driver's side. The purpose of this endeavor is quite simply, *to drive the operator of the car insane*! With a bit of practice any fairly ambitious backseat driver has the potential to fill the average medium to full-sized mental institution within the vicinity to the brink in a matter of weeks.

In order to assure greater success it helps to be related to the driver. As a matter of fact, the closer the backseat driver is related to the driver, the quicker the guarantee of watching such a driver get picked up by "the friendly folks in white coats." For this reason spouses are excellent backseat drivers, being accomplished in the art of "auto-speak" and its subsequent resultant state of complete lunacy on the part of the driver. I suspect it is not malice which motivates the backseat driver but rather the desire to proudly feature at least one member of the family who is stark raving mad.

To become an efficient backseat driver, here is how you should operate:

(1) First, assume that the driver of the car has never ever operated a motor vehicle before in his or her life (it doesn't matter that the target person somehow makes it "out" on a regular basis, or may have driven some vehicle for a while, as evidenced by various fluid leaks or residue left behind where the car was previously parked overnight).

(2) Once you enter the car, always presuppose that the driver has had a bout of amnesia causing him or her to temporarily lose any memory of automobile operating experience, including the purpose for the mysterious round, wheel-shaped object located up-front. Therefore from the moment the doors are shut, the functions of each piece of equipment, device or mechanism must

be explained slowly and thoroughly to the driver and repeated often throughout the trip.

(3) Since the driver's attention will be occupied with digesting new and important information about the car, supplied by you, the driver will be left completely unaware of the functions of the highways, and it would be necessary to make the driver aware of this fact each and every time, mostly by yelling ever so often "Watch out, there is a car!"

(4) Of course you may also consider it prudent to pound on the dashboard screaming in fright, as soon as traffic slows down in front. After all the driver is most probably incapable of concluding that brakes must be engaged to avoid a possible crash.

(5) Naturally, you are aware that most times the driver of the car is also utterly void of any sense of direction. Therefore an unremitting expression of mistrust in the driver's ability to find the way home is necessary and will increase the enormous state of confusion caused by this inaptitude.

(6) Not one successful backseat driving session has ever been completed without explaining the importance of colors to the driver. Especially elucidating the difference between red and green at each and every traffic light will go a long way in producing bite-marks in the steering wheel later on.

(7) It may be necessary to repeat these sessions on a regular basis, employing a variety of techniques, and then sooner or later the driver will enter into a state of total helplessness, and can then be spoon-fed and diapered accordingly. And although excessive drooling and wild babbling might be bothersome for a while, you will now be faced with a complete blank slate, which will make the re-training of the driver possible, and the driver can then begin to approach the superior driving skills that you, the backseat driver are fortunately blessed with.

HOW ABSENT-MINDED CAN YOU BE?

A few days ago a friend of mine reported that he had observed a woman at a gas station driving off with the gas hose still attached to her tank. What kind of imbecile does a dumb thing like that, he wondered? What kind? Who? Well, someone like me of course! I admit it. It happened not once but *twice* in my long career of pouring gas into my cars via a hose. As far as I know, around here I'm the only one who has succeeded in accomplishing such an endeavor multiple times.

But I assume—hope actually—that anyone is capable of doing something like that. In my opinion, forgetting to place the gas nozzle back unto its holder, and the inability to complete the appropriate transaction is not really restricted to imbeciles or any other intelligence-challenged individuals. There is no law which states that you have to fail an IQ test, qualifying you to do something stupid. Also, there are no sex, age or race restrictions either. All that's required is that you are eligible to operate a motor vehicle, and you find yourself in possession of such a machine while the same necessitates a stop at the local gas station. Perhaps the only other prerequisite you need has something to do with your capability to be easily distracted. Someone who suddenly gets up in the middle of the State Bar exams to watch birds eating worms for breakfast outside the window would definitely be a candidate. Or have you ever been absorbed in a book or a TV show, while soup was boiling over in the kitchen? There was a book some years ago named "The man who mistook his wife for a hat." I can see that such a person would be prone to make similar mistakes.

In my case, I was mulling things over in my head, problems demanding immediate action, while idling in a gas station. In my experience, what usually comes next is a peculiar "pop" sound, an unwanted noise that suddenly elicits enormous curiosity amongst bystanders, as they stare and point at you while you get out to inspect the source. The subsequent reaction is quite predictable, as any seasoned gas station attendant will eagerly tell you, since all the culprits have a similar modus operandi—you, or me in this case—mouth ajar, saliva dripping, staring at the end of the unconnected hose, then at the gas column where it had recently been attached. The amount of time wasted, plunked in the middle of the street, holding the nozzle in complete awe while eyes dart back and forth, depends on the subject and his understanding of how the world is put together—usually, one would assume, with duct tape.

But you learn quickly, as you sheepishly enter the gas station store, that mere duct tape would be quite insufficient to put things together in this situation. No, the repair to re-connect the hose will set you back to the tune of hundreds. But don't think the experience stops with your handing over a big chunk of your hard-earned money. That's just the beginning. You will be subjected to contemptuous whisperings around you for a long time to come afterwards. It will typically start with something like, "Oh, that's the guy who . . ." More often than not you might overhear a disdainful word or two, like "dumb", "moron" and "stupid" along with smirks, giggles and guffaws.

But how does the mishap of detached gas hoses compare to people who put coffee cups, briefcases and small infants on top of their cars and drive off? As I understand it, luckily in this last case someone, completely horrified, managed to stop the guy before a tragedy happened. It goes without saying, we just have to become more diligent, pay more attention to things at hand and . . . wait a minute . . . what's that burning smell? Oh, for crying out loud . . . my dinner!

THE BEST WAY TO MANAGE TRAFFIC ON THE FREEWAY

Last week I was meandering down a stretch of highway during a pleasant, warm summer day, minding no one's business but my own, when suddenly I was attacked by fish! Well, actually it was a fish-tank to be exact. It had fallen off a truck a couple of lanes next to me, bounced off the road, hit several cars and burst into a thousand pieces, a few of which hit my windshield, scraping a long line halfway across. Lucky for me I had the window rolled up otherwise I could easily have turned into a scary-looking guy named "Scar-face."

At this time I had not even thought of lunch, but angered by this assault, I knew that I would take horrible revenge on fish in general, and eat the cousins of whatever had been housed in that horrible tank. *I would take great pleasure filleting the creatures and chewing on them bit by bit.* But then I realized that I was probably directing my anger at the wrong target. How could I blame innocent creatures without hands and opposable thumbs, when the real culprit was the driver of the truck? I'm sure that when confronted with the task of transporting a fish-tank in an open truck, he should have been conscientious enough to tie down the item properly. Fortunately for this motor vehicle operator, as I looked around for a place to have lunch, there were only burger places, hotdog, and chicken restaurants lining the highway and not one place featuring the hindquarters of dim-witted truck drivers. I'm sure there are many of us who would gladly sink a fork into any of the folks who cause us to be late during the morning rush hour because of their unsafe driving habits (a situation which is becoming increasingly regular). Or, at the very least, perhaps we would consider using any available cutting utensil to surgically remove the ailing "brain matter" that compels people to engage in perilous maneuvers on the freeway, endangering everyone around them.

Perhaps we should learn from fish, how to behave while swiftly moving around in large crowds. Next time you find yourself at a large aquarium just look at a school of fish, consisting of dozens, maybe hundreds of fish gliding through water and then suddenly switching direction, continuing to swim effortlessly through their liquid highway system. Do you ever see any fish bumping into the other? If that ever happened, I'm sure there would be sharks just waiting by the wayside to grab a hold of the dummies. No insurance would cover any such fool and more than likely the rest of the School would want to teach the erring fish a lesson anyway and gladly hand him over as shark food (in fact, it might be in the interest of the School to raise a certain number of dunces in order to keep the sharks occupied and fed, and to keep unwanted attention away from other fish).

You might think that we have a similar setup, with cops waiting for wayward drivers on the sides of the freeways, but that very fact does not seem as *great* a deterrent as giant sharks looking for prey! Just imagine yourself sauntering along and then suddenly watching a 15-foot eating machine zooming alongside of you, waiting for any improper move or anything out of the ordinary. Maybe *that's* what we need during high volume commuter traffic—big city busses equipped with teeth running up and down the freeway shoulder on a constant lookout for traffic-offenders, and immediately pouncing upon anyone who cuts in front of us or tailgates. Therefore whenever you find yourself in traffic, it might be best to stick to the rules you learned in traffic school because you don't want to end up as one of the dummies invoking the eating frenzy of scar-faced menacing sharks.

HIGHWAY HYPNOSIS

A good indication that it is time to pull over, after speeding on the freeway for hours on your vacation trip, is the moment you wake up and start criticizing your wife's erratic driving and then suddenly realize that it is *you* who is sitting in the driver's seat. Of course it is not your fault if, as a result, you should find yourself an integrate part of the structure of the motor vehicle that was in front of you just a moment before, as you can shift all the blame on "highway hypnosis." It might take a bit of work on your part afterwards though, to convince your insurance company that you were the victim of some kind of mysterious alien power that lulled you to sleep mesmerizing you with advanced techniques of hypnosis.

Why would an alien power be interested in hypnotizing you? Well, of course it is all part of a "grand highway conspiracy", involving all kinds of businesses and industries, including the greasy spoon eateries dotting the exits of freeways, beckoning you to come in for a visit. You realize suddenly that the only option other than paying higher insurance premiums and hospital bills after a collision is to step into one of the many coffee shops for some hot, black, bitter liquid to help you break that magic spell and wake up. I don't want to alarm you but as you can see, it is a "win-win" situation for commerce and, I suspect, there must be these twelve sinister men in dark suits—the ones imbued with equally sinister hypnotic powers—sitting somewhere directing it all. Since they get their money either way, and they seem to allow you at least some choice, you could either opt for a mild heartburn at a cut-rate eating-place, or else you could shell out big bucks for chiropractors in case of an accident.

The term "coffee shop" is a bit of a misnomer in my opinion, and should be changed to "cheese shop." Although you will find yourself floating back into the parking lot on gallons of coffee after your off-the-highway lunch, cheese is the main ingredient of each and every item on the menu in such eateries. Everything is made with cheese—cheese in your sandwiches, cheese on your potatoes, cheese in your salad and in your soup. Even the cream for your coffee usually has turned into some kind of flaky cheese, not to mention the cheesy grins of the waiters and waitresses greeting you.

As for those waiters and waitresses, certainly, dealing with grumpy drivers whose spouses might just have read them the riot act because of their driving skills just moments before, is not an easy task. And that is why probably the professional way-side restaurant waiter's manual confidentially advises them to address everyone with the endearing expression of "honey." How can you possibly get mad at someone calling you "honey", even though the coffee is lukewarm and it takes an eternity for the chefs in the kitchen to finally find the cow, slaughter it and chop off a nice piece for a cheeseburger?

Another sure giveaway that we are dealing with alien conspirators is the fact that not only do waiters and waitresses in every such coffee shop act in the same manner, but they also look exactly alike. More than likely they have been cloned by these "twelve sinister men" and trained to entice us after a calorie-rich meal to ingest "just one more" gigantic slice of artery-clogging cheesecake! And in this case, you are not permitted—due to said advanced techniques of hypnotic suggesting—any other choice, but must consume more calories than your body could safely process, even if you end up pushing your car down the road instead of riding in it. This then tends to make you drowsy again just a few miles down the road and then you begin to repeat the very same scenario as before. And you thought there was no conspiracy?

If you doubt the validity of my very plausible account about aliens and their twelve sinister men, then *you* go on a mind-numbing ten-hour drive yourself and let's see what kind of crazy schemes you come up with.

PARKING IN SAN FRANCISCO

I have no idea why the Lewis & Clark Expedition is being hyped as such a huge achievement. What was the big deal? They ventured into unknown territory and what did they stumble upon—nothing but parking spaces! How miraculous is that? And they had the assistance of scouts. I would dare them to make it into San Francisco any time on a weekday and find even one single parking space without the service of an experienced local guide. Oh sure, you might find parking space in one of those fancy garages but, not only do they cost the equivalent of the Louisiana Purchase price, you will also be required to hand over your keys to someone whose idea of fun might be to enter your vehicle in a NASCAR race while you're doing your business.

On the City streets parking spots are as rare as outhouses were at the time of the Lewis & Clark excursion. But at least at that time, folks had an alternative to tight, smelly enclosures—they had the big outdoors. Today, if you decide to park your car outdoors in the City, you run the risk of getting towed or getting "the boot"—a treatment similar to one you would get if you mistook Mr. Clark's sleeping bag for an outhouse (and why when we say "City" in the Bay Area, do we always automatically assume we're referring to San Francisco? Antioch, Walnut Creek and Concord *are* cities. Pittsburg is a city and I believe—counting income tax-exempt residents like cats and dogs—Brentwood might be one too. Why then has only San Francisco earned the moniker "City"?)

When exactly did parking become a problem in San Francisco? It appears that as soon as Lewis & Clark returned from their trip in the early 1800s, everyone packed up and suddenly started racing West, not stopping until they almost ran into the Pacific Ocean. Smart people (those who settled in Antioch eventually) would have backed up inland a little, but the future inhabitants of the City dropped their luggage where they stood—right at the edge of the ocean, at the end of a peninsula, mind you—and started to build San Francisco. Of course they ran out of space soon after, which made them even more determined to build their houses on top of each other and on the sides of mountains in a determined pursuit to retain their City identity. But even in those horse and buggy days, parking was still a problem, mostly because of the conundrum of how to park a horse sideways on a steep hill without tipping over (nobody seemed to understand that the problem could have been solved quite easily by raising horses with longer legs on one side).

But I'm not the one to tell them how to improve things in San Francisco, since those hoity-toity know-it-all people of "The City" get all upset when you make suggestions. For example, it makes sense if you need parking lots to *build some*. They have this gigantic unused space, called the Golden Gate Park, with nothing but trees and grass. All you have to do is plow it over and pour concrete on it—voila—more parking. See how easy it is? Squirrels don't need all this space. Just like their human brethren in that city, why couldn't they sacrifice a little and move in together? Instead of only one squirrel per tree, why not five, ten or a hundred? Their cousins, the rats, are already thriving quite well in that kind of system. It's their own fault anyway. With a little foresight, these critters could have prevented this development. A few quick bites targeting chosen areas of early San Francisco residents (who were busy using the outdoors as outhouses), might have scared them away—leaving us with plenty of parking today, and a range of other towns we could refer to as "The City" as well.